Chapter 1

June 5th, 1:15 a.m.
Fairfax County, Virginia - Suburbs of Washington, DC

The phone rang.

Luke Stone lay somewhere between asleep and awake. Images flashed in his mind. It was night on an empty rain-swept highway. Someone was injured. A car wreck. In the distance, an ambulance approached, moving fast. The siren wailed.

He opened his eyes. Next to him on the bed table, in the dark of their bedroom, the phone was ringing. A digital clock sat on the table next to the phone. He glanced at its red numbers.

"Jesus," he whispered. He had been asleep for maybe half an hour.

His wife Rebecca's voice, thick with sleep: "Don't answer it."

A tuft of her blonde hair poked out from under the blankets. Soft blue light filtered into the room from a nightlight in the bathroom.

He picked up the phone.

"Luke," a voice said. The voice was deep and gruff, with the slightest hint of a Southern twang. Luke knew the voice all too well. It was Don Morris, his old boss at the Special Response Team.

Luke ran a hand through his hair. "Yeah?"

"Did I wake you?" Don said.

"What do you think?"

"I wouldn't have called you at home. But your cell phone was off."

Luke grunted. "That's because I turned it off."

"We got trouble, Luke. I need you on this one."

"Tell me," Luke said.

He listened as the voice spoke. Soon, he had that feeling he used to get—the feeling that his stomach was in an elevator rapidly descending fifty stories. Perhaps this was why he had quit the job. Not because of too many close calls, not because his son was growing up so fast, but because he didn't like this feeling in his stomach.

It was the knowing that made him sick. The knowing was too much. He thought of the millions of people out there, living their happy lives, blissfully unaware of what was going on. Luke envied them their ignorance.

1

"When did it happen?" he said.

"We don't know anything yet. An hour ago, maybe two. The hospital noticed the security breach about fifteen minutes ago. They have employees unaccounted for, so right now it looks like an inside job. That could change as better intel comes in. The NYPD has gone nuts, for obvious reasons. They called in two thousand extra cops, and from where I sit, it's not going to be nearly enough. Most of them won't even get in until the shift change."

"Who called NYPD?" Luke said.

"The hospital."

"Who called us?"

"The Chief of Police."

"He call anybody else?"

"No. We're it."

Luke nodded.

"Okay, good. Let's keep it that way. The cops need to lock down the crime scene and secure it. But they need to stay outside the perimeter. We don't want them stepping on it. They also need to keep this away from the media. If the newspapers get it, it's going to be a circus."

"Done and done."

Luke sighed. "Assume a two-hour head start. That's bad. They're way out ahead of us. They could be anywhere."

"I know. NYPD is watching the bridges, the tunnels, the subways, the commuter rails. They're looking at highway tollbooth data, but it's a needle in a haystack. No one has the manpower to deal with this."

"When are you going up there?" Luke said.

Don didn't hesitate. "Now. And you're coming with me."

Luke looked at the clock again. 1:23.

"I can be at the chopper pad in half an hour."

"I already sent a car," Don said. "The driver just called in. He'll be at your place in ten minutes."

Luke placed the receiver back in its cradle.

Rebecca was half awake, her head propped up on one elbow, staring at him. Her hair was long, flowing down her shoulders. Her eyes were blue, framed in thick eyelashes. Her pretty face was thinner than when they first met in college. The intervening years had lined it with care and worry.

Luke regretted that. It burned him to think that the work he did had ever caused her pain. That was another reason why he had left the job.

2

He remembered how she was when they were young, always laughing, always smiling. She was carefree then. A long time had passed since he had seen that part of her. He thought that maybe this time away from work would coax it to the fore again, but progress was slow. There were flashes of the real Becca, sure, but they were fleeting.

He could tell that she didn't trust the situation. She didn't trust *him*. She was waiting for that phone call in the middle of the night, the one he would have to answer. The one where he would hang up the phone, get out of bed, and leave the house.

They'd had a good night tonight. For a few hours, it had seemed almost like old times.

Now this.

"Luke..." she began. Her scowl was not friendly. It told him this was going to be a difficult conversation.

Luke got out of bed and moved fast, partly because circumstances demanded it, partly because he wanted to leave the house before Becca organized her thoughts. He slipped into the bathroom, splashed water on his face, and glanced at himself in the mirror. He felt awake but his eyes were tired. His body looked wiry and strong—one thing all this time off had meant was he was in the gym four days a week. *Thirty-nine years old*, he thought. *Not bad.*

Inside the walk-in closet, he pulled a long steel lockbox down from a high shelf. From memory, he punched in the ten-digit combination. The lid popped open. He took out his Glock nine-millimeter and slid it into a leather shoulder holster. He crouched down and strapped a tiny .25 caliber pistol to his right calf. He strapped a five-inch serrated fold-out blade to his left calf. The handle doubled as brass knuckles.

"I thought you weren't going to keep weapons in the house anymore."

He glanced up and of course Becca was there, watching him. She wore a robe pulled tight around her body. Her hair was pulled back. Her arms were folded. Her face was pinched, and her eyes were alert. Gone was the sensual woman from earlier tonight. Long gone.

Luke shook his head. "I never said that."

He stood and began to dress. He put on black cargo pants and dropped a couple extra magazines for the Glock into the pockets. He pulled on a tight dress shirt and strapped the Glock on over it. He slid steel-toed boots onto his feet. He closed the weapon box again and slid it back onto its perch near the top of the closet.

3

"What if Gunner found that box?"

"It's up high, where he can't see it and he can't reach it. Even if he somehow got it down, it's locked with a digital lock. Only I know the combination."

A garment bag with two days of clothing changes hung on the rack. He grabbed it. A small bug-out bag packed with travel-size toiletries, reading glasses, a stack of energy bars, and half a dozen Dexedrine pills sat on one of the shelves. He grabbed that, too.

"Always ready, right, Luke? You've got your box with your guns and your bags with your clothes and your drugs and you're just ready to go at a moment's notice, whenever your country needs you. Am I right?"

He took a deep breath.

"I don't know what you want me to say."

"Why don't you say: *I've decided not to go. I've decided that my wife and son are more important than a job. I want my son to have a father. I don't want my wife to sit up for nights on end anymore, wondering if I'm alive or dead, or if I'm ever coming back.* Can you do that, please?"

At times like these, he felt the growing distance between them. He could almost see it. Becca was a tiny figure in a vast desert, dwindling toward the horizon. He wanted to bring her back to him. He wanted it desperately, but he couldn't see how. The job was calling.

"Is Dad going away again?"

They both turned red. There was Gunner at the top of the three steps that led to his room. For a second, Luke's breath caught in his throat at the sight of him. He looked like Christopher Robin from the *Winnie the Pooh* books. His blond hair poked up in tufts. He wore blue pajama pants covered with yellow moons and stars. He wore a *Walking Dead* T-shirt.

"Come here, monster."

Luke put his bags down, went over, and picked up his son. The boy clung to his neck.

"You're the monster, Dad. Not me."

"Okay. I'm the monster."

"Where are you going?"

"I need to go away for work. Maybe a day, maybe two. But I'll be back as soon as I can."

"Is Mom going to leave you like she said?"

Luke held Gunner out at arm's length. The boy was getting big and Luke realized that one day soon he wouldn't be able to hold him like this anymore. But that day hadn't come yet.

"Listen to me. Mom isn't going to leave me, and we're all going to be together for a long, long time. Okay?"

"Okay, Dad."

He disappeared up the steps and toward his room.

When he was gone, the two of them stared across at each other. The distance seemed smaller now. Gunner was the bridge between them.

"Luke..."

He held up his hands. "Before you speak, I want to say something. I love you, and I love Gunner, more than anything in this world. I want to be with you both, every day, now and forever. I'm not leaving because I feel like it. I don't feel like it. I hate it. But that call tonight... people's lives are at stake. In all the years I've been doing this, the times that I've left in the middle of the night like this? The situation was a Level Two threat exactly twice. Most of the time, it was Level Three."

Becca's face had softened the tiniest amount.

"What threat level is this?" she asked.

"Level One."

Chapter 2

1:57 am

McLean, Virginia - Headquarters of the Special Response Team

"Sir?" someone said. "Sir, we're here."

Luke snapped awake. He sat up. They were parked at the gate of the helipad. A light rain was falling. He looked at the driver. It was a young guy with a crew cut, probably just out of the military. The kid was smiling.

"You dozed off, sir."

"Right," Luke said. The weight of the job settled on him again. He wanted to be home in bed with Becca, but he was here instead. He wanted to live in a world where murderers didn't steal radioactive materials. He wanted to sleep and dream of pleasant things. At the moment, he couldn't even imagine what those pleasant things might be. His sleep was poisoned by knowing too much.

He climbed out of the car with his bags, showed the guard his identification, and stepped through the scanner.

A sleek black helicopter, a big Bell 430, sat on the pad, rotors turning. Luke crossed the wet tarmac, ducking low. As he approached, the chopper's engine kicked into another gear. They were ready to leave. The door to the passenger compartment slid open and Luke climbed inside.

There were six people already on board, four in the passenger cabin, two up front in the cockpit. Don Morris sat next to the closest window. The seat facing him was empty. Don gestured to it.

"Glad you could come, Luke. Have a seat. Join the party."

Luke strapped into the bucket seat as the chopper lurched toward the sky. He looked at Don. Don was old now, his flat-top hair gone gray. The stubble of his beard was gray. Even his eyebrows were gray. But he still looked like the Delta Force commander he once was. His body was hard and his face was like a granite bluff—all rocky promontories and sharp drop-offs. His eyes were twin lasers. He held an unlit cigar in one of his stone hands. He hadn't lit one in ten years.

As the helicopter gained altitude, Don gestured at the other people in the passenger cabin. He quickly made the introductions. "Luke, you're at the disadvantage, because everybody here already knows who you are, but you might not know them. You do know Trudy Wellington, science and intel officer."

Luke nodded to the pretty young woman with the dark hair and the big round glasses. He had worked with her many times. "Hi, Trudy."

"Hi, Luke."

"Okay, lovebirds, that's enough. Luke, over here is Mark Swann, our tech officer on this job. And with him is Ed Newsam, weapons and tactics."

Luke nodded to the men. Swann was a white guy, sandy hair and glasses, could be thirty-five, could be forty. Luke had met him once or twice before. Newsam was a black guy Luke had never seen, probably early-thirties, bald, close-cropped beard, stacked and chiseled, broad chest, tattooed twenty-four-inch pythons bulging from a white T-shirt. He looked like he'd be hell in a gunfight, and even worse in a street fight. When Don said "weapons and tactics," what he meant was "muscle."

The helicopter had reached cruising altitude; Luke guessed about ten thousand feet. It leveled off and started moving. These things tapped out at about 150 miles per hour. At that speed, they were looking at a solid hour and a half to New York City.

"Okay, Trudy," Don said. "What do you got for us?"

The smartpad in her hands glowed in the darkness of the cabin. She stared into it. It gave her face an eerie quality, like a demon.

"I'm going to assume no prior knowledge," she said.

"Fair enough."

She began. "Less than an hour ago, we were contacted by the New York Police Department counter-terrorism unit. There is a large hospital on the upper east side of Manhattan called Center Medical Center. They store a great deal of radioactive materials onsite, in a containment vault six stories below street level. Mostly, the materials are waste products from radiation therapy for cancer patients, but they also stem from other uses, including radiographic imaging. Sometime in the last few hours, unknown persons infiltrated the hospital, breached the security system, and removed the radioactive waste housed there."

"Do we know how much they got?" Luke said.

Trudy consulted her pad. "Every four weeks, the materials are removed by truck and are transported to a radioactive containment facility in western Pennsylvania jointly controlled by the Department of Homeland Security and the Pennsylvania

Department of Environmental Protection. The next delivery was scheduled for two days from now."

"So about twenty-six days of radioactive waste," Don said. "How much is that?"

"The hospital doesn't know," Trudy said.

"They don't *know*?"

"They inventory the waste and track it in a database. The database was accessed and erased by whoever stole the material. The amounts differ from month to month, based on treatment schedules. They can recreate the inventory from treatment records, but it's going to take several hours."

"They don't back up that database?" said Swann, the tech guy.

"They do back it up, but the backup was also wiped clean. In fact, records for the past year were wiped."

"So someone knows what they're doing," Swann said.

Luke spoke up. "How do we know this is an emergency if we don't even know what was taken?"

"Several reasons," Trudy said. "This was more than a theft. It was a well-coordinated and planned attack. The video surveillance cameras in strategic parts of the hospital were turned off. This includes several entrances and exits, stairwells and freight elevators, the containment vault, and the parking garage."

"Did anyone talk to the security guards?" Luke said.

"The two security guards who manned the video console were both found dead inside a locked equipment closet. They were Nathan Gold, fifty-seven-year-old white male, divorced, three children, no known ties to organized crime or extremist organizations. Also Kitty Faulkner, thirty-three-year-old black female, unmarried, one child, no known ties to organized crime or extremist organizations. Gold worked at the hospital for twenty-three years. Faulkner worked there eight years. The corpses were undressed, their uniforms missing. They were both strangled, with obvious facial discoloration, swelling, neck trauma, and ligature marks associated with death by garroting or similar technique. I have photos if you want to take a look."

Luke held up a hand. "That's okay. But let's assume for the moment that it was men who did this. Does a man kill a female security guard and then put on her uniform?"

"Faulkner was tall for a woman," Trudy said. "She was five foot ten, and heavyset. A man could easily fit into her uniform."

"Is that all we have?"

Trudy went on. "No. There's a hospital employee who was on shift and is currently unaccounted for. That employee is a custodial staff member named Ken Bryant. He's a twenty-nine-year-old black male who spent a year in pre-trial detention on Rikers Island, and then thirty months at Clinton Correctional Center in Dannemora, New York. He was convicted of robbery and simple assault. Upon release, he completed a six-month jail diversion and job training course. He's worked at the hospital for nearly four years, and has a good record. No attendance issues, no disciplinary issues.

"As a custodian, he has access to the hazardous waste containment vault, and may have knowledge of hospital security practices and personnel. He once had ties to drug traffickers and to an African-American prison gang called the Black Gangster Family. The drug traffickers were low-level street dealers in the neighborhood where he grew up. He probably affiliated himself with the prison gang for personal protection."

"You think a prison gang, or a street gang, was behind this?"

She shook her head. "Absolutely not. I mention Bryant's affiliations because he's still a loose end. To access and erase a database, as well as hijack a video surveillance system, requires technical expertise not generally associated with street or prison gangs. We're thinking the level of sophistication and the materials stolen suggest a terrorist sleeper cell."

"What can they do with the chemicals?" Don said.

"It has radiological dispersion device written all over it," Trudy said.

"Dirty bomb," Luke said.

"Bingo. There's no other reason to steal radioactive waste. The hospital doesn't know the amounts that were taken, but they know what the stuff was. The chemicals include quantities of iridium-192, caesium-137, tritium, and fluorine. Iridium is highly radioactive, and concentrated exposure can cause burns and radiation sickness within minutes or hours. Experiments have shown that a tiny dose of caesium-137 will kill a forty-pound dog within three weeks. Fluorine is a caustic gas dangerous to soft tissue like the eyes, skin, and lungs. At very low concentrations, it makes eyes water. At very high concentrations, it inflicts massive lung damage, causing respiratory arrest and death within minutes."

"Wonderful," Don said.

"The important takeaway here," Trudy said, "is high concentrations. If you're a terrorist, for this to work, you don't want a wide dispersal area. That would limit exposure. You want to pack

9

a bomb with the radioactive material and a conventional explosive like dynamite, and you want to set it off in an enclosed space, preferably with a lot of people around. A crowded subway train or subway station at rush hour. Commuter hubs like Grand Central Terminal or Penn Station. A large bus terminal or airport. A tourist attraction like the Statue of Liberty. The enclosed space maximizes radiation concentrations."

Luke pictured the narrow, claustrophobic stairwell that climbed to the top of the Statue of Liberty. On any given day, it was mobbed with people, often school children on field trips. In his mind's eye he saw Liberty Island filled with ten thousand tourists, the ferries jammed with even more people, like refugee boats from Haiti.

Then he saw the subway platforms of Grand Central Terminal at 7:30 a.m., so crowded with commuters that there was nowhere to stand. A hundred people would be lined up on the stairs, waiting for a train to come in and the platform to clear so the next group of people could descend. He pictured a bomb going off amongst that crowd.

And then the lights going out.

A wave of revulsion passed through him. More people would die in the panic, in the crush of bodies, than in the initial explosion.

Trudy went on. "The problem we face is there are too many attractive targets to watch them all, and the attack doesn't have to take place in New York. If the theft happened as long as three hours ago, then we're already looking at a possible operations radius of at least a hundred fifty miles. That includes all of New York City and its suburbs, Philadelphia, and major cities in New Jersey like Newark, Jersey City, and Trenton. If the thieves remain at large for another hour, you can expand that radius to include Boston and Baltimore. The whole region is a population center. In a radius that large, we could be looking at as many as ten thousand possible soft targets. Even if they stick with high-profile, big-name targets, we're still talking about hundreds of places."

"Okay, Trudy," Luke said. "You gave us the facts. Now what's your gut?"

Trudy shrugged. "I think we can assume this is a dirty bomb attack, and that it's sponsored by a foreign country, or possibly an independent terrorist group like ISIS or Al-Qaeda. There may be Americans or Canadians involved, but operational control is elsewhere. It's definitely not a homegrown domestic group, like environmentalists or white supremacists."

10

"Why? Why not domestic?" Luke said. He already knew why, but it was important to air it, to take things one step at a time, to not overlook anything.

"The leftists burn down Hummer dealerships in the middle of the night. They spike logging forests, and then paint the spiked trees so no one gets hurt. They have zero history of attacking populated areas or murdering anyone, and they hate radioactivity. The right-wingers are more violent, and Oklahoma City demonstrated they will attack civilian populations as well as symbols of government. But neither group likely has the training for this. And there's another good reason why it probably isn't them."

"Which is?" Luke said.

"Iridium has a very short half-life," Trudy said. "It'll be mostly useless in a couple of days. Also, whoever stole these chemicals needs to act fast before they get radiation sickness themselves. The Muslim holy month of Ramadan begins tonight at sunset. So I think we have an attack designed to coincide with the start of Ramadan."

Luke nearly breathed a sigh of relief. He had known and worked with Trudy for a few years. Her intel was always good, and her ability to spin scenarios was exceptional. She was right far more often than she was wrong.

He looked at his watch. It was 3:15. Sunset was probably around eight o'clock tonight. He did a quick calculation in his head. "So you think we have more than sixteen hours to track these people down?"

Sixteen hours. Looking for a needle in a haystack was one thing. But having sixteen hours to do it, with the most advanced technology and the very best people, was quite another. It was almost too much to hope for.

Trudy shook her head. "No. The problem with Ramadan is it starts at sunset, but whose sunset? In Tehran, sunset tonight will be at 8:24 p.m., which is 10:54 a.m. here. But what if they pick the start of Ramadan worldwide, for example in Malaysia or Indonesia? We could be looking at something as early as 7:24 a.m., which makes some sense because that's the start of the morning rush hour."

Luke grunted. He stared out the window at the vast lighted megalopolis below him. He glanced at his watch again. 3:20. Up ahead, on the horizon, he could see the tall buildings of Lower Manhattan, and the twin blue lights cutting high into the sky where

11

the World Trade Center once stood. In three hours, the subways and train stations would begin filling up with commuters.

And out there, somewhere, were people planning to make those commuters die.

Chapter 3

3:35 a.m.
East Side of Manhattan

"It looks just like rats," Ed Newsam said.

The chopper came in low over the East River. The dark water was beneath them, flowing fast, tiny swells rising and falling. Luke could see what Ed meant. The water looked like a thousand rats running under a black shimmering blanket.

They dropped slowly down to the 34th Street heliport. Luke watched the lights of the buildings to his left, a million twinkling jewels in the night. Now that they were here, a sense of urgency surged through him. His heart skipped a beat. He had stayed calm during the long flight because what else was he going to do? But the clock was ticking, and they needed to move. He could almost jump out of the helicopter before it landed.

It touched down with a bump and a shudder, and instantly everyone in the cabin unbuckled. Don wrenched the door open. "Let's go," he said.

The blast gate to the street was twenty yards from the pad. Three SUVs waited just outside the concrete barriers. A squad of New York SRT guys ran to the helicopter and off-loaded the equipment bags. A man took Luke's garment bag and his bug-out bag.

"Careful with those," Luke said. "The last time I came up here, you guys lost my bags. I'm not going to have time for a shopping trip."

Luke and Don climbed into the lead SUV, Trudy sliding in with them. The SUV was stretched to create a passenger cabin with facing seats. Luke and Don faced forward while Trudy faced backward. The SUV rolled out almost before they sat down. Within a minute they were inside the narrow canyon of FDR Drive, racing north. Yellow taxis zoomed all around them, like a swarm of bees.

No one spoke. The SUV raced along, hugging the concrete curves, passing through tunnels beneath crumbling buildings, banging hard over potholes. Luke could feel his heart beat in his chest. The driving wasn't what made his pulse race. It was the anticipation.

"It would have been nice to come up here for a little fun," Don said. "Stay in a fancy hotel, maybe see a Broadway show."

"Next time," Luke said.

13

Outside his window, the SUV was already exiting the highway. It was the 96th Street exit. The driver barely paused at a red light, then turned left and floored it down the empty boulevard.

Luke watched as the SUV roared into the circular driveway of the hospital. It was a quiet time of night. They pulled directly in front of the bright lights of the emergency room. A man in a three-piece suit stood waiting for them.

"Sharp dresser," Luke said.

Don poked Luke with a thick finger. "Say, Luke. We got a little treat for you tonight. When was the last time you put on a hazmat suit?"

Chapter 4

4:11 a.m.
Beneath Center Medical Center, Upper East Side

"Not too tight," Luke said around a mouthful of plastic thermometer.

Trudy had placed the sensor of a portable blood pressure monitor on Luke's wrist. The sensor squeezed his wrist hard and then harder still, then slowly released it in stages, making gasping sounds as it did so. Trudy tore back the Velcro on the wrist sensor and in almost the same motion, pulled the thermometer from his mouth.

"How does it look?" he said.

She glanced at the readouts. "Your blood pressure is up," she said. "138 over 85. Resting heart rate 97. Temperature 100.4. I'm not going to lie to you, Luke. These numbers could be better."

"I've been under a little stress lately," Luke said.

Trudy shrugged. "Don's numbers are better than yours."

"Yeah, but he takes statins."

Luke and Don sat together in their boxers and T-shirts on a wooden bench. They were in a sub-basement storage facility beneath the hospital. Heavy vinyl drapes hung all around them, closing off the area. It was cold and dank down here, and a shiver raced along Luke's spine. The breached containment vault was two stories further below them.

People milled around. There were a couple of SRT guys from the New York office. The SRT guys had set up two folding tables with a series of laptops and video displays across them. There was the guy in the three-piece suit, who was an intelligence officer from the NYPD counter-terrorism unit.

Ed Newsam, the big weapons and tactics guy Luke had met on the chopper, pushed through the vinyl curtains with two more SRT guys behind him. Each SRT man carried a sealed clear package with bright yellow material inside.

"Attention," Newsam said in a loud voice, cutting through the chatter. He pointed two fingers at his own eyes. "Don and Luke, eyes on me, please."

Newsam held a bottle of water in each hand. "I know you've both done this before, but we're going to treat it like the first time, that way there's no mistakes. These men behind me are going to

15

inspect your suits for you, and then they're going to help you put them on. These are Level A hazmat suits, and they're solid vinyl. It's going to get hot inside of them, and that means you're going to sweat. So before we begin, I need you to start drinking these bottles of water. You will be glad you did."

"Has anyone been down there before us?" Luke said.

"Two guards went down after the security breach was discovered. The lights are knocked out. Swann has tried to bring them back on, but no luck. So it's dark down there. The guards had flashlights, but when they found the vault open and canisters and drums strewn around, they backed out in a hurry."

"They get any exposure?"

Newsam smiled. "A little. My daughters are going to use them as nightlights for a few days. They didn't have suits on, but they were only there for a minute. You're going to be down there longer."

"Will you be able to see what we see?"

"Your hoods have mounted videocams and LED lights. I'll see what you're seeing, and I'll be recording it."

It took twenty minutes to get dressed. Luke was frustrated. It was hard to move inside the suit. He was covered head to toe in vinyl, and it was already getting hot inside. His face plate kept fogging up. It seemed like time was flying past them. The thieves were far out ahead.

He and Don rode the freight elevator together. It creaked slowly downward. Don carried the Geiger counter. It looked like a small car battery with a carry handle.

"You guys hear me okay?" Newsam said. It sounded like he was inside Luke's head. The hoods had built-in speakers and microphones.

"Yeah," Luke said.

"I hear you," Don said.

"Good. I hear you both loud and clear. We're on a closed frequency. The only people on here are you guys, me, and Swann up in the video control booth. Swann has access to a digital map of the facility and those suits are outfitted with tracking devices. Swann can see you on his map, and he's going to direct you from the elevator to the vault. You with me, Swann?"

"I'm here," Swann said.

The elevator lurched to a stop.

"When the doors open, step out and turn left."

The two men moved awkwardly down a wide hallway, guided by Swann's voce. Their helmet lights played against the walls, throwing shadows in the dark. It reminded Luke of shipwreck scuba dives he had done in years past.

Within a few seconds, the Geiger counter started to click. The clicks came spaced apart at first, like a slow heartbeat.

"We have radiation," Don said.

"We see it. Don't worry. It's not bad. That's a sensitive machine you're carrying."

The clicks started to speed up and grow louder.

Swann's voice: "In a few feet, turn right, then follow that hallway maybe thirty feet. It will open into a large square chamber. The containment vault is on the other side of the chamber."

When they turned right, the Geiger counter began to click loud and fast. The clicks came in a torrent. It was hard to tell one from the next.

"Newsam?"

"Step lively, gentlemen. Let's try to do this in five minutes or less."

They moved into the chamber. The place was a mess. On the floor, canisters, boxes, and large metal drums were knocked over and left randomly. Some of them were open. Luke trained his light on the vault across the room. The heavy door was open.

"You seeing this?" Luke said. "Godzilla must have passed through here."

Newsam's voice came in again. "Don! Don! Train your light and your camera on the ground, five feet ahead. There. A few more feet. What's that on the floor?"

Luke turned toward Don and focused his light in the same place. About ten feet from him, amid the wreckage, were sprawled what looked like a pile of rags.

"It's a body," Don said. "Shit."

Luke moved over to it and trained his light on it. The person was big, wearing what looked like a security guard's uniform. Luke kneeled beside the body. There was a dark stain on the floor, like a bad motor oil leak under a car. The head was sideways, facing him. Everything above the eyes was gone, his forehead blown out in a crater. Luke reached around to the back of the head, feeling for a much smaller hole. Even through the thick chemical gloves, he found it.

"What do you have, Luke?"

"I have a large male, 18 to 30 years old, of Arab, Persian, or possibly Mediterranean descent. There's a lot of blood. He's got entry and exit wounds consistent with a gunshot to the back of the head. It looks like an execution. Could be another guard or it could be one of our subjects had an argument with his friends."

"Luke," Newsam said. "In your utility belt, you've got a small digital fingerprint scanner. See if you can dig it out and get a print off that guy."

"I don't think that's going to be possible," Luke said.

"Come on, man. The gloves are cumbersome, but I know where the scanner is. I can walk you to it."

Luke pointed his camera at the man's right hand. Each finger was a ragged stump, gone below the first knuckle. He glanced at the other hand. It was the same way.

"They took the fingerprints with them," he said.

Chapter 5

Luke and Don, dressed in street clothes again, walked quickly down the hospital corridor with the sharp dresser from the NYPD counter-terrorism unit. Luke hadn't even caught the guy's name. He thought of him as Three-Piece. Luke was about to give the guy his orders. They needed things to happen, and for that they needed the city's cooperation.

Luke was taking charge, like he always tended to do. He glanced at Don, and Don nodded his assent. That's why Don brought Luke on: to take charge. Don always said that Luke was born to play quarterback.

"I want Geiger counters on every floor," Luke said. "Somewhere away from the public. We didn't hit any radiation until six levels down, but if it starts to move upward, we need everyone out, and fast."

"The hospital has patients on life support," Three-Piece said. "They're hard to move."

"Right. So start putting those logistics in place now."

"Okay."

Luke went on. "We're going to need an entire hazmat team down there. We need that body brought up, no matter how contaminated, and we need it done fast. The clean-up can wait until after we have the body."

"Got it," Three-Piece said. "We'll put it in a lead-lined casket, and bring it to the coroner in a radiation containment truck."

"Can it be done quietly?"

"Sure."

"We need a match for dental records, DNA, scars, tattoos, surgical pins, whatever we can find. Once you have the data, pass it on to Trudy Wellington on our team. She's got access to databases your people won't have."

Luke pulled out his phone and speed-dialed a number. She picked up on the first ring.

"Trudy, where are you?"

"I'm with Swann on Fifth Avenue, in the back of one of our cars, on our way down to the command center."

"Listen, I've got..." He looked at Three-Piece. "What's your name?"

"Kurt. Kurt Myerson."

19

"I've got Kurt Myerson from the NYPD here. He's with the counter-terrorism unit. They're going to bring the body up. I need you to connect with him for dental records, DNA, any identifiers at all. When you get the data, I want this guy's name, age, country of origin, known associates, everything. I need to know where's he been and what he's been doing for the past six months. And I need all of this yesterday."

"Got it, Luke."

"Great. Thank you. Here's Kurt, he's going to give you his direct number."

Luke handed Kurt the phone. The three men pushed through a set of double doors, barely slowing down. In a moment, Kurt handed the phone back to Luke.

"Trudy? You still with me?"

"Would I ever be anywhere else?"

Luke nodded. "Good. One more thought. The surveillance cameras are off here at the hospital, but there's got to be cameras all over this neighborhood. When you get to the command center, grab a few of our people. Have them access anything they can find within a five-block radius of this place, and pull video from, let's say, 8p.m. until 1a.m. I want to get a look at every commercial or delivery vehicle that came near the hospital during that time. Highest priority is small delivery vans, bread trucks, hot dog trucks, anything along those lines. Anything small, convenient, that can carry a concealed payload. Lower priority is tractor trailers, buses, or construction vehicles, but don't overlook them. Lowest priority is RVs, pickup trucks, and SUVs. I want screen captures of license plates, and I want ownership of the vehicles tracked. If you find one that looks fishy, you search more cameras for that vehicle on an expanding radius, and find out where it went."

"Luke," she said, "I'm going to need more than a few people for that."

Luke thought about it for two seconds. "Okay. Wake up some people back home, bring them in to SRT headquarters, and forward the license plate data to them. They can track ownership down there."

"Got it."

They hung up. Luke reoriented himself to the present moment, and a new thought occurred to him. He glanced at Kurt Myerson.

"Okay, Kurt. Here's the most important thing. We need this hospital locked down. We need the employees who were on shift

20

tonight gathered up and sequestered. People are going to talk, I understand that, but we've got to keep this out of the hands of the media for as long as we can. If this gets out, there's going to be panic, there's going to be ten thousand false leads called in to the police, and the bad guys will get to watch the entire investigation unfold on television. We can't let it happen."

They pushed through another set of double doors and into the main lobby of the hospital. The entire front face of the lobby was glass. Several security guards stood near the locked front doors.

Outside was a mob scene. A crowd of reporters pushed up against police barriers on the sidewalk. Photographers pressed against the windows, taking interior shots of the lobby. News trucks were parked ten deep on the street. As Luke watched, three different TV reporters filmed segments directly in front of the hospital.

"You were saying?"

Chapter 6

5:10 a.m.
Inside a van

Eldrick was sick.

He sat in the rear passenger seat of the van, hugging his knees, wondering what he had gotten himself into. He had seen some bad shit in prison, but nothing like this.

In front of him, Ezatullah was on the phone, shouting something in Farsi. Ezatullah had been making calls for hours now. The words didn't mean anything to Eldrick. It all sounded like gibberish. The real deal, Ezatullah had trained in London as a chemical engineer, but instead of getting a job, he had gone to war. In his early 30s, a wide scar across one cheek, to hear him tell it, he had waged jihad in half a dozen countries—and had come to America to do the same.

He screamed into the phone again and again before he got through. When he finally reached someone, he launched into the first of several shouted arguments. After a few minutes, he settled down and listened. Then he hung up.

Eldrick's face was flushed. He had a fever. He could feel it burning through his body. His heart was racing. He hadn't thrown up, but he felt like he was going to. They had waited at the rendezvous point on the South Bronx waterfront for over two hours. It was supposed to be a simple thing. Steal the materials, drive the van ten minutes, meet the contacts and walk away. But the contacts never showed.

Now they were...somewhere. Eldrick didn't know. He had passed out for a while. He was awake again, but everything seemed like a vague dream. They were on the highway. Momo was driving, so he must know where they were going. A technology expert, Momo, skinny with no muscle tone, looked the part. He was so young the smooth skin of his face didn't have a single line. He looked like he couldn't grow a beard if Allah himself depended on it.

"We have new instructions," Ezatullah said.

Eldrick groaned, wishing he was dead. He didn't know it was possible to feel this sick.

"I have to get out of this van," Eldrick said.

"Shut up, Abdul!"

22

Eldrick had forgotten: his name was Abdul Malik now. It felt weird to hear himself being called Abdul, he, Eldrick, a proud black man, a proud American for most of his life. Feeling as sick as he did now, he wished he'd never changed it. Converting in prison was the dumbest thing he'd ever done.

All that shit was in the back. There was a lot of it, in all kinds of canisters and boxes. Some of it had leaked out, and now it was killing them. It had killed Bibi already. The dummy had opened a canister when they still were down in the vault. He was immensely strong and he wrenched the lid off. Why did he do that? Eldrick could picture him holding the canister up. "There's nothing in here," he'd said. Then he'd held it to his nose.

Within a minute, he started coughing. He just sort of sank down to his knees. Then he was on all fours, coughing. "I have something in my lungs," he said. "I can't get it out." He started gasping for air. The sound was horrible.

Ezatullah walked up and shot him in the back of the head.

"Believe me, I did him a favor," he'd said.

Now, the van was passing through a tunnel. The tunnel was long and narrow and dark, with orange lights zooming by overhead. The lights made Eldrick dizzy.

"I have to get out of this van!" he shouted. "I have to get out of this van! I have to…"

Ezatullah turned around. His gun was out. He pointed it at Eldrick's head.

"Quiet! I'm on the phone."

Ezatullah's sliced up face was flushed red. He was sweating.

"You gonna kill me the way you did Bibi?"

"Ibrahim was my friend," Ezatullah said. "I killed him out of mercy. I will kill you just to shut you up." He pressed the muzzle of the gun against Eldrick's forehead.

"Shoot me. I don't care." Eldrick closed his eyes.

When he opened them again, Ezatullah had turned back around. They were still in the tunnel. The lights were too much. A sudden wave of nausea passed through Eldrick, and a great up-rushing spasm gripped his body. His stomach clenched and he tasted acid in his throat. He bent over and threw up on the floor between his shoes.

A few seconds passed. The stench wafted up into his face, and he wretched again.

Oh God, he begged silently. *Please let me die.*

Chapter 7

5:33 a.m.
East Harlem, Borough of Manhattan

Luke held his breath. Loud noises were not his favorite thing, and one hell of a loud noise was coming.

He stood completely still in the bleak light of a tenement building in Harlem. His gun was out, his back pressed to the wall. Behind him, Ed Newsam stood in almost the exact same pose as his. In front of them in the narrow hallway, half a dozen helmeted and flak-jacketed SWAT team members stood on either side of an apartment door.

The building was dead quiet. Dust motes hung in the air. Moments before, a small robot had slid a tiny camera scope beneath the door, looking for explosives attached to the other side. Negative. Now, the robot had retreated.

Two SWAT guys stepped up with a heavy battering ram. It was a swing-type, an officer holding the handle on each side. They didn't make a sound. The SWAT team leader held up his fist. His index finger appeared.

That was one.

Middle finger. Two.

Ring finger…

The two men reared back and swung the ram. BAM!

The door exploded inward as the rammers ducked back. The four others swarmed in, suddenly shrieking, "Down! Down! Get DOWN!"

Somewhere down the hallway, a child started crying. Doors opened, heads peeped out, then ducked back in. It was one of those things around here. Sometimes the cops came and broke down a neighbor's door.

Luke and Ed waited about thirty seconds until SWAT had secured the apartment. The body was on the floor in the living room, much as Luke suspected it might be. He barely looked at it.

"All clear?" he said to the SWAT leader. The guy glared at Luke just a little bit. There had been a brief argument when Luke commandeered this team. These guys were NYPD. They weren't chess pieces for the feds to move around on a whim. That's what they wanted Luke to know. Luke was fine with that, but a terrorist attack was hardly one man's whim.

"All clear," the team leader said. "That's probably your subject right there."

"Thank you," Luke said.

The guy shrugged and looked away.

Ed kneeled by the body. He carried a fingerprint scanner with him. He took prints from three of the fingers.

"What do you think, Ed?"

He shrugged. "I preloaded Ken Bryant's prints from the police database on here. We should know if we have a match in a few seconds. Meanwhile, you've got obvious ligature marks and swelling. The body is still somewhat warm. Rigor mortis has set in, but is not complete. The fingers are turning blue. I'd say he died the same way as the security guards at the hospital, of strangulation, roughly eight to twelve hours ago."

He looked up at Luke. There was a glint in his eyes. "If you want to take his pants down for me, I can get a rectal temperature reading, and narrow the time a little better."

Luke smiled and shook his head. "No thanks. Eight to twelve hours is fine. Just tell me: is it him?"

Ed glanced at his scanner. "Bryant? Yeah. It's him."

Luke pulled his phone and dialed Trudy. On the other end, her phone rang. Once, twice, three times. Luke glanced around at the dreary bleakness of the apartment. The living room furniture was old, with ripped upholstery, and stuffing coming out of the arms of the sofa. A threadbare rug was splayed on the floor, and empty takeout boxes and plastic utensils were strewn across the table. Heavy black curtains were tacked over the windows.

Trudy's voice came on, alert, almost musical. "Luke," she said. "What's it been? Half an hour?"

"I want to talk about the missing janitor."

"Ken Bryant," she said.

"Right. He's not missing anymore. Newsam and I are at his apartment. We have a positive ID on him. He died about eight to twelve hours ago. Strangled, like the guards."

"Okay," she said.

"I want you to access his bank accounts. He probably had direct deposit from his job at the hospital. Start with that one and work your way out from there."

"Um, I'm going to need a warrant for that."

Luke paused. He understood her hesitancy. Trudy was a good officer. She was also young and ambitious. Breaking the rules had derailed many a promising career. But not always. Sometimes breaking the rules led to fast-track promotions. It all depended on which rules you broke, and what happened as a result.

"You have Swann there with you?" he said.

"Yes."

"Then you don't need a warrant."

She didn't answer.

"Trudy?"

"I'm here."

"We don't have time to execute a warrant. There are lives at stake."

"Is Bryant a suspect in this case?"

"He is a person of interest. Anyway, he's dead. We are hardly violating his rights."

"Am I right that this is an order from you, Luke?"

"This is a direct order," he said. "This is my responsibility. If you want to take it that far, this is me telling you that your job depends on this. You do what I say, or I will initiate disciplinary proceedings. Is that understood?"

She sounded petulant, almost like a child. "Fine."

"Good. When you access his account, look for anything out of the ordinary. Money that doesn't belong there. Large deposits or large withdrawals. Wire transfers. If he has a savings account or investments linked, take a look at those. We're talking about an ex-con with a custodial job. He shouldn't have that much money. If he does, I want to know where it came from."

"Okay, Luke."

He hesitated. "How are we doing on license plates?"

"We are going as fast as we can," she said. "We accessed overnight video footage from cameras at Fifth Avenue and 96th Street, as well as Fifth Avenue and 94th Street, and a few others around the neighborhood. We are tracking a 198 vehicles, 46 of which are high priority. I should have an initial report from headquarters in about fifteen minutes."

Luke glanced at his watch. Time was getting tight. "Okay. Good work. We'll be down there as soon as we can."

"Luke?"

"Yes."

"The story is all over the news. They have three live feeds on the big board here right now. They're all leading with it."

He nodded. "I figured."

She went on. "The mayor has scheduled an announcement for 6a.m. It sounds like he's going to tell everyone to stay home today."

"Everyone?"

"He wants all nonessential personnel to stay out of Manhattan. All office workers. All cleaning workers and store clerks. All school children and teachers. He is going to suggest that five million people take the day off."

Luke put his hand to his mouth. He took a breath. "That should do a lot for morale," he said. "When everyone in New York stays home, the terrorists just might hit Philadelphia."

Chapter 8

Eldrick stood alone, about ten yards from the van. He had just thrown up again. It was mostly dry heaves and blood now. The blood disturbed him. He was still lightheaded, still feverish and flushed, but with nothing left in his stomach, the nausea was mostly gone. Best of all, he was finally out of the van.

Somewhere over the dirty horizon, the sky was just starting to brighten, a pale sickly yellow. Down here on the ground, it was still dark. They were parked in a desolate parking lot along a bleak waterfront. A highway overpass soared twenty stories above their heads. Nearby was an abandoned brick industrial building with twin smokestacks. Its windows were broken black holes like dead eyes. The building was surrounded by a barbed wire fence with signs posted every thirty feet: KEEP OUT. There was a visible hole in the fence. The area around the building was overgrown with bushes and tall grass.

He watched Ezatullah and Momo. Ezatullah peeled off one of the large magnetic decals that said Dun-Rite Laundry Services, carried it to the water's edge, and hurled it over the side. Then he came back and peeled off the other side. It never occurred to Eldrick that the signs came off. Meanwhile, Momo kneeled at the front of the van with a screwdriver, removing the license plate and replacing it with a different one. A moment later, he had moved to the back, doing the same with the rear plate.

Ezatullah made a gesture toward the van. "Voilà!" he said. "Totally different vehicle. Catch me now, Uncle Sam." Ezatullah's face was bright red and sweaty. He seemed to be wheezing. His eyes were bloodshot.

Eldrick glanced at their surroundings. Ezatullah's physical state had given him an idea. The idea flashed in his mind like lightning, here and gone in an instant. It was the safest way to think. People could read thoughts in your eyes.

"Where are we?" he said.

"Baltimore," Ezatullah said. "Another of your great American cities. And a pleasant place to live, I imagine. Low crime, natural

28

beauty, and the citizens are all healthy and wealthy, the envy of people everywhere."

In the night, Eldrick had been delirious. He had passed out more than once. He had lost track of time, and of where they were. But he had no idea they had come this far.

"Baltimore? Why are we here?"

Ezatullah shrugged. "We are on our way to our new destination."

"The target is here?"

Now Ezatullah smiled. The smile seemed out of place on his radiation-poisoned face. He looked like death itself. He reached out with a trembling hand and gave Eldrick a friendly pat on the shoulder.

"I'm sorry I was angry with you, my brother. You've done a good job. You delivered everything you promised. If Allah wills it, I hope you are in paradise this very day. But not by my hand."

Eldrick just stared at him.

Ezatullah shook his head. "No. Not Baltimore. We are traveling south to strike a blow that will give joy to the suffering masses throughout the world. We are going to enter the lair of the Devil himself and cut off the beast's head with our own hands."

Eldrick felt a chill all over his upper body. His arms broke out in goose bumps. He noticed that his own shirt was soaked in sweat. He didn't like the sound of this. If they were headed south and they were in Baltimore, then the next city was…

"Washington," he said.

"Yes."

Ezatullah smiled again. Now the smile was glorious, that of a saint standing at the gates of heaven, ready to be granted entrance.

"Kill the head and the body will die."

Eldrick could see it in Ezatullah's eyes. The man had lost his mind. Maybe it was the sickness, or maybe it was something else, but it was obvious he wasn't thinking clearly. All along, the plan had been to steal the materials and drop off the van in the South Bronx. It was a dangerous job, very difficult to pull off, and they had done it. But whoever was in charge had changed the plan, or had lied about it since the beginning. Now they were traveling to Washington in a radioactive van.

To do what?

Ezatullah was a seasoned jihadi. He must know that what he was hinting was impossible. Whatever he thought they were going

29

to do, Eldrick knew they weren't even going to come close. He pictured the van, riddled with bullet holes, three hundred yards from the White House or Pentagon or Capitol Building fence.

This wasn't a suicide mission. It wasn't a mission at all. It was a political statement.

"Don't worry," Ezatullah said. "Be happy. You've been chosen for the greatest honor. We will make it, even though you cannot imagine how. The method will become clear to you in time." He turned and slid open the side door of the van.

Eldrick glanced at Momo. He was finishing up the rear license plate. Momo hadn't spoken in a while. He probably wasn't feeling too well himself.

Eldrick took a step backwards. Then he took another. Ezatullah busied himself with something inside the van. His back was turned. The funny thing about this moment was another one like it might never come. Eldrick was just standing there in a vast open lot, and no one was looking at him.

Eldrick had run track in high school. He was good at it. He remembered the crowds inside the 168th Street Armory in Manhattan, the standings on the big board, the buzzer going off. He remembered that knotted up feeling in his stomach right before a race, and the crazy speed on the new track, skinny black gazelles jockeying, pushing off, elbows high, moving so fast that it seemed like a dream.

In all the years since, Eldrick had never run as fast as he did back then. But maybe, with one focused burst of energy and everything riding on it, he could match that speed right now. No sense in hesitating, or even thinking much more about it.

He turned and took off.

A second later, Momo's voice behind him:

"EZA!"

Then something in Farsi.

The abandoned building was ahead. The sickness came roaring back. He wretched, blood spurting down his shirt, but he kept going. He was already out of breath.

He heard a clack like a stapler. It echoed faintly against the walls of the building. Ezatullah was shooting, of course he was. His gun had a silencer.

A sharp sting went through Eldrick's back. He fell to the pavement, skinning his arms on the broken asphalt. A split second

30

later, another shot echoed. Eldrick got up and kept running. The fence was right here. He turned and went for the hole.

Another sting went through him. He fell forward and clung to the fence. All the strength seemed to flow out of his legs. He hung there, supporting himself with the death grip of his fingers through the chain links.

"Move," he croaked. "Move."

He dropped to his knees, forced the ripped fence aside and crawled through the hole. He was in deep grass. He stood, stumbled along for a few steps, tripped over something he couldn't see, and rolled down an embankment. He didn't try to stop rolling. He let his momentum carry him to the bottom.

He came to rest, breathing heavily. The pain in his back was unreal. His face was in the dirt. It was wet here, muddy, and he was right along the riverbank. He could tumble into the dark water if he wanted to. Instead, he crawled deeper into the underbrush. The sun hadn't come up yet. If he stayed here, didn't move, and didn't make a sound, it was just barely possible...

He touched a hand to his chest. His fingers came away wet with blood.

*

Ezatullah stood at the hole in the fence. The world spun around him. He had become dizzy just trying to run after Eldrick.

His hand held the chain link of the fence, helping him stand. He thought he might vomit. It was dark back in those bushes. They could spend an hour looking for him in there. If he made it into the big abandoned building, they might never find him.

Moahmmar stood nearby. He was bent over, hands on his knees, breathing deeply. His body was shaking. "Should we go in?" he said.

Ezatullah shook his head. "We don't have time. I shot him twice. If the sickness doesn't finish him, the bullets will. Let him die here alone. Perhaps Allah will take pity on his cowardice. I hope so. Either way, we must continue without him."

He turned and started back toward the van. It seemed like the van was parked far away. He was tired, and he was sick, but he kept putting one foot after the other. Each step brought him closer to the gates of Paradise.

31

Chapter 9

6:05 a.m.
Joint Counter-Terrorism Command Center - Midtown Manhattan

"Luke, the best thing to do is get your people together and go back to Washington," the man in the suit said.

Luke stood inside the swirling chaos of the command center's main room. It was already daytime, and weak light filtered in from windows two stories above the working floor. Time was passing too quickly, and the command center was a clusterfuck in progress.

Two hundred people filled the space. There were at least forty workstations, some of them with two or three people sitting at five computer screens. On the big board up front, there were twenty different television and computer screens. Screens showed digital maps of Manhattan, the Bronx, Brooklyn, live video streams of the entrances to the Holland and Lincoln Tunnels, mug shots of Arab terrorists known to be in the country.

Three of the screens currently showed Mayor DeAngelo, at six-foot-three dwarfing the aides that flanked him, standing at the microphone and telling the brave people of New York to stay home and hug their kids. He was reading from prepared remarks.

"In a worst-case scenario," the mayor said, his voice coming from speakers located around the room, "the initial explosion would kill many people and create mass panic in the immediate area. Radiation exposure would cause widespread terror throughout the region and probably the country. Many people exposed in the initial attack would become sick, and some would die. The clean-up costs would be enormous, but they would be dwarfed by the psychological and economic costs. A dirty bomb attack on a major train station in New York City would cripple transportation along the Eastern seaboard for the foreseeable future."

"Pleasant," Luke said. "I wonder who writes his material."

He scanned the room. Everyone was represented here, everyone jockeying for position. It was alphabet soup. NYPD, FBI, NSA, ATF, DEP, even CIA. Hell, the DEA was here. Luke wasn't sure how stealing radioactive waste constituted a drug crime.

Ed Newsam had gone to track down the SRT staff among the crowd.

"Luke, did you hear me?"

Luke turned back to the matter at hand. He was standing with Ron Begley of Homeland Security. Ron was a balding man in his late 50s. He had a large round gut and pudgy little fingers. Luke knew his story. He was a desk jockey, a man who had come up through the government bureaucracy. On September 11, he was at Treasury running a team analyzing tax evasion and Ponzi schemes. He slid over to counter-terrorism when Homeland Security was created. He had never made an arrest, or fired a gun in anger, in his life.

"You said you want me to go home."

"You're stepping on toes here, Luke. Kurt Myerson called his boss at NYPD and told him you were at the hospital treating people like your personal servants. And that you commandeered a SWAT team. Really? A SWAT team? Listen, this is their turf. You're supposed to follow their lead. That's how the game is played."

"Ron, the NYPD called us in. I assume that's because they felt they needed us. People know how we work."

"Cowboys," Begley said. "You work like rodeo cowboys."

"Don Morris got me out of bed to come up here. You can talk to Don…"

Begley shrugged. A ghost of a smile appeared on his face. "Don's been recalled. He caught a chopper out twenty minutes ago. I suggest you do the same."

"What?"

"That's right. He's been kicked upstairs on this one. They called him back to do a situation briefing at the Pentagon. Real high-level stuff. I guess they couldn't get an intern to do it, so they're bringing in Don."

Begley lowered his voice, though Luke could still easily hear him. "A word of advice. What does Don have, three more years before retirement? Don's a dying breed. He's a dinosaur, and so is SRT. You know it and I know it. All of these little secret agencies within an agency, they're going by the wayside. We're consolidating and centralizing, Luke. What we need now is data-driven analysis. That's how we're going to solve the crimes of the future. That's how we're going to catch these terrorists today. We don't need macho super-spies and aging former commandos rappelling down the sides of buildings anymore. We just don't. Playing hero ball is over. It's actually a little ridiculous, if you think about it."

"Great," Luke said. "I'll take that under advisement."

"I thought you were teaching college," Begley said. "History, political science, that kind of thing."

Luke nodded. "I am."

Begley put a meaty hand on Luke's arm. "You should stick with that."

Luke shook the hand off and plunged into the crowd, looking for his people.

*

"What do we got?" Luke said.

His team had set up camp in an outlying office. They had grabbed some empty desks and built their own little command station with laptops and satellite uplinks. Trudy and Ed Newsam were there, along with a few of the others. Swann was off in a corner by himself with three laptops.

"They called Don back," Trudy said.

"I know. Have you talked to him?"

She nodded. "Twenty minutes ago. He was just about to take off. He said keep working this case until he personally calls it off. Politely ignore anyone else."

"Sounds good. So where are we?"

Her face was serious. "We're moving fast. We've narrowed it down to six high-priority vehicles. All of them passed within a block of the hospital last night, and have details that are funky or don't match up."

"Give me an example."

"Okay. One is a food vendor truck registered to a former Russian paratrooper. We were able to follow him on surveillance cameras, and as near as we can tell, he's been cruising around Manhattan all night, selling hot dogs and Pepsi to sex workers, pimps, and johns."

"Where is he now?"

"He's parked on 11th Ave, south of the Jacob Javits Convention Center. He hasn't moved in a while. We're thinking he might be asleep."

"Okay, sounds like he just became low priority. Pass him on to NYPD, just in case. They can roust him and toss his truck, find out what else he's selling in there. Next."

Trudy ran down her list. A minivan operated as an Uber car by a disgraced former nuclear physicist. A forty-ton tractor trailer with an insurance claim that it was demolished in an accident and scrapped. A delivery van for a commercial laundry service, with license plates registered to an unrelated flooring business in Long Island. An ambulance reported stolen three years ago.

"A stolen ambulance?" Luke said. "That sounds like something."

Trudy shrugged. "Usually it's the illegal organ trade. They harvest from newly deceased patients within minutes of death. They have to harvest the organs, pack them, and get them out of the hospital quickly. No one looks twice at an ambulance waiting around in a hospital parking lot."

"But tonight, maybe they weren't waiting for organs. Do we know where they are?"

She shook her head. "No. The only location we have is the Russian. This is still more of an art than a science. Surveillance cameras aren't everywhere yet, especially once you get out of Manhattan. You see a truck pass a camera, then you might not see it again. Or you might pick it up on another camera ten blocks away, or five miles away. The tractor trailer crossed the George Washington Bridge into New Jersey before we lost it. The laundry van went over the 138th Street Bridge into the South Bronx and disappeared. Right now, we're tracking them all down using other means. We've contacted the trucking company, Uber, the flooring company, and the laundry service. We should know something on those soon. And I've got eight people at headquarters sifting through hours of video feeds, looking for the ambulance."

"Good. Keep me posted. What's going on with the bank stuff?"

Trudy's face was stone. "You should ask Swann about that."

"Okay." He took a step toward Swann's little fiefdom in the corner.

"Luke?"

He stopped. "Yeah."

Her eyes darted around the room. "Can we talk? In private?"

*

"You're going to fire me because I won't break the law for you?"

"Trudy, I'm not going to fire you. Why would you even think that?"

"It's what you said, Luke."

They were standing in a tiny utility room. There were two empty desks in here and one small window. The carpeting was new. The walls were white with nothing on them. There was a small video camera mounted in one corner, near the ceiling.

It looked like the room had never been used. The command center itself had been open for less than a year.

Trudy's big eyes stared at him intently.

Luke sighed. "I was giving you an out. I thought you would understand that. If trouble comes down, you can blame it on me. All you did was what I told you to do. You were afraid you'd lose your job if you didn't follow my orders."

She took a step closer to him. In the confines of the room, he could smell her shampoo, and the understated cologne she often wore. The combination of scents did something to his knees. He felt them tremble the slightest amount.

"You can't even give me a direct order, Luke. You don't work at SRT anymore."

"I'm on a leave of absence."

She took another small step toward him. Her eyes were focused on him like twin lasers. There was intelligence in those eyes, and heat.

"And you left… why? Because of me?"

He shook his head. "No. I had my reasons. You weren't one of them."

"The Marshall brothers?"

He shrugged. "When you kill two men in one night, it's a good time to take a pause. Maybe reassess what you're doing."

"Are you saying you never had any feelings for me?" she asked.

He looked at her, stunned by the question. He had always sensed Trudy flirting with him, and he had never taken the bait. There had been a few times, drunk at cocktail parties, after bad fights with his wife, when he had come close. But thoughts of his wife and son had always pulled him back from the brink of doing something stupid.

"Trudy, we work together," he said firmly. "And I'm married."

She came even closer.

"I'm not looking for a marriage, Luke," she said softly, leaning in, inches away.

She pushed herself against him now. His arms were at his sides. He felt the heat from her, and that old uncontrollable urge when she was near, the excitement, the energy... the lust. She reached up to lay her hands on his chest, and as soon as her palms touched his shirt, he knew he had to act now or give in to her completely.

With one final act of supreme self-discipline, Luke stepped back and gently pushed her hands away.

"I'm sorry, Trudy," he said, his voice raspy. "I care about you. I really do. But this is not a good idea."

She frowned, but before she could say anything, a heavy fist banged against the wooden door.

"Luke? You in there?" It was Newsam's voice. "You should come out and look at this. Swann's got something."

They stared at each other, Luke feeling guilty as hell as he thought of his wife, even though he hadn't done anything. He peeled himself away before anything more could happen and couldn't help wondering how this would affect their working together.

He also, worst of all, couldn't help but admit, deep down, that he didn't want to leave the room.

*

Swann sat a long table with his three video monitors arrayed in front of him. With his thinning hair and glasses, he reminded Luke of a NASA physicist at mission control. Luke stood behind him with Newsam and Trudy, the three of them hovering over Swann's narrow shoulders.

"This one is Ken Bryant's checking account," Swann said, moving his cursor around on the center screen. Luke absorbed the details: deposits, withdrawals, total balance, a date range from April 28th to May 27th.

"How secure is this connection?" Luke said. He glanced around the room and out the door. The main room of the command center was just down the hall.

"This?" Swann said. He shrugged. "It's independent of the command center. I'm connected to our own tower and our own satellites. It's encrypted by our guys. I suppose CIA or NSA could have somebody trying to break it, but why bother? We're all on the same team, right? I wouldn't worry about that. Instead, I would focus on this bank account. Notice anything funny?"

"His balance is over $24,000," Luke said.

"Right," Swann said. "A janitor has a pretty sizeable chunk of money in his checking account. Interesting. Now let's go back a month. March 28th to April 27th. The balance goes as high as $37,000, and he starts spending it down. There are transfers here from an unnamed account, $5,000, then $4,000, then, oh well, forget the whole IRS reporting problem… give me $20,000."

"Okay," Luke said.

"Go back another month. Late February to late March. His beginning balance is $1,129. By the end of the month, it's over $9,000. Go back another month, late January to late February, and his balance never reached $2,000 the whole time. From there, if you go back three years, you see that his balance rarely went above $1,500. Here was a guy living month to month, who suddenly started getting large wire transfers in March."

"Where are they coming from?"

Swann smiled and raised a finger. "Now for the fun part. They're coming from a small offshore bank specializing in anonymous numbered accounts. It's called Royal Heritage Bank, and it's based on Grand Cayman."

"Can you hack it?" Luke said. He glanced sidelong at Trudy's disapproving look.

"I don't have to," Swann said. "Royal Heritage is owned by a CIA asset named Grigor Svetlana. He's a Ukrainian who used to be in the Red Army. He got himself in deep with the Russians twenty years ago, after some old Soviet weaponry disappeared and then turned up on the black markets in West Africa. I'm not talking about guns. I'm talking about anti-aircraft, anti-tank, plus some low-altitude cruise missiles. The Russians were ready to hang him upside down. With nowhere to turn, he turned to us. I have a friend at Langley, and the accounts at Royal Heritage Bank, far from being anonymous, are in fact an open book to the American intelligence community. Of course, this isn't something most Royal Heritage customers are aware of."

"So you know who owned the account making the transfers."

"I do."

"Okay, Swann," Luke said. "I understand. You're very clever. Now get to the point."

Swann gestured at the computer screens. "Bryant himself owned the account that was making the transfers. That's the account on my left monitor there. You can see it has about $209,000 in it right now. He was transferring a little bit here and there from the numbered account to his local checking account, probably for his own personal use. And if we scroll back a few months, you can see that Bryant's offshore account was created on March 3rd by a $250,000 transfer from another Royal Heritage account, the one on the right monitor here."

Luke looked at the account on the right. There was more than forty-four million dollars in it.

"Someone got a bargain hiring Bryant," he said.

"Exactly," Swann said.

"Who is it?"

"It's this man." On the screen, a photo identification card appeared. It showed a middle-aged man with dark hair fading to white. "This is Ali Nassar. Fifty-seven years old. Iranian national. Born in Tehran to an influential and wealthy family. Studied at the London School of Economics, then Harvard Law School. Went home and got another law degree, this one from the University of Tehran. As a result, he can practice law in both the United States and Iran. He's been involved in international trade negotiations for much of his career. He lives here in New York and is currently an Iranian diplomat to the United Nations. He has full diplomatic immunity."

Luke stroked his chin. He could feel the short stubble growing there. He was starting to get tired. "Let me get this straight. Nassar paid Ken Bryant, presumably for access to the hospital, as well as information about security measures and how to circumvent them."

"Presumably, yes."

"So he's likely running a terrorist cell here in New York, he's an accessory to the theft of hazardous materials and at least four murders, and he can't be prosecuted under American law?"

"It certainly appears that way."

"Okay. You're in the account already, right? Let's see where else he's been sending money."

"It'll take me a little while."

"That's fine. I have an errand to run in the meantime."

Luke glanced at Ed Newsam. Newsam's face was hard, his eyes flat and blank.

"Say, Ed? You feel like taking a ride with me? Maybe we should go pay Mr. Ali Nassar a visit."

Newsam smiled, looking more like a scowl.

"Sounds like fun."

Chapter 10

6:20 a.m.
Congressional Wellness Center - Washington, DC

It was not easy to find.

Jeremy Spencer stood in front of a set of locked gray steel doors in a sub-basement of the Rayburn House Office Building. The doors were tucked away in a corner of the underground parking lot. Few people knew this place existed. Even fewer knew where it was. He felt foolish, but he knocked on the door anyway.

Someone buzzed him in. He pulled back the door, feeling that old familiar sense of uncertainty in his stomach. He knew that the Congressional Gym was off-limits to everyone but the members of the United States Congress. And yet, despite the breach of long-standing protocol, he had been invited inside.

Today was the biggest day of his young life. He had been in Washington for three years, and he was moving up.

Seven years ago, he was an upstate New York trailer park redneck. Then he was a student on a full scholarship at the State University of New York at Binghamton. Rather than kick back and enjoy the free ride, he became president of the campus Republicans and a commentator on the school newspaper. Soon he was posting on Breitbart and Drudge. Now, what seemed like a deep breath later, he was a beat reporter for Newsmax, covering the Capitol.

The gym was not fancy. There were a few cardio trainers, some mirrors, and some free weights on a rack. An old man in sweat pants and a T-shirt, with headphones on, walked on a treadmill. Jeremy entered the quiet locker room. He turned a corner, and in front of him was the man he had come to see.

The man was tall, mid-fifties, with silver hair. He stood at an open locker, so Jeremy saw him in profile. His back was straight, and his large jaw jutted forward. He wore a T-shirt and shorts, both soaked from a work-out. His shoulders, arms, chest, and legs, everything was muscular and defined. He looked like a leader of men.

The man was William Ryan, nine-term Representative from North Carolina, and Speaker of the House. Jeremy knew everything about him. His family was old money. They had owned tobacco plantations since before the Revolution. His great-great grandfather

41

was a United States Senator during Reconstruction. He had graduated first in his class at the Citadel. He was charming, he was gracious, and he wielded power with a sense of confidence and entitlement so complete that few people in his party considered opposing him.

"Mr. Speaker, sir?"

Ryan turned, saw Jeremy there, and flashed a bright smile. His T-shirt was dark blue, with red and white letters. PROUD AMERICAN was all it said. He held out his hand for a shake. "Sorry," he said. "Still a little sweaty."

"No problem, sir."

"Okay," Ryan said. "Enough with the sirs. In private, you call me Bill. If that feels too hard, call me by my title. But I want you to know something. I requested you, and I'm giving you an exclusive. Late this afternoon, I may end up giving a press conference with all the media. I don't know yet. But until then, all day long, my thoughts on this crisis are going to be under your byline. How does that feel?"

"It feels great," Jeremy said. "It's an honor. But why me?"

Ryan lowered his voice. "You're a good kid. I've been following you for a long while. And I want to give you a piece of advice. Totally off the record. After today, you're no longer an attack dog. You're a seasoned journalist. I want you to print what I'm about to say word for word, but starting tomorrow, I want you to become slightly more... nuanced, let's say. Newsmax is great for what it is, but a year from now I see you at the *Washington Post*. That's where we need you, and it will happen. But first, people need to believe you've matured and grown into a so-called fair and balanced, mainstream reporter. Whether you have or not isn't important. It's all about perceptions. Do you understand what I'm telling you?"

"I think I do," Jeremy said. His blood roared in his ears. The words were exciting and terrifying all at once.

"We all need friends in high places," the Speaker said. "Including me. Now fire away."

Jeremy took out his telephone. "Recorder is on... now. Sir, are you aware of the massive theft of radioactive material that took place in New York City overnight?"

"I am more than aware," Ryan said. "Like all Americans, I am deeply concerned. My aides woke me at four a.m. with the news. We are in close contact with the intelligence community, and we

42

are monitoring the situation closely. As you well know, I have been working to pass a Congressional Declaration of War against Iran, which the President and his party have been blocking at every turn. We are in a situation where Iran is occupying our ally, the sovereign nation of Iraq, and our own personnel have to pass through Iranian checkpoints to enter and leave our embassy there. I don't believe there has been a series of events so humiliating since the Iran hostage crisis in 1979."

"Do you believe this theft was carried out by Iran, sir?"

"First off, let's call it what it is. Whether or not a bomb goes off on a subway train, this is a terrorist attack on American soil. At least two security guards were murdered, and the great city of New York is in a state of fear. Second, we don't have enough information yet to pinpoint who the terrorists are. But we know that weakness on the world stage encourages these sorts of attacks. We need to show our true strength, and we need to come together as a country, both right and left, to defend ourselves. I invite the President to join with us."

"What do you think the President should do?"

"At the very least, he needs to declare a nationwide state of emergency. He should issue temporary special powers to law enforcement, until we track these people down. These powers should include warrant-less surveillance, as well as random search and seizure at all train stations, bus terminals, airports, schools, public squares, malls, and other hubs of activity. He also needs to act immediately to safeguard all other stockpiles of radioactive material, everywhere in the United States."

Jeremy stared into Ryan's fierce eyes. The fire there was almost enough to make him turn away.

"And here's the main thing. If the attackers do turn out to be from Iran, or sponsored by Iran, then he either needs to declare war, or step out of the way and let us do it. If this is indeed an Iranian attack, and in the face of that information, the President continues to block our efforts to protect our country and our allies in the Middle East... then what choice does he leave me? I myself will initiate the impeachment proceedings."

Chapter 11

6:43 a.m.
Seventy-Fifth Street near Park Avenue - Manhattan

Luke sat in the back of one of the agency SUVs with Ed Newsam. They were across the quiet, tree-lined street from a fancy high-rise, modern, with glass double doors and a white-gloved doorman at the entrance. As they watched, the doorman held the door open for a thin blonde woman in a white suit, who came out walking a dog. He hated buildings like this.

"Well, there's at least one person in this city who doesn't seem too worried about a terror attack," Luke said.

Ed slumped way back in his seat. He seemed half asleep. With Ed's beige cargo pants and the white T-shirt painted on to his chiseled features, his cue ball head, and his close-cropped beard, he didn't look like anyone's idea of a federal agent. He certainly didn't look like anyone this building would allow in.

As Luke thought about Ali Nassar, he was annoyed at his diplomatic immunity. He hoped that Nassar didn't try to make a big deal about it. Luke had no patience to negotiate.

Luke's phone rang. He glanced at it. He pressed the button.

"Trudy," he said. "How can I help you?"

"Luke, we just got a piece of intel," she said. "The body you and Don found in the hospital."

"Tell me."

"Thirty-one-year-old Ibrahim Abdulraman. Libyan national, born in Tripoli to a very poor family. Little if any formal education. Joined the army at eighteen. Within a short time, he was transferred to Abu Salim prison, where he worked for several years. He has been implicated in human rights violations at the prison, including torture and murder of government political opponents. In March 2011, as the regime began to collapse, he fled the country. He must have seen the writing on the wall. A year later, he turned up in London, working as a bodyguard for a young Saudi prince."

Luke's shoulders slumped. "Hmmm. A Libyan torturer working for a Saudi prince? Who then ends up dead while stealing radioactive materials in New York? Who was this guy, really?"

"He had no history of extremist ties, and doesn't seem to have had strong political beliefs. He was never an elite soldier for any military, and appears not to have undergone any advanced training. It looks to me like he was an opportunist, hired muscle. He disappeared from London ten months ago."

"Okay, give me that name again."

"Ibrahim Abdulraman. And Luke? You need to know something else."

"Tell me."

"I didn't find out this information. It's on the big board in the main room. This guy Myerson at NYPD didn't give me the identifiers when he had them, and they did their own search. They released the information to everybody without even telling us. They're boxing us out."

Luke looked at Ed and rolled his eyes. The last thing he wanted was to get involved in an interagency pissing contest. "All right, well..."

"Listen, Luke. I'm a little worried about you. You're running out of friends here, and I doubt an international incident is going to help. Why don't we pass the bank transfer details up the line, and let Homeland make this call? We can apologize for the hack, say we got overzealous. If you go see that diplomat now, you're putting yourself way out on a limb."

"Trudy, I'm already there."

"Luke—"

"Trudy, I'm hanging up now."

"I'm trying to help you," she said.

After he hung up, he looked at Ed.

"You ready?"

Ed barely moved. He gestured at the building.

"I was born to do this."

*

"Can I help you gentlemen?" the man said as they walked in.

A glittering chandelier hung from the ceiling in the front lobby. To the right, there was a sofa and a couple of designer chairs. There was a long counter along the left wall, with another doorman standing behind it. He had a telephone, a computer, and a bank of video screens. He also had a small TV set showing the news.

The man appeared about forty-five. His eyes were red and veiny, not necessarily bloodshot. His hair was slicked back. He looked like he had just stepped out of the shower. Luke guessed he had worked here so long, he could drink all night and do the job in his sleep. He probably knew by sight every single person who ever came in or out of this place. And he knew that Luke and Ed didn't belong.

"Ali Nassar," Luke said.

The man picked up his telephone. "Mr. Nassar. The penthouse suite. Who may I say is calling?"

Without saying a word, Ed slid over the counter and pressed the handle on the receiver, severing the man's connection. Ed was big and strong like a lion, but when he moved, he was fluid and graceful, like a gazelle.

"You may not say anyone is calling," Luke said. He showed the doorman his badge. Ed did the same. "Federal agents. We need to ask Mr. Nassar a few questions."

"I'm afraid that won't be possible at this moment. Mr. Nassar doesn't accept callers before 8a.m."

"Then why did you pick up the telephone?" Newsam said.

Luke glanced at Ed. That was a snappy answer. Ed didn't seem like the debate team type, but he might have done well.

"You've been watching the news?" Luke said. "I'm sure you've heard about the radioactive waste that's gone missing? We have reason to believe Mr. Nassar may know something about that."

The man stared straight ahead. Luke smiled. He had just poisoned Nassar's well. This doorman was a hub of communication. By tomorrow, every single person in the building was going to know the government had come to question Nassar about his terrorist activities.

"I'm sorry, sir," the man began.

"You don't have to be sorry," Luke said. "All you have to do is grant us access to the penthouse level. If you don't, I will arrest you right now for obstruction of justice, and I will lead you away from here in handcuffs. I'm sure you don't want that, and I don't want to do it. So give us the key or the code or whatever it is, and then go on about your business. Also, know that if you tamper with the elevator once we are inside it, not only will I arrest you for obstruction, I will arrest you as an accessory after the fact to four murders, and the theft of hazardous materials. The judge will set bail at ten million dollars, and you will languish on Rikers Island awaiting trial for the next twelve months. Does that sound appealing to you…" Luke glanced at the man's nameplate.

46

"John?"

*

"Were you really going to arrest that man?" Ed said.

It was a glass elevator, which moved through a round glass tube in the southwest corner of the building. As they rose, the view of the city became breathtaking, then dizzying. Soon, they could catch a vast sweep, the Empire State Building directly across from them, the United Nations building to their left. In the distance, a line of airplanes glinted in the early morning sun on their approach to LaGuardia Airport.

Luke smiled. "Arrest him for what?"

Ed giggled. The elevator kept moving, up and up.

"Man, I'm tired. I was just going to bed when Don called me."

"I know," Luke said. "Me too."

Ed shook his head. "I haven't done this round the clock thing in a while. I don't miss it."

The elevator reached the top floor. A warm tone sounded, and the doors slid open.

They stepped into a wide hallway. The floor was polished stone. Directly in front of them, ten yards ahead, two men stood. They were big men in suits, dark-skinned, perhaps Persian, perhaps some other ethnicity. They were blocking a set of double doors. Luke didn't really care.

"Looks like our doorman called ahead."

One of the men in the hall waved his hand. "No! You must go back. You cannot come here."

"Federal agents," Luke said. He and Ed walked toward the men.

"No! You have no jurisdiction. We refuse your entrance."

"I guess I'm not going to bother showing them the badge," Luke said.

"Yeah," Ed said. "No reason to."

"On my go, okay?"

"Sure."

Luke waited a beat.

"Go."

They were five feet from the men. Luke stepped up to his man and threw the first punch. He was surprised at how slow his own fist seemed to move. The man was five inches taller than Luke. He had the wingspan of a great bird. He blocked the punch easily and grabbed Luke's wrist. He was strong. He pulled Luke closer.

Luke raised a knee to the groin, but the man blocked it with his leg. The man put a big hand to Luke's throat. His fingers clenched like an eagle's talons, digging into the vulnerable flesh.

With his free hand, his left, Luke jabbed him in the eyes. Index and middle fingers, one in each eye. It wasn't a direct hit, but it did the job. The man let go of Luke and stepped backwards. His eyes watered. He blinked and shook his head. Then he smiled.

It was going to be a fight.

Then Newsam was there, sudden, like a ghost. He grabbed the man's head in both hands, and banged it hard against the wall. The violence of it was profound. Some people banged an opponent's head against the wall. Ed Newsam did it like he was trying to break through the wall using the man's head.

Bang!

The man's face winced.

Bang!

His jaw went slack.

Bang!

His eyes rolled.

Luke raised a hand. "Ed! Okay. I think you got him. He's done. Let him down easy. These floors look like marble."

Luke glanced at the other guard. He was already sprawled out on the ground, eyes closed, mouth open, head leaning against the wall. Ed had made short work of them both. Luke hadn't made a dent.

Luke pulled a couple of plastic zip ties from his pocket and kneeled by his man. He bound the man's ankles. He trussed them tight, like a prized pig. Eventually, someone would come and cut these things off. When they did, the guy probably wouldn't have any feeling in his feet for an hour.

Ed was doing the same with his man.

"You're a little rusty, Luke," he said.

"Me? Nah. I'm not even supposed to fight. They hired me for my brains." He could still feel the place on his throat where the man's hand had been. It was going to be sore tomorrow.

Ed shook his head. "I was Delta Force, same as you. I came in two years after the Stanley Combat Outpost operation in Nuristan. People were still talking about it. How they dropped you guys up there and you got overrun. In the morning, only three men were still fighting. You were one of them, right?"

Luke grunted. "I'm not aware of the existence of…"

"Don't bullshit me," Ed said. "Classified or not, I know the story."

Luke had learned to live his life in air-tight compartments. He rarely talked about the forward fire base incident. It took place a lifetime before, in a corner of eastern Afghanistan so remote that just putting some troops on the ground there was supposed to mean something. It was ancient history. His wife didn't even know about it.

But Ed was Delta, so… okay.

"Yeah," he said. "I was there. Bad intelligence put us up there, and it turned into the worst night of my life." He gestured at the two men on the floor.

"It makes this look like an episode of *Happy Days*. We lost nine good men. Just before dawn, we ran out of ammo." Luke shook his head. "It got ugly. Most of our guys were dead by then. And the three of us that made it… I don't know if we ever really came back. Martinez is paralyzed from the waist down. Last I heard, Murphy is homeless, in and out of the VA psychiatric ward."

"And you?"

"I have nightmares about it to this day."

Ed was binding the wrists of his man. "I knew a guy who was on the clean-up detail after they cleared the area. He said they counted 167 bodies on that hill, not including our guys. There were 21 enemy hand-to-hand combat deaths inside the perimeter."

Luke looked at him. "Why are you telling me this?"

Ed shrugged. "You're a little rusty. No shame in admitting that. And you might be smart. And you might be small. But you're also muscle, just like me."

Luke barked laughter. "Okay. I'm rusty. But who you calling small?" He laughed, looking up at Ed's enormous frame.

Ed laughed back. He searched the pockets of the man on the floor. In a few seconds, he found what he was looking for. It was a key card to the digital lock mounted on the wall next to the double doors.

"Shall we go inside?"

"After you," Ed said.

49

Chapter 12

"You can't be in here!" the man shouted. "Out! Get out of my home!"

They were standing in a wide open living area. There was a white baby grand piano in the far corner, near floor to ceiling windows with more spectacular views. Morning light streamed in. Nearby was a modern white sofa and table set, with accent chairs, clustered around a giant flat-panel TV mounted on the wall. On the opposite wall was a massive canvas, ten feet high, with crazy splotches and drips of bright color. Luke knew something about art. He guessed it was a Jackson Pollock.

"Yeah, we've been all through that with the guys out in the hall," Luke said. "We can't be here, and yet... here we are."

The man was not tall. He was thick and stubby, and wearing a white plush robe. He was holding a large rifle and sighting down the barrel at them. It looked to Luke like an old Browning safari gun, probably loading .270 Winchester rounds. That thing would take down a moose at four hundred yards.

Luke moved to the right side of the room, Ed to the left. The man swung the rifle back and forth, unsure who to target.

"Ali Nassar?"

"Who is asking?"

"I'm Luke Stone. That's Ed Newsam. We're federal agents."

Luke and Ed circled the man, moving in closer.

"I am a diplomat attached to the United Nations. You have no jurisdiction here."

"We just want to ask you a couple of questions."

"I've called the police. They will arrive in a few moments."

"In that case, why don't you put the gun down? Listen, it's an old gun. You've got a bolt action on that thing. If you fire it once, you'll never have time to chamber the next round."

"Then I will kill you and let the other one live."

He spun toward Luke. Luke kept moving along the wall. He put his hands up to show he was no threat. He'd had so many guns pointed at him in his life that he had long ago lost track of them all. Still, he didn't feel good about this one. Ali Nassar didn't look like much of a marksman, but if he did manage to get a shot off, it was going to put a big hole in something.

50

"If I were you, I'd kill that big man over there. Because if you kill me, there's no telling what that guy's gonna do. He likes me."

Nassar didn't waver. "No. I will kill you."

Ed was already behind the man and within ten feet. He crossed the distance in a split second. He knocked the barrel of the gun upward, just as Nassar pulled the trigger.

BOOM!

The report was loud in the confines of the apartment. The shot tore a hole through the white plaster of the ceiling.

In one move, Ed snatched the gun away, punched Nassar in the jaw, and guided him to a seat in one of the accent chairs.

"Okay, sit down. Careful, please."

Nassar was jolted by the punch. It took several seconds for his eyes to come back to center. He held a chubby hand to the red welt that was already rising on his jaw.

Ed showed Luke the rifle. "How about this thing?" It was ornate, with a pearl inlaid stock and polished barrel. It had probably been hanging on a wall somewhere a few minutes before.

Luke turned his attention to the man in the chair. He started from the beginning again.

"Ali Nassar?"

The man was pouting. He looked angry in the same way that Luke's son Gunner used to look when he was four years old.

He nodded. "Obviously."

Luke and Ed moved quickly, wasting no time.

"You can't do this to me," Nassar said.

Luke glanced at his watch. It was 7a.m. The cops could show up any minute.

They had him in an office just off the main living room. They had taken away Nassar's robe. They had taken away his slippers. He wore tighty-whitey underwear and nothing else. His large stomach protruded. It was tight like a snare drum. They had him sitting in an armchair, his wrists zip-tied to the arms of the chair, his ankles zip-tied to the legs.

The office had a desk with an old-style tower computer and desktop monitor. The CPU was inside a thick steel box, which itself was anchored to the stone floor. There was no obvious way to open the box, no lock, no door, nothing. To get at the hard drive, a welder would have to cut the box. There wasn't going to be any time for that.

Luke and Ed stood over Nassar.

51

"You have a numbered account at Royal Heritage Bank on Grand Cayman Island," Luke said. "On March 3rd, you made a $250,000 transfer to an account held by a man named Ken Bryant. Ken Bryant was strangled to death sometime last night in an apartment in Harlem."

"I have no idea what you're talking about."

"You are the employer of a man named Ibrahim Abdulraman, who died this morning in a sub-basement of Center Medical Center. He was killed with a gunshot to the head while he was stealing radioactive material."

A flicker of recognition passed across Nassar's face.

"I do not know this man."

Luke took a deep breath. Normally, he would have hours to interview a subject like this. Today he had minutes. That meant he might have to cheat a little.

"Why is your computer bolted to the floor?"

Nassar shrugged. He was beginning to regain his confidence. Luke could almost see it come flooding back. The man believed in himself. He thought he was going to stonewall them.

"There is a great deal of confidential material in there. I have clients who are engaged in business deals involving intellectual property. I am also, as I indicated, a diplomat assigned to the United Nations. I receive communications from time to time that are... how would you call it? Classified. I am in these positions because I am known for my discretion."

"That may be," Luke said. "But I'm going to need you to give me the password so I can take a look for myself."

"I'm afraid that won't be possible."

Behind Nassar, Ed laughed. It sounded like a grunt.

"You might be surprised at what's possible," Luke said. "The fact is, we're going to access that computer. And you're going to give us the password. Now, there's an easy way to do this, and a hard way. The choice is up to you."

"You won't hurt me," Nassar said. "You're already in a great deal of trouble."

Luke glanced at Ed. Ed moved over and kneeled by Nassar's right side. He took Nassar's right hand in his two powerful hands.

Luke and Ed had met for the first time late last night, but they were already starting to work together without verbal communication. It was like they were reading each other's minds. Luke had experienced this before, usually with guys who had been in special operations units like Delta. The relationship usually took longer to develop.

"You play that piano in there?" Luke said.

Nassar nodded. "I'm classically trained. When I was young, I was a concert pianist. I still play a bit for fun."

Luke crouched down so he was at eye level with Nassar.

"In a moment, Ed is going to start breaking your fingers. That'll make it hard to play the piano. And it's going to hurt, probably quite a bit. I'm not sure it's the kind of pain a man like you is accustomed to."

"You won't do it."

"The first time, I'm going to count to three. That will give you a last few seconds to decide what you want to do. Unlike you, we warn people before we hurt them. We don't steal radioactive material and aim to kill millions of innocent people. Hell, you'll be getting off easy compared to what you're doing to the others. But after the first time, there won't be any more warnings. I'll just look at Ed, and he'll break another finger. Do you understand?"

"I will have your job," Nassar said.

"One."

"You are a little man with no power. You will regret ever coming here."

"Two."

"Don't you dare!"

"Three."

Ed broke Nassar's pinky at the second knuckle. He did it quickly, with very little effort. Luke heard the crunch, just before Nassar screamed. The pinky bent out sideways. There was something almost obscene about the angle.

Luke put his hand under Nassar's chin and tilted his head up. Nassar's teeth were gritted. His face was flushed and his breath came in gasps. But his eyes were hard.

"That was just the pinky," Luke said. "The next one is the thumb. Thumbs hurt a lot more than pinkies. Thumbs are more important, too."

"You are animals. I will tell you nothing."

Luke glanced at Ed. Ed's face was hard. He shrugged and broke the thumb. This time it made a loud cracking sound.

Luke stood up and let the man shriek for a moment. The sound was ear-splitting. He could hear it echoing through the apartment, like something from a horror movie. Maybe they should find a hand towel in the kitchen to use as a gag.

He paced the room. He didn't enjoy this sort of thing. It was torture, he understood that. But the man's fingers would heal. If a dirty bomb went off on a subway train, many people would die. The survivors would get sick. No one would ever heal. Weighing the two, the man's fingers and dead people on a train, the decision was easy.

Nassar was crying now. Clear mucus ran from one of his nostrils. He was breathing crazily. It sounded like *huh-huh-huh-huh.*

"Look at me," Luke said.

The man did as he was told. His eyes were no longer hard.

"I see the thumb got your attention. So we'll take the left thumb next. After that, we'll start on the teeth. Ed?"

Ed moved around to the man's left.

"Kahlil Gibran," Nassar gasped.

"What's that? I didn't hear you."

"Kahlil underscore Gibran. It's the password."

"Like the author?" Luke said.

"Yes."

"*And what is it to work with love?*" Ed said, quoting Gibran.

Luke smiled. "*It is to weave the cloth with threads drawn from your own heart, even as if your beloved were to wear that cloth.* We have that on our kitchen wall at home. I love that stuff. I guess we're just three incurable romantics here."

Luke went to the computer and ran his finger across the touchpad. The password box came up. He typed in the words.

Kahlil_Gibran

The desktop screen appeared. The wallpaper was a photo of snow-capped mountains, with yellow and green meadows in the foreground.

"Looks like we're in business. Thanks, Ali."

Luke slipped an external hard drive he had gotten from Swann out of the thigh pocket of his cargo pants. He plugged it into a USB port. The external drive had huge capacity. It should easily swallow this man's entire computer. They could worry later about breaking any encryption.

He started the file transfer. On the screen, an empty horizontal bar appeared. On the left hand side, the bar began to fill up with the color green. Three percent green, four percent, five. Beneath the

54

bar, a blizzard of file names appeared and disappeared as each one was copied to the destination drive.

Eight percent. Nine percent.

Outside in the main room, there was a sudden commotion. The front doors banged open. "Police!" someone screamed. "Drop your weapons! On the ground!"

They moved through the apartment, knocking things over, blasting through doors. It sounded like there were a lot of them. They would be here any second.

"Police! Down! Down! Get down!"

Luke glanced at the horizontal bar. It seemed to be stuck on twelve percent.

Nassar stared up at Luke. His eyes were heavily lidded. Tears streamed from them. His lips trembled. His face was red, and his almost naked body had broken out in sweat. He did not look vindicated or triumphant in any way.

Chapter 13

Eldrick Thomas woke from a dream.

In the dream, he was in a small cabin high in the mountains. The air was clean and cold. He knew he was dreaming because he had never been in a cabin before. There was a stone fireplace with a fire going. The fire was warm and he held his hands to the flames. In the next room he could hear his grandmother's voice. She was singing an old church hymn. She had a beautiful voice.

He opened his eyes to daylight.

He was in a lot of pain. He touched his chest. It was tacky with blood, but the gunshots hadn't killed him. He was sick from radioactivity. He remembered that. He glanced around. He was lying in some mud and was surrounded by thick bushes. To his left was a large body of water, a river or a harbor of some sort. He could hear a highway somewhere close.

Ezatullah had chased him here. But that was... a long time ago. Ezatullah was probably gone by now.

"Come on, man," he croaked. "You gotta move."

It would be easy to just stay here. But if he did that, he was going to die. He didn't want to die. He didn't want to be a jihadi anymore. He just wanted to live. Even if he spent the rest of his life in prison, that would be all right. Prison was okay. He had been in prison a lot. It wasn't as bad as people claimed.

He tried to stand, but he couldn't feel his legs. They were just gone. He rolled onto his stomach. Pain seared through him like a jolt of electricity. He went away to a dark place. Time passed. After a while, he returned. He was still here.

He started to crawl, his hands gripping the dirt and the mud and pulling him along. He dragged himself up a long hill, the hill he had fallen down last night, the hill that had probably saved his life. He was crying from the pain, but he kept going. He didn't give a shit about pain, he was just trying to make it up this hill.

A long time passed. He was lying face down in the mud. The bushes were a little less dense here. He looked around. He was above the river now. The hole in the fence was directly in front of him. He crawled toward it.

56

He got caught on the bottom of the fence while pulling himself through. The pain made him scream.

Two old black men were sitting on white buckets not far away. Eldrick saw them with surreal clarity. He had never seen anyone so clearly before. They had fishing rods, tackle boxes, and a big white bucket. They had a big blue cooler on wheels. They had white paper bags and Styrofoam breakfast platters from McDonald's. Behind them was an old rusty Oldsmobile.

Their lives were paradise.

God, please let me be them.

When he screamed, the men rushed over to him.

"Don't touch me!" he said. "I'm contaminated."

Chapter 14

7:09 a.m.
The White House - Washington, DC

Thomas Hayes, President of the United States, stood in slacks and a dress shirt at the counter in the family kitchen of the White House. He peeled a banana and waited for the coffee to brew. When he was alone, he preferred to quietly come in here and make himself a simple breakfast. He hadn't even put on his tie yet. His feet were bare. And he was tormented with dark thoughts.

These people are eating me alive.

The thought was an unwelcome intruder in his mind, the kind of thing that occurred to him more and more these days. Once upon a time, he had been the most optimistic person he knew. From his earliest days, he had always been the top performer, everywhere he found himself. High school valedictorian, captain of the rowing team, president of the student body. Summa cum laude at Yale, summa cum laude at Stanford. Fulbright Scholar. President of the Pennsylvania State Senate. Governor of Pennsylvania.

He had always believed that he could find the right solution to any problem. He had always believed in the power of his leadership. What's more, he had always believed in the inherent goodness of people. Those things were no longer true. Five years in office had beaten the optimism out of him.

He could handle the long hours. He could handle the various departments and the vast bureaucracy. Until recently, he had been on decent terms with the Pentagon. He could live with the Secret Service around him twenty-four hours a day, intruding on every aspect of his life.

He could even handle the media, and the lowbrow ways they attacked him. He could live with the way they mocked his "country club upbringing," and how he was a "limousine liberal," supposedly lacking the common touch. The problem wasn't the media.

The problem was the House of Representatives. They were immature. They were moronic. They were sadistic. They were a mob of vandals, intent on dismantling him and taking him away, one piece at a time. It was as if the House was a student congress at a junior high school, but one where the children had elected the school's worst juvenile delinquents to office.

The mainstream Republicans were a rampaging horde of medieval barbarians, and the Tea Partiers were bomb-throwing anarchists. Meanwhile, closer to home, the House Minority Leader was eyeing his own future run for the Oval Office, and made it no secret that he was willing to throw the current President under the bus. The Blue Dog Democrats were two-faced traitors—glad-handing country cousins one minute, angry white men railing about Arabs and immigrants and inner-city crime the next. Every morning, Thomas Hayes woke secure in the knowledge that his pool of friends and allies was growing smaller by the hour.

"You with me, Thomas?"

Hayes looked up.

David Halstram, his chief of staff, stood across from him, fully dressed, looking like he always did—awake, energetic, fully alive, in the battle and eager for more. David was 34 years old, and he had only been in the job nine months. Give him time.

"When did the story come out?" Hayes said.

"About twenty minutes ago," David said. "It's already trending on social media, and the TV stations are scrambling to line up guests to debate it on the 8a.m. shows. It has legs. Between Speaker Ryan and the Iran debacle and terrorists in New York, we are in a bad place right now."

Hayes made a fist with his right hand. He had punched exactly two people in his entire life. Both had happened long ago, when he was a kid in school. At this moment, he would like to make Representative Bill Ryan number three.

"We were scheduled to have lunch tomorrow," he said. "I thought that might be a step forward. Not that we would iron out everything in one meeting, but…"

David waved that idea away. "He caught us flat-footed. You have to admit it was a pretty savvy move. He basically calls for your impeachment because you won't start World War Three. And he does it with a friendly reporter in an outlet like Newsmax, where there will be no critical commentary opposing it, no balance in the article itself, the whole thing can get tweeted and blogged by the conservative echo chamber all day, and he doesn't have to say another word. It's already taking on a life of its own. Meanwhile, we have to act like adults. We have to hold a press conference to address the threat of a terror attack, and the possibility it was sponsored by Iran. We have to answer questions about whether

59

there's a groundswell of support for your impeachment, and what we're doing to safeguard radioactive materials across the country."

"What are we doing?"

"About radioactive materials?"

"Yes."

David shrugged. "That depends on what you mean. The policy is that radioactive waste is stored securely, but it isn't always true. Okay, the vast majority of it gets dealt with reasonably well. There are places, like Center Medical Center by the way, that are pretty good about handling it and removing it to secure sites. But even they ship the stuff in containment trucks without security personnel, using public roads. Then there are the hospitals that store the radioactive stuff with the biohazard material. There are even a handful of hospitals, especially in the south, that appear to just throw it all out with the regular garbage. I'm not kidding. And don't get me started on the nukes. Originally, all spent nuclear fuel rods were supposed to be transferred to secure storage facilities, but it never happened. The facilities were never developed. The vast majority of spent fuel rods in the United States, going back to the early 1970s, are stored onsite at the reactors where they were used. And there's evidence to suggest that almost ninety percent of the reactors in the country are leaking, some of them into the neighboring groundwater."

President Hayes stared at his chief of staff. "Why don't I know about these things?"

"Well, technically, you do know about them. You've been briefed, but it's never been a high priority before now."

"When was I briefed?"

"You want me to get you the dates?"

"I want dates, personnel, content of the briefings. Yes."

David's shoulders dropped. He paused. "Thomas, I can do that for you. Then what? Are you going to reread a Nuclear Regulatory Commission briefing from three years ago? I think we've got bigger fish to fry right now. We've got an ongoing crisis in the Middle East, and a drumbeat for war in the media and in the halls of Congress. We've got stolen radioactive material and a potential terrorist attack unfolding in New York City. We're losing the right flank in our own party. They may well go over to the other side en masse by this afternoon. And the second most powerful man in Washington just called for your impeachment. We are standing on an island, and the water is rising all around us. We need to take action, and we need to do it today."

Hayes had never felt so lost. It was all too much. His wife and daughters were on vacation in Hawaii. Good for them. He wished he was there instead of here.

He reached for David Halstram like the man was a life preserver tossed to him in a stormy sea.

"What do we do?"

"We circle the wagons," David said. "Your cabinet is still firm. They have your back. I took the liberty of calling a meeting for later this morning. We're going to get all the big brains in here and build a unified front. Kate Hoelscher at Treasury. Marcus Jones at the State Department. Dave Delliger at Defense can't be here for obvious reasons, but he's going to call in on the secure line. And Susan Hopkins is flying in from the West Coast as we speak."

"Susan," Hayes began.

He couldn't even get past the name. For more than half a decade, he had done everything in his power to distance himself from his running mate and Vice President. The whole situation with Susan, the reality of her, embarrassed him. She had begun life as a fashion model. When she retired from that at age twenty-four, she married a technology billionaire. When her kids reached school age, she launched herself into politics with her husband's money.

People loved her because she was beautiful. She had stayed fit and healthy and enthusiastic into early middle-age. A woman's magazine had recently photographed her out jogging in bright orange yoga pants and a tank top. She was a decent public speaker. She was unstoppable at ribbon-cuttings and cook-offs. Her issues were breast cancer awareness (as if somehow people were not already aware of breast cancer), lifelong exercise, and childhood obesity.

Eleanor Roosevelt she wasn't.

David raised a hand. "I know, I know. You think Susan is lightweight, but you've never given her a chance. She was a two-term Senator from California, Thomas. She is the first female Vice President in the history of the United States. These are not small achievements. She's smart, and she's good with people. Most of all, she is on your side. You need all hands on deck right now, and I believe she can help you."

"What can she possibly do? We're not holding a beauty pageant."

David shrugged. "Your most recent approval rating was 12%. That was taken three days ago, before this latest disaster. You could be in single digits by next week. Your nemesis Bill Ryan isn't doing too much better. He's at 17%, mostly because he's been unable to ram through a declaration of war. He'll probably get a temporary bump from threatening to impeach you."

"Okay. People are unhappy with the government."

David raised a finger. "Mostly true. Except for Susan. This Iran thing hasn't touched her. Her overall rating is 62%, and she's rock solid among all women except the religious right. Liberal and independent men adore her. She's the most popular politician in America, and it's possible she can loan you some of that popularity."

"How?"

"By being here in the White House, working side by side with you on the most pressing issues confronting this country, while we photograph it. By making public appearances with you, and quite literally looking up at you on the podium for leadership, as though you are her hero."

"Jesus, David."

"Dismiss it at your peril, Thomas. This is where we are. I talked to her on the plane just before I walked in here. She understands what's at stake, and she is ready to do these things. She is also ready to take whatever statements we want to make, then stump them on the talking head shows and out in the countryside."

Hayes stroked his chin. "I just have to decide if I'm willing to do this."

David shook his head. "The time for deciding about Susan is long past. We need her, and the truth is you haven't treated her very well. Frankly, you should be glad she's still willing to speak to you."

Chapter 15

7:12 a.m.
Ali Nassar's Apartment - Manhattan

"Down! Stay down!"

Luke was face down on the stone floor of Nassar's office. They had taken the gun from his shoulder holster. A cop's shoe was on the back of his neck. The cop was heavyset, over two hundred pounds. His bulk could snap Luke's neck, if that's what the man decided to do.

With one hand, Luke held his badge above his head. "Federal agents!" he shouted, trying to match the volume of the cops.

"FBI! FBI!" Ed screamed beside him. This was the dangerous moment, when good guys tended to shoot other good guys by mistake.

Someone snatched Luke's badge away. Rough hands pulled his arms behind his back and cuffed him tight. He felt the cold steel bite into his wrists. He made no attempt at resistance. In other rooms of the apartment, cops were still surging through, screaming and shouting.

"Stone, what are you doing?"

Luke recognized the voice. He craned his head around to see who it was. Ron Begley of Homeland Security stood over him, surrounded by uniformed cops. He stared down at Luke with an expression probably calculated to convey disgust, or maybe pity. Begley wore a long trench coat. With his big gut and his coat, he looked like a TV producer's idea of an alcoholic Irish detective. Standing with him was Three-Piece, the NYPD counter-terrorism officer from this morning, the one who didn't like being treated like a servant. It took Luke a moment to remember his name. Myerson. Kurt Myerson.

In a sense, Luke was glad to see them.

"The man in the chair has been operating a terrorist cell located here in New York. We have evidence tying him to the group who stole radioactive materials from Center last night."

Begley crouched near Luke's head. "The man is no longer in the chair. We just cut him loose. I guess you must know that he's a diplomat attached to the Iranian United Nations contingent, right?"

"He's hiding behind diplomatic immunity," Luke said. "That's what allows him to—"

"We're on the verge of war with Iran, Stone. That much is true. But starting the war is outside of your job description." Begley paused. The squat seemed to take his breath away, but he stuck with it.

"Can you even imagine the amount of shit that's about to come down from this? The United States of America is going to have to issue a public apology to Iran. This is because you took it upon yourself to invade a diplomat's home, strip him to his underwear, and subject him to questioning that at first glance appears to meet the international definition of torture. The President is going to choke on his Wheaties when he hears about this. And a rogue agent from a secretive FBI unit no one has ever heard of is going to go around and around in the twenty-four-hour news loop, just in case there was anyone left in the country who thought government spying wasn't out of control."

"Ron, listen."

"I'm done listening to you, Stone. What good does it do? You're out of your mind. Right now, I've got people contacting Don Morris. Since he's the only person you seem to listen to, he's going to personally relieve you of your command. At this point, you're way past worrying about job security. That man in the next room is very likely to press charges, and if he does, I think you're going to see some jail time. No one is going to protect you. No one is going to stand up for you."

Begley lowered his voice. "I'll be honest with you. People are already questioning Don's judgment for bringing you up here. The Special Response Team is Don's pet project, right? The whole thing could get broken up and scattered to the winds faster than I even thought it would. You did me a favor today."

Begley rose from his crouch. "Get the cuffs off these guys," he said to someone nearby. "Then walk them out of here. Straight out to the elevator, then down to the street. No pauses, no chit-chatting, no looking right or left. If they give you any trouble at all, shoot them both in the head."

"Sir?"

Begley shrugged. "That's my little joke."

Two men pulled Luke to his feet. He caught a glimpse of Begley and Myerson leaving the room. The cops uncuffed Luke, then handed him his gun and his badge. Ed Newsam stood just to his left, receiving the same treatment.

Luke glanced at the computer, his external hard drive still attached to it. The horizontal bar was almost entirely green. The file transfer was nearly done. Luke caught Ed's attention. Ed's eyebrows arched for a split second.

"Let's go," a cop said. "Out."

Ed walked first, Luke following. Ed's broad back filled Luke's field of vision. They took two steps out of the room. To the right, Ali Nassar sat in an accent chair. He was back inside his plush white robe, talking on his cell phone. A female cop injected a local anesthetic into his hand, and immediately began setting his fingers in temporary splints. Nassar made exaggerated winces from the pain.

Suddenly Ed dropped to the ground. His head hit the floor with a thud. His eyes rolled back, showing the whites. A violent tremor went through his body. His head and arms jerked. Within a few seconds, a trickle of white foam began to flow from his mouth.

"Oh, Jesus," Luke said. He kneeled by Ed's side.

Begley had turned around. "Get out of there, Stone!"

Luke stood and backed away, his hands in the air. The cops moved in.

"What's the matter with him?" Begley said.

"He has a seizure disorder. He was in a Humvee that took a direct hit in Afghanistan, and he sustained a serious head injury. Slight brain damage, altered brain waves. I'm not really sure. You just have to keep his airways clear. It should pass in a few minutes."

"You guys have an agent in the field that gets seizures?"

"I don't make these decisions, Ron."

"Okay, step back. These guys know what they're doing. They'll take care of it."

Luke took a step back. Then another. A circle of cops kneeled and stood around Ed. A few seconds passed, and Begley returned to his conversation with Myerson. Luke floated backwards slowly, as though he were standing still. He retreated into the office. He darted to the computer, pulled out his hard drive, and dropped it into the thigh pocket of his cargo pants. He picked up a blue pen off the desk.

He turned. A cop stood in the doorway.

Luke held up the pen. "Almost forgot my pen."

The cop gestured out the door. "Come on."

In the main room, Ed had stopped foaming at the mouth. He lay on his side, barely moving. His eyes closed, and then slowly opened. A couple of cops helped him to a sitting position. He blinked his eyes again. He seemed like a person who did not know where he was.

"You okay?" someone said. "You hit your head pretty hard."

Ed took a deep breath. He was clearly embarrassed to be vulnerable in front of all these macho cops. "I don't know, man. The stress. The lack of sleep. This only happens when I'm rundown."

Luke glanced around the room. To his right, Nassar was off the phone. He stood talking to the cop who had splinted his fingers. Luke made a beeline for him.

"Stone!"

Luke held out his left hand to Nassar, as though he wanted to shake hands. Nassar, grim-faced, ignored the gesture. Luke reached out, grabbed him by his robe, and pulled him close. They were face to face, close enough to kiss.

"I know what you did," Luke said. "And I'm going to take you down."

"You will be unemployed by this afternoon," Nassar said. "I will see to it."

Then the cops were everywhere, separating them. A big burly cop put Luke in a full nelson and swung him around.

"Enough!" Begley shouted. "Get these clowns out of here!"

In the elevator down, they were surrounded by cops. It was quiet, everyone watching the numbers descending rapidly.

"You okay?" Luke said.

Ed shrugged. "I'm tired. I haven't had one of these in a couple of years. They wipe me right out. My whole body is still shaking."

On the street, the cops let them go. They walked side by side along the tree-lined street, back to the waiting SUV. Luke didn't speak until they were fifty yards away from the cluster of cops.

"A seizure?" he said. "You've never had a seizure in your life."

Ed smiled. "Seizures are my standby. But to make it work, you have to sell it."

"You sold it, all right. When I heard your head hit the ground, even I wasn't sure. I swear I felt it in my feet."

"Right. Good thing I have a hard head. And I always keep a couple of foaming pills on me to double it down. How'd you do?"

66

Luke shrugged. "I got the hard drive. And that last little bit? The confrontation with Nassar? That's an old pickpocket move." He reached into his cargo pants and pulled out a new smartphone in a white plastic case. "I took the man's cell phone out of his robe."

Chapter 16

7:20 a.m.
Site R - Blue Ridge Summit, Pennsylvania

"Gentlemen, the meeting will now come to order."

Fourteen men had gathered in a quiet chamber deep beneath the surface of the earth. The chamber was mostly bare, with a large conference table in the center, a poured concrete floor, and rounded stone walls and ceiling. LED lights were mounted in recessed ceiling fixtures. Oxygenated air was pumped into the room through several small vents. The complete lack of windows gave the room the sense of being the dead end of a cave, which is exactly what it was. A claustrophobic wouldn't last five minutes in there.

There was no audio or recording equipment in the chamber. An intercom attached to the facility-wide communications system had been removed a decade before. Built into one wall was an old interactive computer projection screen, which at one time would display both a map of the world and a map of the United States. It could be used to plot the location of troop deployments, aircraft, even missile launches. Theoretically, the device still worked, but the theory was untested. No one had turned it on since 1998.

The chamber was behind a double-thick steel door at the end of a metal catwalk. The catwalk teetered three stories above a dim and cavernous command and control room operated around the clock by a skeleton crew of military personnel. This was the deepest part of the sprawling facility, first opened in 1953, and hardened to withstand repeated direct hits from Soviet-era nuclear ballistic missiles.

Ten of the men sat in padded office chairs around the conference table. The men represented various intelligence organizations and branches of the American military, both traditional and special operations. Against one wall, four more men sat in folding chairs. These men represented four broad civilian industries, including coal mining, oil and natural gas, banking and finance, and aerospace and defense.

The group operated in secrecy, even from itself. No one in the room wore identifying markers of any kind. There were no name plates, no indications of rank, and no combat ribbons or medals in evidence. Indeed, there were no uniforms. The military men all wore dress shirts and slacks. Although most of the men knew one another to some degree, two of the men were strangers, and had affiliations that were unclear to the rest of the group.

A silver-haired four-star general, once a commander in the Army Special Forces, stood at the head of the table. He rubbed an old, long-faded scar on his forehead.

"You all know me," he said. "You know my role here. So I'll get right to it. Events have moved forward quickly in the past twenty-four hours, faster than we could have anticipated. In response to these events, and to ensure continuity in the event of a major attack or disruption, we have updated the evacuation plans for all high-level elected and appointed civilian government personnel. The plans are in effect as of 0600 hours, approximately one hour and twenty minutes ago. They will remain in effect until further notice. Please pay attention because they are a departure from previous plans."

He glanced at a single sheet of paper in front of him on the desk.

"During an attack or disruption, President Thomas Hayes and Vice President Susan Hopkins will be evacuated by helicopter to the secure Mount Weather civilian government facility near Bluemont, Virginia. In the event of the death of President Hayes, Vice President Hopkins is number two in the line of succession and will take the Oath of Office at Mount Weather. Civilian cabinet members, including the Secretary of the Treasury, the Secretary of State, and the Secretary of Education, will be evacuated to Mount Weather, either by helicopter or military convoy, depending on circumstances and availability of aircraft. These individuals represent numbers five, six, and eight in the line of succession, respectively."

He glanced at his notes again.

"In an attack, the Speaker of the House of Representatives will be evacuated by helicopter to this facility, Site R. The Speaker is currently William Ryan of North Carolina. In the event of the deaths of both the President and Vice President, Speaker Ryan is number three in the line of succession, and will be administered the Oath of Office here as our guest."

He looked around the room, meeting each set of eyes in turn.

"In the case of an attack or disruption, the Senate President Pro Tem will board the Airborne Communications Command aircraft, codename Nightwatch, at Joint Base Andrews. The aircraft will remain at a cruising altitude of forty thousand feet, with an escort of fighter jets, for the duration of the crisis. In the unlikely event of the deaths of the President, the Vice President, and Speaker of the House, the Senate President is number four in the line of succession, and will take the Oath of Office aboard the airplane. The Senate President Pro Tem is Senator Edward Graves of Kansas, current Chairman of the Congressional Armed Forces Committee."

A hand at the table was raised. The general recognized a man much older than himself, a former Navy admiral, a man so ancient that once upon a time he led a Marine Corps unit through the shit storm at Pusan Reservoir during the start of the Korean War. There was an iconic photograph from the event, which had never been declassified, but which the general had seen. It showed the admiral at nineteen years of age, shirtless in a muddy trench, his eyes wild, his face and upper body painted dark red with the blood of dead communists.

"Yes?"

"You haven't mentioned the Secretary of Defense. Normally, he would board the Airborne Command."

The general shrugged. "The Secretary of Defense will come here."

"Do you anticipate that will cause any problems?"

The general picked up the paper in front of him and began to carefully shred it into long narrow strips. "We don't anticipate," he said, "any problems at all."

Chapter 17

7:40 a.m.

Joint Counter-Terrorism Command Center - Midtown Manhattan

"How the hell did Begley know where we were?"

Luke stood in the doorway of the small room SRT controlled at the command center. Trudy and Swann were here, along with a few guys from the New York office. They stared at him with big doe eyes. Someone in the room was playing innocent. That, more than anything, made Luke see red.

"What?" Trudy said.

"Begley. He turned up at the Iranian's apartment with the police. Nobody called him. He just showed up. How did he do that?"

Swann shook his head. He gestured at his machines. "This stuff is encrypted. I'm on my own network. There's no way Begley's people could break the code in the short time we've been here."

"Trudy?"

She put her hands in the air as if he had pulled a gun. "No way, Luke. Don't even go there. I despise Begley. You think I'm going to rat you out to him?"

Ed slipped by him and into the room. "I think you want to stay focused, man. No sense chasing rabbits into holes in the ground. I don't believe anybody here sold you down the river."

Luke nodded. Ed had a point. "All right." He walked over to Swann and placed the contents of his pockets on Swann's table. "I copied the hard drive from his computer. This is his cell phone. I need you to pull the data from it, then destroy the phone and make it disappear. Do that first."

Swann shrugged. "They'll know anyway. It's an iPhone. They'll trace its location right to us. They probably already have."

"That's fine," Luke said. "But let's not be holding it in our hands when they come looking for it. Okay?"

"Okay, Luke."

Luke glanced at the doorway, half expecting to find Begley standing there. "What have you found in the bank account?"

"A lot. Ali Nassar is a busy man. There are a ton of transactions going on with that account. Money comes in, money

71

goes out. Geneva, Nassau, Tehran, Paris, Washington. A lot of it is anonymous, impossible to trace. Well, not impossible, but it would take more time than we have."

"Anything interesting that we can see?"

"There's this. Over the past six months, Nassar has paid more than eight million dollars to something called the China Aerospace Science and Technology Corporation, which is a company owned and operated by the Chinese government. They build military-grade robotic drones, pretty high-end stuff. The drones can carry air-to-surface missiles and bomb payloads, do surveillance, satellite data links, you name it. And China sells them dirt cheap, to people who probably shouldn't have them. North Korea comes to mind. African dictators. Non-state actors. Their CH-3A drone is similar in mission capability to our MQ-9 Reaper, but has a price tag under a million dollars. You see the picture?"

Luke saw. "Could you put a dirty bomb on board one of those things, and say... crash it into something?"

Swann pursed his lips. "Maybe. But keep in mind it would be hard to fly a large payload drone in an area like Manhattan, with so many tall buildings around. These aren't backyard hobbyist drones. They're big. We're talking about eight to ten meter wingspans, depending on the aircraft. These drones need room to maneuver. They take off, fly, and land like airplanes. They have three-mile ceilings, but if you flew one that high, air traffic control would pick it up on radar in a minute."

Luke tapped the hard drive with Nassar's computer files on it. "See if he's got anything on it in here."

"Before or after I do the phone?"

"Phone first, but move quickly."

Swann sighed. "No one at this job has ever told me to move slowly. Relax, Swann. Take your time and do a thorough job. Those are words I never hear."

"If you want to hear those magic words, I think you better go work in the private sector."

Swann made a face. "What? And make five times the salary? I won't hear of it."

"Luke?" Trudy said.

He turned to her. Her eyes were wide. She held a cell phone out to him.

"It's Don," she said. "For you."

72

Chapter 18

Luke held the phone to his ear and walked out into the hall. The buzz of conversation echoed to him from the main control room. He didn't want to take this call. Part of the reason was he didn't want to go home, not now, not after everything that had happened this morning, not when so much was at stake. But there was more to it than that, a lot more.

Luke remembered the day he met Don. Luke was a twenty-seven-year-old Army captain. He had made captain six months before, and he had just been accepted into Delta Force, the Army's elite special operations and counter-terrorism unit. It was his first day, and Luke was nervous. Don was his new commanding officer. Don was giving him some instructions, as Luke stood at ease in front of Don's desk.

"Yes sir, Colonel," Luke said at one point.

Don sighed heavily. "Son, let's get one thing perfectly clear. You're not in the regular Army anymore. This is Delta Force. We're going to live together, we're going to fight together, and one day we might die together. So you call me Don, or you call me Morris. You can call me fuck-head. I don't care. But two things you don't call me are sir and Colonel. You save that for dealing with the other branches of the military. You understand?"

"Yes…" Luke caught himself before he said sir again. "Don."

Don smiled. "Good. Fuck-head will come in time."

Years later, when Don left Delta to form the Special Response Team, Luke was among his first employees.

"Don?" he said now.

"Luke. How are you holding up?"

"Good. I'm good. How did the briefing go?"

"It hasn't gone yet. We just got off the chopper ten minutes ago. It looks like I'm going to be here a while before anything happens. You know how these things go. Hurry up and wait."

"Right," Luke said.

"I think they're going to put me out to pasture," Don said.

Luke nodded. "Yeah. I know."

"The Director called me a little while ago. Ron Begley's boss at Homeland called him. I heard all about the diplomat."

"Don, I got a little carried away. If you lose SRT over it, I will feel badly about that. But I'm not sorry I did it."

"Relax, son. Why do you think I called you last night? So you could come in and play by the rules? If that's what I wanted, I would have let you sleep. We've got plenty of those guys in government. More than we need. No, I'm not concerned about that. I wouldn't have expected any less from you."

"Begley knew where I was," Luke said. "He came waltzing in with the city cops."

"Of course he did. We've had an internal leak for a while. Six months, maybe more."

Luke ran a hand through his hair. A leak was bad news. He looked up and down the hallway. At the end of the hall, near the water foundations, a small knot of intelligence agents were gathered, murmuring quietly. One of them glanced his way, then covered what he was saying with his hand.

Luke was growing tired. He needed to find his bug-out bag. It was almost time for an eye opener.

"Who is it?" he said.

Don seemed reluctant to speak. "Luke…"

"Come on, Don. I'm a big boy. I can take it."

"I haven't been able to nail it down. But I have my suspicions. The writing's been on the wall about SRT for months. We've got a couple of people who might be looking to jump ship before we go under."

"Name one."

"Trudy Wellington."

"Don…"

Don cut him off. "Right. I know what you're going to say. She's our best intel officer. You're right about that. And you were sleeping with her for a while. I know all about it. So was I. I regret that now. If Margaret ever found out, I think I would die. But it's more than that. I told Trudy some things I shouldn't have. Pillow talk. I assume you know how that goes. I'm afraid I might have made SRT an open book for others to read. Believe me, I feel very foolish."

Luke didn't respond. He couldn't think of a single thing to say.

"Luke, I feel old."

"Don—"

"There may be others," Don said. "Besides Trudy. Things have gotten out that even she couldn't have known. We sweep headquarters for bugs every week. We encrypt all of our communications. Our network is locked down. And still…"

His voice trailed off for a moment.

"SRT has become a viper's nest, Luke. There's no one I can trust anymore. You know what? Part of why I called you last night was so we could ride together again. I wanted it to feel like old times. Maybe we would fly in and put the smack-down on the bad guys one last time."

Luke took a deep breath. He felt like this phone call could go on for another hour, and he might not say another word.

"So here's the part you've been waiting for," Don said. "Know that I have no choice in this whatsoever. It comes from on high."

Don's voice changed. Suddenly, he sounded like he was reading from prepared remarks. "Luke, you're suspected of committing multiple felonies in the course of performing your duties. As such, you are formally relieved of your command at the Special Response Team, effective immediately. You have been placed on administrative suspension pending an investigation into your actions. You may be subpoenaed to testify on your own behalf. Your salary and benefits are intact during this time, but that's conditional and depends on your full cooperation with the investigation."

Luke finally found his voice. "I was on a leave of absence," he said.

"You've been the best investigator, the best counter-terrorism agent, and one of the best soldiers I've ever worked with," Don said. "Please surrender your badge and your service firearm to Trudy. Any personal firearms in your possession will require the use of a private concealed carry license, if you have one."

"I do," Luke said.

"I'm sorry about this, Luke. I really am."

The call ended. Seconds later, Luke couldn't recall how he had signed off. He might have just hung up. He stood in the hallway for a few moments, the phone still pressed to his ear. Then he floated back into the office. He didn't seem to be in control of his legs. His feet were far away.

Trudy was there. She stared at him.

"What did Don say?"

A war of emotions raged inside him, and he needed to get it under control. He didn't want to be that person. Jealous. Angry.

Hurt. But it was him. He was that person. He was a married man, and yet he felt burned by this woman. He had thought there was something between them. The idea that she was just maneuvering... The idea that she was also with Don, maybe even at the same time... Who else was she with? Where was she passing agency secrets? He needed time to digest all of this.

Luke faked a smile, and the smile, all by itself, rallied him a little. It almost felt real. "Don said to hang in there and keep plugging. They want to suspend me, but he's decided to fight it. You know Don. He's a tough old bird."

"He did?" she said. "He decided to fight your suspension?"

Reading her face was almost too easy. She didn't believe a word of it.

"Yeah," Luke said. "He changed his mind about the whole thing while we were talking. He knows it's wrong. Don and I go way back, and he's not just going to let that history drop. So I'm still in the game, at least for now. What do you have for me?"

She hesitated. "Well..."

Luke snapped his fingers. "Trudy, our backs are against the wall. We need to stay sharp. Vans, trucks, what happened with all that?"

She picked up her smartpad. "There's been movement. The local cops tossed the hot dog truck. You were right. The Russian was operating a full-service restaurant for pimps and prostitutes. Hot dogs, Italian sausages, potato chips, Red Bull, Pepsi, Mountain Dew. Also oxycontin, methamphetamine, ecstasy, tranquilizers, diazepam... you name it. They found him in the back of the truck on a mattress with two prostitutes. Don't get too excited. All three of them were asleep with their clothes on."

"What else?"

"The stolen ambulance turned up in the parking lot of a meat warehouse in Newark, New Jersey. The Newark police went in. Ghastly. The warehouse doubled as a storage facility for human organs, mostly livers and kidneys. In a room at the back, they found two sets of lungs being kept alive inside sealed plastic domes. An apparatus forced oxygenated air into the lungs and the lungs were breathing. One cop described it as"—she glanced at her pad—"like giant pink meat wings."

"What about the laundry truck?"

"Nothing so far. We called the company, Dun-Rite Laundry Services. The owner was there. He went outside and counted his trucks. He said they were all accounted for. Twenty-one trucks. He also said they only use step-up vans—he bought an entire fleet of converted bread trucks. They don't use small delivery vans like the one we picked up on video. He invited us to send someone out and take a look."

"Did we?"

She nodded. "An agent is on his way out there now."

"So someone copied his company logo and put it on their own van."

"Yes. And Dun-Rite has a contract at Center. So a van with that logo wouldn't necessarily arouse suspicion if it was parked at the hospital."

"We need to find that van," Luke said.

"We're looking, Luke."

"Look harder."

He walked away from her. The move was abrupt and gave away too much. It told her everything she needed to know. He moved over to Swann's station. Swann was still working three screens simultaneously.

"What do you got, Swann?"

"The plot thickens," Swann said. "Ali Nassar has an entire folder in his computer dedicated to drone technology. He's got PDF files of full-color brochures. He's got hundreds of photographs and bird's-eye point-of-view videos. He's got spreadsheet comparisons of specs, payloads, weaponry, speed, altitude. He's either been buying drones or writing a term paper on them."

"How about the phone?"

Swann nodded. "The phone. His call history has been completely wiped. He's got an app that erases his history automatically as he goes. We can get it back, but we'd have to go to his service provider with a warrant."

"You can't hack them?"

"I could, but what's the point? It would take me twelve hours, and by then whatever's going to happen will have already happened. Anyway, we've got a more pressing matter. Just after midnight last night, Nassar bought a one-way plane ticket to Venezuela. It's for 2:30 afternoon, JFK nonstop to Caracas, executive class. The boarding pass was on his phone. The receipt and an extra copy of the boarding pass were on his computer hard drive."

"Venezuela?" Luke said.

Swann shrugged. "We don't have an extradition treaty with Venezuela."

"Sure, but why not go home to Iran?"

Swann turned around. His eyes goggled behind his glasses. "What if the attack fails? Last I heard, they still have firing squads in Iran. That gives getting fired for incompetence a whole different meaning."

"The point is he's leaving the country," Luke said.

"Yes he is. Today."

"And he bought the ticket right around the time someone was stealing the radioactive materials."

Swann nodded. "My guess is he bought it right after he learned they had successfully pulled off the heist."

"We got him," Luke said. He clapped Swann on the shoulder. "Good work."

Luke turned, and Begley was standing in the doorway. Two large men in suits flanked him. Luke glanced around the room. Ed Newsam stood in a corner by the window, scanning the street below and drinking a bottle of orange juice. Trudy was simultaneously on her pad and her cell phone. A couple of local SRT guys were at desks, pecking away at laptops.

"Stone, why are you here?" Begley said. The room quieted when he spoke. Everyone looked at him.

Luke smiled. "Ron, for once I'm glad to see you. We've had a breakthrough. Ali Nassar made a quarter of a million dollar bank transfer from an offshore account to Ken Bryant, the dead janitor at Center. Nassar has been spending millions of dollars on military-grade robotic drones. And last night, while the thieves were hitting Center, he booked a plane ticket to Venezuela for this afternoon."

Begley shook his head. "None of that impresses me."

"We need to bring him in, Ron. We can't let him leave the country. If he makes it to Venezuela, it's going to be hard to get him back here."

Begley looked at Ed. "A seizure, Newsam? That's funny. I had them check your personnel record. You don't have a seizure disorder. You were never even injured in Afghanistan."

Ed barely moved. He raised his index finger. "Incorrect. I was injured twice. Cracked ribs, a concussion, and a broken arm one time when our Humvee hit an IED and rolled. The guy next to me lost his leg." He shrugged. "Shot in the calf the other time. The bullet ripped a nice chunk out. They had to take meat from my ass to rebuild the muscle. To this day, the ass meat is a different shade of brown from the leg meat. You can see the line where they're attached. You want to look at it?"

Begley said nothing.

"Anyway, those sound like injuries to me. I've got two Purple Hearts, so I guess Uncle Sam agrees."

"I meant you never had a brain injury."

Ed looked out the window again. "That's different."

"Begley, are you listening to me?" Luke said. "We have the man who bankrolled the terror cell. And we know what the delivery system is. It's a drone attack. And that means there's a good chance it won't happen here. There's no room in Manhattan to fly the kind of drones we're talking about. We're looking at a very targeted attack, a dirty bomb delivered to a specific enclosed place by a drone. And the drone will probably fly low, beneath radar detection."

Begley smiled. "You have no idea what you're talking about, Stone. The whole thing would be funny if you weren't so serious about it. We have the intel we need. We know what the targets are. Ibrahim Abdulraman, remember him? The man with no fingerprints? His cousin happens to be in prison in Egypt. They've been interrogating him for over an hour."

"Torturing him," Stone said.

"Not much different from what you two did, is it?"

"It is different," Stone said. "We broke a man's fingers to get a computer password, which was instantly verifiable information."

"There are three possible targets," Begley said. "The chosen target is up to the discretion of the attackers, and depends on conditions at the site of attack. The first target is the below-ground restaurant level of Grand Central Terminal at lunch time. It's always wall-to-wall people. We're treating this as the most likely scenario. We've got men with Geiger counters at every entrance to the terminal."

Luke shook his head. "You can't trust it. They waterboard people in Egypt. You know that. They electrocute them. They hang them from the wrists. They impale them on iron rods. The subjects will say anything to make it stop."

Begley went on, ignoring him. "Second most likely is the PATH train from Hoboken to Manhattan. Those trains are crowded, and they're under the Hudson River for a long time. Same deal. We have Geiger counters in place at all entrances on both sides of the river. The third target involves causing a car accident in the Midtown Tunnel, then setting off the bomb after the traffic backs up. We're checking all cars on both sides of the tunnel, but this is the least likely target. There are really too many variables at play to make an attack feasible. See what I mean, Stone? We've got the whole thing under control."

"You're wrong, Begley. You can't trust intel you get from torture."

"No. You're wrong. You know why I told you the targets? Just so you would see exactly how wrong you are. You've been chasing phantoms. You're out of the loop, and you're under suspension. So go home and let the grown-ups handle this, okay?"

Begley turned to the two men flanking him. "I want this man, and the man over by the window, escorted from the building. Give them three minutes to gather up whatever belongings they have, and then get them out of here."

Begley left, leaving silence in his wake.

Luke stood in the middle of the room, staring at the two men who would escort him out. The men watched him, their faces impassive. Luke glanced around the room. Everyone was looking at him.

Chapter 19

"I guess we're not high priority anymore," Ed Newsam said.

The black SUV sat parked just outside the concrete barriers of the 34th Street heliport, where they had come in nearly five hours before. Morning traffic buzzed past them on FDR Drive. The chopper wasn't on the pad, so they sat in the back seat of the SUV and waited. As they watched, a big white Sikorsky came in over the river, an executive helicopter.

It landed, and a group of outrageous young people climbed out. One man wore tight black jeans and no shirt. His hair was blue and spiked, and the entirety of his scrawny upper body was covered in tattoos. Another very thin man wore an electric blue suit, with a matching bowler hat on top. The three women with them were dressed like prostitutes from two decades before, in mini-skirts, halter tops, and five-inch heels. The whole group were stumbling, laughing, and dropping things. They seemed drunk.

Two very large older men, one white and one black, both completely bald, walked behind the young people. The big men were conventionally dressed in black T-shirts and blue jeans.

They all piled into a white stretch limousine. In a moment, the limo pulled into traffic and disappeared. Their helicopter was already gone. It had touched down, disgorged them, and taken off again.

"You worried?" Luke said.

Newsam was slumped back in the seat, his normal downtime look. "About what?"

Luke shrugged. "I don't know. Losing your job?"

Newsam smiled. "I don't think they'll fire me. It's politics, man. Somebody high up is protecting Ali Nassar, that's all. Listen, we got the right guy. You know it and I know it. If a dirty bomb goes off today, God forbid, heads will roll, but they won't be our heads. A couple of people in the Middle East will die in air strikes. Ali Nassar will turn up smoked in an alleyway in Caracas. None of it will make the newspapers. You and I will quietly get bonuses to help us keep our mouths shut. We'll never understand any of it,

81

mostly because it doesn't make sense. And the person pulling the strings will go on the same as before."

Luke grunted. Cynical talk was widespread among intelligence agents. It wasn't something that Luke usually got into. He had always tried to keep it simple. We were the good guys. Over there were the bad guys. That worldview was the protective veil that he wrapped around himself. He had to admit it was getting a workout this morning.

"And if a bomb doesn't go off?"

Ed's smile broadened. "I guess they'll say we worked over a nice man who's just trying to make the world a better place. What does it matter? You saw those kids come in a minute ago? Rock stars, TV stars, who knows? My little girls would probably know them on sight. You see those big guys with them? Bodyguards. I did a little bit of that when I first came back stateside. The hours are terrible because the kids are like werewolves. They only come out at night. But the money is good. I would do it again, if I had to. A man like me, who doesn't get rusty, has a lot of options in this world."

Luke's phone rang. He glanced at the number. It was Becca.

"It's my wife. I'm going to take this."

"Go ahead," Ed said. "I'm gonna take a nap."

"Hi, babe," Luke said as he hit the green button. He tried to put on a cheerful voice, more for her benefit than his own.

"Luke?"

"Yeah," he said. "Hi."

"Sweetheart, it's good to hear your voice," she said. "I've been worried about you, but I didn't want to call. It's been all over the television. That's your case, right? The stolen nuclear materials?"

"Yes. It is."

"How is it going?"

"I'm off the case as of twenty minutes ago. I'm actually on my way home."

"I'm glad to hear it. Is that good or bad?"

"It's office politics, I guess you'd say. But it'll definitely be nice to get back and put this night behind me. What are you up to?"

"Well, Gunner and I have decided to take the day off and have a play date. He had a lot of trouble getting back to sleep last night, and so did I. We want you here with us, Luke. We want you to quit that silly job once and for all. So I figured Gunner has missed a total of four days of school all year, and I have plenty of personal days, so why not call in as well?"

"Sure," Luke said. "Why not? What are you guys going to do?"

"We were going to go downtown. I wanted to go to the Air and Space Museum, and he wanted to go to the Spy Museum, naturally."

Luke smiled. "Of course."

"But now with this whole terror thing, I don't know. Apparently they're doubling security everywhere, especially tourist sites. It's kind of scary. So I'm letting him sleep in for another hour, while I figure out something else to do. I guess we'll have a late breakfast and then… what? Go to the movies? I doubt the terrorists will attack a movie theater in the suburbs during a matinee. Right?"

Now he almost laughed. "Ah… yeah. I don't think they'd go to all this trouble if that was their target."

"Maybe we'll go to the indoor climbing gym after that, then get some crab cakes for lunch."

"It sounds like a nice day."

"Should we wait for you?" she said.

"I'd love to. But I'm waiting for a helicopter. I can't predict when I'll get home. Anyway, I haven't slept in twenty-four hours."

After they hung up, Luke closed his eyes and allowed himself to doze. Was Ed snoring next to him? It sure sounded like it. Luke imagined his future. The college semester was over now. He had taught a couple of adjunct classes, and he had enjoyed it. He could picture doing more of that, maybe going back for a master's degree, and picking up a full professorship somewhere. A man like him, a former 75th Rangers and Delta Force special operations commando with worldwide deployments and combat experience, a former FBI counter-terrorism agent, there would be a place for him.

He pictured this upcoming summer. He and Becca had a small summer house on Chesapeake Bay. The house had been in her family for generations. It was in a beautiful spot, on a bluff overlooking the water. A rickety staircase hugged the bluff down to their boating and swimming dock. In the summers, Luke kept an old motorboat there. Gunner was an age now where Luke could teach him some things. Maybe Luke would get him out on water skis this year. Maybe he'd teach him how to drive the boat.

Luke created an image in his mind. It was of the three of them, sitting at the table on the back patio at the summer house, as the sun set over the water toward the west. It was the end of a long day of swimming and boating. They were eating steamed mussels, and a bottle of chilled white wine was open on the table. He could see it all in vivid detail. As they all sat and laughed, an air raid siren shattered the quiet. It howled and howled, the shriek of it rising and falling.

He opened his eyes. His phone was ringing.

"Are you going to answer that?" Ed Newsam said. "Or you want me to?"

Luke picked it up without looking to see who was calling.

"Stone," he said.

"Luke, it's Trudy. Listen, I know you lied to me. I know you're suspended. That's an issue for another time."

"Okay."

"Some information just came in. It's up on the big board right now. A man was brought into Baltimore Memorial Hospital in critical condition about forty minutes ago. He has acute radiation poisoning and at least two gunshot wounds in his back. He was found by two fishermen under a highway overpass along the Baltimore waterfront."

"Who is he?"

"His name is Eldrick Thomas. Also known as LT. Also known as Abdul Malik. Twenty-eight-year-old African American. Born and raised in the Brownsville section of Brooklyn. Substantial rap sheet, with multiple prison sentences over the past ten years. Assault, armed robbery, weapons possession. He is one strike away from going inside for a long time."

"All right, he's been a bad boy," Luke said.

"More to the point, he was incarcerated with Ken Bryant on two occasions. Once for five months at Rikers Island, and once for almost two years at Clinton Correctional Center. He was affiliated with the same prison gang as Bryant, the Black Gangster Family. He converted from Christianity to Islam while in prison, and took on the Abdul Malik name. He had three disciplinary infractions where fights broke out because he was proselytizing to other inmates, especially about the need for jihad within the borders of the United States. One of these landed him in solitary confinement for a month."

Luke was becoming alert. He glanced at Ed. Ed had picked up on Luke's body language and sat up straight in his seat.

"Here's the kicker," Trudy said. "Eldrick Thomas and Ken Bryant were friends in prison. Their appearances were so similar that the other inmates, and the guards, often referred to them as the Twins. I'm looking at mug shots of them on Swann's screen. They could be brothers. In fact, if you really wanted to take it that far, they could be mistaken for the same man."

"Why is he in Baltimore?" Luke said.

"No one knows."

"Has anyone spoken to him?"

"Negative. He was unconscious when they brought him in. He's in surgery at this moment, getting the bullets removed. He's under general anesthesia."

"Is he going to live?"

"They expect him to survive surgery. Beyond that is anyone's guess."

"Why are you telling me all this?"

He could feel her smile on the other end of the phone. "I just thought you might want to know."

"Who are my chopper pilots?" Luke said.

"Rachel and Jacob," Trudy said. "I ordered them special for you."

"Friendlies," Luke said.

"That's right."

The call ended. Luke glanced out at the water. A black Bell helicopter was coming in. That was their ride. His bug-out bag was at his feet. He opened it and pawed around for his Dexedrine pills. He found them and held the bottle up for Ed's inspection.

"Dexies," Ed said. "I used to live on them in Afghanistan. Take 'em long enough and they'll kill you, ya know."

Luke nodded.

"I know."

He opened the bottle and carefully poured two capsules into his palm. One half of each capsule was reddish-brown, the other half clear.

"It looks like we have one more shot at this, if we want it. You up for bending a few more rules this morning?"

Ed took a capsule from between Luke's fingers. He popped it in his mouth and swallowed. He glanced at his watch.

"I think I can make some time."

85

Chapter 20

Zero Hour
Between Alive and Dead

He drifted, listening to the sounds.

Music was playing, some kind of quiet classical music with violins and piano. The people gathered around him were talking in mechanical voices.

"Scissors. Scalpel. Suction. I said suction! Can't you clear that out some more?"

"Yes, Doctor."

Then: "He was lucky. An inch to the left and it would have nicked his aorta. He'd have been dead in a couple of minutes."

Eldrick wasn't interested in the doctors, and he wasn't interested in the body on the table. They were all below him now, and he caught a glimpse of the thing the doctors were working so hard to save. It reminded him of a dead dog by the side of the road. It didn't seem like something worth saving.

He turned and through the doorway he saw his grandmother in the next room, standing at the stove and stirring a pot. Something smelled really good.

"LT, get your butt in here."

He ran in there. It was afternoon, the sun was shining outside the windows of their apartment, and he wanted to go down to the park and play some ball. But the smell of dinner was enough to make him shake with anticipation. It was a happy time, before everything had gone so wrong.

"You finish your homework, honey?"

"Yes, Grandma."

"You wouldn't lie to me, would you?"

He smiled.

She turned to him, and her face was serious. "You've done a bad thing, haven't you?"

He wasn't a child after all. He was a grown man, and she was the little old lady she became before breast cancer took her away.

He nodded. "I did a bad thing."

"Can you make it right?"

He shook his head. "I don't know if anything will ever be right again."

9:30 a.m.

Johns Hopkins Bayview Medical Center - Baltimore, Maryland

"Here come a couple of them," Luke said.

He and Ed stood in a hospital corridor, about twenty yards from a door marked PHARMACY. A few moments before, Luke had tried to open it. It was locked. Up the hall, two men in blue scrubs and white lab jackets walked toward them. They were chatting and laughing about something.

There were surveillance cameras every at every corner. It didn't matter. Luke planned to act fast. He was already in trouble. What was a little more?

"Excuse me, guys," Luke said. "Are you men doctors?"

"Yes we are," one said, a fit middle-aged guy in wire frame glasses. "What's the trouble?"

Luke stepped close to the man. His gun was out. He pressed it to the man's stomach, down low, away from the video cameras. He put a friendly hand on the man's shoulder. "Don't say a word, either of you."

Ed stepped in close behind the second man. Luke could see a gun in Ed's hand. He pressed the muzzle hard into the small of the second doctor's back.

"We're not going to hurt you, if you do exactly what I say."

The first doctor, so confident a moment before, was trembling. "I..." he said. He couldn't speak.

"It's okay," Luke said. "Don't talk. I need you to open the door to the pharmacy over there. That's all I need you to do. Open the door and come inside with me for a few minutes."

The second doctor was calmer. He was balding, with thick glasses, more heavyset than the first. "That's fine. If you need drugs, that's fine. We'll get you what you need. But there are security cameras everywhere. You're not going to get very far."

Luke smiled. "We're not going very far."

The men turned as a group and went to the door. The second doctor swiped his key card against the reader and the light turned green. Luke opened the door. Inside the room were numerous locked cabinets.

"What do you need?" the doctor said.

"Ritalin," Luke said. "Two injections."

"Ritalin?" the man said.

"Yes. Quickly now, I don't have a lot of time."

The doctor paused. "Sir, you won't get high from Ritalin. If you have an attention deficit, you can easily get it with a prescription. You don't have to go to all this trouble. There are programs that will help you pay. And anyway, Ritalin isn't the preferred—"

Luke shook his head. "We're not in school anymore, Doc. Let's just assume I know what I'm doing, and you don't know what I'm doing. Okay?"

The doctor shrugged. "Suit yourself." He opened a cabinet, showed Luke the bottle, and prepared the injections. While he worked, Ed placed four plastic zip ties on the counter. He opened a drawer and found a couple of small hand towels and some surgical tape. He put the items next to the zip ties.

The doctor finished preparing the injections, and passed the syringes across the counter.

"Very good," Luke said. "Thank you. Now I need you to do one more thing before we leave."

"All right," the doctor said.

"Take off your clothes," Luke said. "Both of you."

*

Luke and Ed, dressed in surgical gowns and gloves, walked through the crowd of police officers standing outside the door to Eldrick Thomas's room. They paused and put their surgical masks on before they went in.

A yellow and black triangular sign was affixed to the door. DANGER: RISK OF RADIATION.

Beneath that was another sign. It was a series of instructions.

A. Visits limited to 1 hour per day. No pregnant women or persons under age 18 should visit the patient.

B. Visitors should remain at least 6 feet from the patient.

C. Visitors must be protected with gowns, shoe covers, and gloves. Visitors should not handle any items in the room.

D. Visitors must not smoke, eat, or drink while in the patient's room.

A cop touched Luke on the arm. "When can we expect him to wake up?"

Luke gave him the serious doctor face. "You mean *if* he wakes up. We're doing the best we can. You guys just need to wait a little longer."

They went inside. Thomas lay flat on a hospital bed, asleep. Random spots on his face and neck were flushed a deep, dark red. His wrists and ankles were fastened to the metal rails of the bed with plastic flex cuffs. Various machines monitored his vital signs. Two cops in surgical masks and gloves stood in one corner, as far from Thomas as the room would allow.

"Guys, can you please give us a few minutes with the patient?" Ed said.

"We're not supposed to leave the room," one cop said.

Ed said the magic words, the ones that would start a bureaucratic shoving match if the patient weren't radioactive. "I'm sorry, but your presence conflicts with the provision of medical care." Then he smiled. "Anyway, the guy is tied to the bed. He's not going anywhere. Just give us a minute, okay?"

The cops went out, probably happy to get away.

Luke walked straight to Thomas's side. He took the cap off the syringe, turned Thomas's left arm, found the thick vein at the crook of his elbow, and gave him the injection.

"Ritalin, huh?" Ed said.

Luke shrugged. "It brings people right out of general anesthesia. Not exactly FDA approved, but it works like a charm."

He stepped back. "Shouldn't be long."

A minute passed, then two minutes. Halfway through the third minute, Luke thought he saw a slight flutter in the eyelids.

"Eldrick," he said. "Wake up."

Eldrick's eyes slowly opened. He blinked. He looked very tired. He looked like he was a hundred years old.

"My chest hurts," he said, his voice rising just above a whisper. He glanced slowly around without moving his head. "Where am I?"

Luke shook his head. "It doesn't matter where you are. You were in New York last night. You stole radioactive materials from Center Medical Center. You were working with Ken Bryant and Ibrahim Abdulraman. They were both murdered. So were two security guards."

Memory flooded into the man's face. He barely moved a muscle. He seemed so weak that he could die any minute. But his eyes were hard. "Cops?" he said.

Luke nodded. "We need to know where and when the bomb goes off."

Eldrick Thomas looked at Ed. He made a gesture with his head toward Luke. "Hey, bro. Get this white devil pig out of here."

He closed his eyes slowly, then opened them again. "After that, I'll tell you whatever I know."

*

Luke waited in the hall, fifty yards down from the wall of cops. It wasn't long before Ed came out. He walked quickly.

"Come on, man. Let's go."

Luke walked fast, keeping up with Ed's pace. "What's up?"

"I think he had a heart attack," Ed said. "Maybe the Ritalin was too much for him. I don't know. I hit the alarm before I left."

"Did he say anything?"

"Yeah. He did."

"What was it?"

"I don't know if I can believe it."

Luke stopped. Ed stopped, too.

"We need to keep walking," Ed said.

Luke shook his head. "What's the target?"

Above their heads, the hospital intercom came on. A woman's voice, calm, mechanical, almost robotic. *Code Blue, Code Blue. Third Floor, Room 318. Third Floor, Room 318. Code Blue...* Frantic doctors and staff ran past them in the halls, bumping shoulders.

"It's timed for the start of Ramadan in Iran. 8:24 p.m., which is 10:54 a.m. here." He looked at his watch. "Just over one hour from now."

"Where?" Luke demanded.

Ed stared back grimly. For the first time, Luke saw despair on Ed's face.

"The White House."

Chapter 21

10:01 a.m.
The skies between Baltimore and Washington DC

The pilots were bad-asses.

The chopper flew low and fast. The landscape buzzed by below them, almost close enough to touch. Luke barely noticed. He shouted into the telephone. He kept losing the call. The hand-off process from one cell tower to the next was iffy at over a hundred miles per hour.

"We need to evacuate the White House," he said. "Trudy! Do you hear me?"

Her voice cut through the static. "Luke, there's a warrant for your arrest. You and Ed. It just came through."

"Why? Because of the doctors? We didn't hurt them."

There was a burst of static. The call dropped.

"Trudy? Trudy! Shit!"

He looked at Ed.

"He told me they were in the Dun-Rite Laundry van," Ed said. "The signs were magnetic decals. They took them off in Baltimore, and changed the license plates. There may be surveillance cameras near where Thomas was found. They might pick up the trail on the van's location that way."

Luke's phone rang. He picked it up.

"Trudy."

"Luke, before you say another thing, let me speak. Eldrick Thomas is dead. He had a massive heart attack. You and Ed are on video surveillance. It's clear in the video that you gave Thomas a shot of some kind."

"Ritalin, to wake him up," Luke said.

"Ed leaned in close just before Thomas died."

"Trudy, Thomas was giving Ed the information. Do you understand? Eldrick Thomas is not the issue right now. The attack is planned for the White House. All the evidence points to a drone attack. They were in the Dun-Rite Laundry van. They changed the markings. We need to find the van and we need to get everyone out of the White House. *Now*."

Another burst of static came in.

91

"They're not going to… Luke? Luke?"

"I'm here."

"They're watching Grand Central and the Hoboken PATH station. They closed the Midtown Tunnel. I spoke with Ron Begley. They don't believe it's the White House. They think you killed Eldrick Thomas. The arrest warrant is for murder."

"What? Why would I murder Eldrick Thomas?"

The phone cut out again.

Luke looked at Ed. "We'll get the pilots to radio it in."

Ed shook his head. "No good. Nobody's going to believe us. And if we tell the pilots to radio it in, everybody's going to know where we are. No. We have to go in ourselves. And we have to go in stealth."

Luke went up to the cockpit and poked his head inside.

He knew these two—Rachel and Jacob. They were old friends of his, and they'd flown together for years. Both of them were former U.S. Army 160th Special Operations Aviation Regiment. Luke and Ed were used to flying with people like this. The 160th SOAR were the Delta Force of helicopter pilots.

Rachel was as tough as they came. You don't join an elite group of Army special operations pilots as a woman. You brawl your way in. Which was perfect for Rachel—her off-work hobby was cage fighting. Meanwhile, Jacob was as steady as a rock. His calm under fire was legendary, almost surreal. His hobby was mountaintop meditation retreats. The two of them might know Luke was suspended. They might even know there was a warrant for his arrest. But they also knew Luke was Delta, and they weren't the types to ask too many questions.

"How close can you get us to the White House?" Luke said.

"You got a lunch date?" Rachel said.

Luke shrugged. "Come on."

"South Capitol Street heliport," Jacob said. "It's a DC Metro Police pad, closed to all other traffic, but I know them. I can squeeze us in there. They're about three miles from the White House."

"I need an SRT car waiting for us," Luke said. "No driver, just the car. Okay?"

"Got it," Rachel said. She glanced back at him.

"I'll tell you all about it later," he said.

Luke went back to the hold. Ed stood by the open cargo door.

Luke shouted at him. "We got a helipad three miles from the White House, and we'll have a car there that we drive."

Ed nodded. "That sounds right."

The phone rang again. Luke looked at the caller ID. He didn't want to talk about arrest warrants anymore, or about who believed what. This time, when he answered, he barely spoke to her.

"Trudy, put Mark Swann on the phone."

Chapter 22

"We're never going to make it."

Luke drove the company SUV toward the White House through mid-morning traffic. It was stop and go. They were running out of time.

The phone was plastered to his ear. It rang and rang. Finally, it picked up. For the third or fourth time in a row, he got her voicemail. She had told him that she and Gunner planned on going to the movies.

Her voice was vibrant and bright. He pictured her: beautiful, smiling, optimistic, and energetic. "Hi, this is Becca. I can't answer your call right now. Please leave a message after the tone, and I'll call you back as soon as I can."

"Becca!" he said. He took a breath. He didn't want to alarm her. "I need you to do something for me. I don't have time to explain. When you get this message, drive straight to the country house. Don't go home. Don't stop to pick up anything. Just get on the highway and go. If you need anything, you can always get it over there. I'll meet you there as soon as I can." He paused. "I love you both so much. Do this for me. Don't hesitate. Just go now, as soon as you hear this."

He hung up. Next to him, Ed sat ramrod straight. A thick vein stuck out on Ed's forehead. He was sweating.

"We gotta get around this traffic somehow," Luke said.

Ed reached into the glove compartment and pulled out an LED siren light. He mounted it on the dashboard, turned it on, and then hit the siren switch. Outside the car, the shriek of the siren was impossibly loud.

WAH-WAH-WAH-WAH-WAH.

"Go!" Ed said.

Luke pulled into oncoming traffic and laid on the horn. He tapped the accelerator, raced to the next light, then veered back into his own lane. He stomped on it now and the car took off like a missile.

"Go, man! Go!" Ed screamed.

Up ahead, cars at the next light pulled off to the right like a herd of animals. Luke blew through the intersection, going seventy miles per hour.

The phone rang.

"Swann?"

The voice had a subtle twang. "Luke, it's Don Morris."

"Don, I have to keep this line clear."

"Son, what are you doing? They told me you killed a man in a hospital in Baltimore."

Luke shook his head. "I didn't kill anyone. They're going to attack the White House. That's what this has been all along."

"That's not true, Luke. In the past ten minutes, they arrested two Arab kids, one at Grand Central and one in Hoboken. They were both carrying pressure cooker bombs in knapsacks. NSA is tracking down their identities and affiliations right now."

"Pressure cookers aren't dirty bombs!" Luke said. He heard the shrillness in his own voice. He sounded like a crazy person. He had barely slept in twenty-four hours. He knew that. His perceptions might be off. But this far off? Could it be? He glanced at the speedometer. They were going eighty-five miles an hour on city streets.

"The pressure cookers were cat's paws," Don said. "The bombs weren't even operational. The bad guys sent the kids in to see what the response would be. Now they know the targets are compromised."

Luke tried to slow his voice down, so that he and Don could have a rational conversation. He wanted to make Don understand what Luke thought was painfully clear. "Don, we talked to Eldrick Thomas. He was one of the thieves. We didn't kill him. He died of radiation poisoning. He told us the target is the White House."

"Luke, I know who he was. The intel we have is that besides everything else, Eldrick Thomas was a professional conman. He was playing you, that's all. That's what conmen do. They play people right up to the end. He tells you it's the White House. Security gets beefed up, and people think he's cooperating. If he lives, maybe he gets a better plea deal. The man was in and out of prison his entire life. But he knows the target is the White House. Do you think the people behind this would trust a low-level hoodlum with that kind of information?"

Luke didn't say a word.

95

"You can still call this off," Don said. "Come back to headquarters. I'll meet you there. If you say you didn't kill him, I believe you. I'll do whatever I can to protect you. We'll get a psychiatrist in. He'll say you had a PTSD episode. A psychotic break. Your combat record will support that. You might have to do a few days in-patient stay, but you will get out of this."

Luke couldn't believe the things he was hearing.

"I have to keep this line clear," he said.

"You're all the way out there now, Luke. If you go much further, you're going to be by yourself."

A call was coming through.

"Don, I have to run."

"Luke! Don't you dare hang up this phone."

Ahead was the gate to the White House. Ed turned off the bubble light and the siren. Luke slowed the SUV. He held his phone out so he could see the screen. The person trying to call through was Swann.

Luke toggled the call in. "Swann. Did you get us the Secret Service clearance?"

Swann was hesitant. "I think so."

"You *think* so?"

"You both have murder warrants, Luke. Give me a break. Yeah, it looks like you have Yankee White clearance, Category One. You're cleared to work directly with the President and Vice President. But it's fake. In thirty seconds, the Secret Service database could cross-reference the crime database and kick you out again. Someone could double-check it and find that the clearance was approved in the past five minutes. I can't guarantee anything. I'd say it's fifty-fifty at best. How soon will you be there?"

"We're there now. We're pulling into the driveway."

"Well, all right then. I guess we're about to see how good I am."

Luke hung up. He toggled back to Don.

"Don?"

The line was dead.

The guardhouse was up ahead. It was protected by concrete barriers. There was both a STOP sign and a DO NOT ENTER sign. Four men in suits loitered by the entrance. NOTICE, another sign read. RESTRICTED AREA. 100% ID CHECK.

Luke turned to Ed. Ed's face was slick and shiny with sweat.

"Ready?" Luke said.

96

"Ready for anything."

Luke felt a trickle of sweat inside his shirt. They were about to bluff their way into the White House. They would get as far as they could on fake security clearances, then bull through the rest of the way. They were going to try to override the entire Secret Service security apparatus and evacuate the President on their own orders, two men from a different agency, and who had been suspended from duty hours ago. And all of this was on the say-so of a dead career criminal who may or may not have been lying.

For a brief moment, Luke could almost see Don's point. From the outside, this must seem like a crazy idea.

A guard appeared at Luke's left elbow. Luke had driven up to the gatehouse on autopilot. Numb, he handed the man his identification along with Ed's. The man went away, but came back a minute later.

"I'm sorry," he said. "These are both rejected. You don't have clearance."

"Maybe it's a sign," Ed said.

"Run them again, please," Luke said.

Ahead of them, the gate opened. The security guard reappeared.

"Sorry about that," he said. "Must be a glitch in the system."

Luke drove slowly through the White House gate.

*

Swann was good. He was very, very good.

They entered the West Wing, passed through an identification check, then moved quickly down a hall lined with Greek-style columns. Their footsteps echoed on the marble floor. They turned right, and the entrance to the Oval Office was just ahead.

Two Secret Service men stood outside the door.

"Hi, fellas," one of them said. "That's far enough."

Luke raised his badge. "FBI. We have Yankee White security clearance. We need to talk to President Hayes."

"The President is in a meeting."

"He'll want to hear what we have to say."

The guy shook his head. "We weren't told anything about this. You'll have to wait while we check it out."

Ed didn't hesitate. He punched the first man in the throat, then spun and caught the second man across the jaw with an elbow. The

97

first man went to the floor clutching at his throat. Ed crouched, slammed his head against the stone floor, then was back up again. The second man was reaching for his gun when Ed punched him in the face. The man was unconscious before he hit the floor.

Luke and Ed burst through the door to the Oval Office.

Across the room from them, the President was there, and so was the Vice President. They were poring over what looked like a giant map draped on the President's desk. Behind them, three tall windows looked out on the Rose Garden. A man was taking photographs. A young man with thinning hair stood nearby. Half a dozen other people were in the room.

When Luke and Ed came in, the President stood up straight. He was very tall.

Four Secret Service agents drew their guns.

"Freeze! On the ground!"

In the middle of the room, the cream-colored carpet had a round Seal of the President. Luke stepped into it. He raised his hands.

"FBI," he said. "I have an important message for the President."

He was tackled from behind. In a second, his cheek was against the carpet. His arms were twisted painfully behind him. A man's foot was on his face. A few feet away, Ed was in the same position.

"FBI!" Luke screamed. "Federal agents!"

They had his badge and ID. They took his gun from its holster. He felt them pull up his pants legs and take away his extra gun and his knife.

"What is going on here?" the President said.

Three men held Luke down. A heavy arm was against his neck. It hurt to move. It was hard to speak. "Sir. I'm Agent Stone with the FBI Special Response Team. This is Agent Newsam. You are in danger. We have reliable intelligence suggesting there is a plot to attack the White House with a dirty bomb. That attack is scheduled to coincide with the start of Ramadan in Tehran, less than fifteen minutes from now."

President Hayes moved closer. He towered over Luke.

"It isn't true," a female voice said.

Luke craned his neck enough to see Susan Hopkins, the Vice President. She was very pretty, like a veteran television announcer. She wore a gray pin-striped suit and her blonde hair in a short bob.

"We just received a report that the threat was contained to New York City, and has been neutralized."

"There isn't enough time to tell you everything," Luke said. "We have to evacuate the entire building, and we're almost out of time. If we're wrong, that's very embarrassing. The White House had a bomb scare and was evacuated for no reason. But if you're wrong… I don't want to think about that."

Everyone looked at the President. He was a man accustomed to making difficult decisions. He paused for all of seven seconds.

"Get everyone out," he said. "Initiate evacuation protocols for all staff. Ten minutes from now, I don't want a single person inside this building."

Chapter 23

10:50 a.m.
Beneath the White House

They rode an elevator deep into the bowels of the earth. Ten people were on board: the President, the Vice President, the President's young chief of staff, Ed and Luke, and five Secret Service agents. One of the agents carried a black leather satchel, secured to his wrist with a metal clasp. Somewhere above them, an alarm was going off.

"How sure of this are you?" the President said.

Luke's face was rug burned. The back and side of his neck was sore. He could feel a welt rising on his jaw. His mouth was bleeding.

"I'm not sure of anything, sir."

"If you're wrong, you're going to be in a lot of trouble."

"Sir, I think you may not appreciate the full extent of that trouble."

The elevator doors opened. They exited into to a cavernous lighted chamber, disappearing into the distance. Two black limousines were lined up just outside the elevator. Luke found himself in the second car, with Ed, the Vice President, and two Secret Service agents.

Ed's face was a mess. His right eye was swollen half shut. The lid was cut and bleeding.

The car sped through the tunnel, yellow lights zooming overhead.

"I, for one, hope that you're wrong," Susan Hopkins said.

"So do I," Luke said. "More than anything."

At the far end of the tunnel, they took another elevator to the surface. They came out at a helipad. A big gray Sikorsky was on the pad, its rotors already turning. They climbed aboard and the helicopter took off.

As they rose, Luke saw that they were rising from a wooded area about half a mile from the White House. They hovered at a distance. The President stared at the building. Luke did, too.

"If something were going to happen, it would be happening right around now," the President said. "Isn't that right?"

Luke glanced at his watch. "It's 10:53."

"A dirty bomb tends to be small," Ed said. "We might not see anything from this distance."

"It may be a drone attack," Luke said. "If so, we might—"

Suddenly, his words were cut off as the Oval Office exploded.

A flash of red and yellow light appeared behind the tall windows. The glass shattered. The walls seemed to bulge, then blew outward onto the lawn.

Another, larger explosion destroyed the West Wing.

As they watched, the roof caved in.

A series of explosions walked down the Colonnade toward the main Residence in the center. Everyone watched the flames consume one of the enduring symbols of the United States. A huge explosion, the largest one yet, ripped through the Residence. A huge chunk of masonry flew upwards, spinning end over end. Luke watched its arc as it disintegrated in the air.

Suddenly the helicopter shuddered. It dropped sickeningly before the pilots caught it, and it started its ascent again.

"It's a shockwave," Luke said. "We're okay."

The helicopter turned and headed west. They all flew in silence, exchanging dazed looks. Luke looked at Ed's damaged face. He looked like a boxer who had just lost a fight. There was nothing left to say.

Behind them, the White House burned.

PART TWO

Chapter 24

11:15 a.m.

Mount Weather Emergency Operations Center - Bluemont, Virginia

"Weapons?" a man said to Luke.

Twenty Secret Service men were on the pad when the helicopter came down. They operated smoothly and efficiently, separating Luke and Ed from the main group, and hustling the President and Vice President toward the gaping maw of the open tunnel. The entrance was two stories high, framed in corrugated metal.

Overhead, helicopter gun ships filled the air like dragonflies. The President's helicopter had flown out here with a ten-chopper escort.

Luke and Ed stood isolated on the tarmac, about twenty feet apart. They were fenced in by barbed wire. The Secret Service searched them roughly. Two men held Luke's arms while others reached inside his clothes. His clothes rippled with the wind from helicopter rotor blades.

"Weapons?" the man said again.

Luke was in a fog. The White House had blown up. The Oval Office, then the entire West Wing, the Colonnade, all the way to the Presidential Residence. He had expected... something. But not the thing he had witnessed. He was too tired right now to make sense of it.

It occurred to him that he hadn't reached Becca. She would be worried about him. He hoped she had gotten out to the country house. It was over on the Maryland Eastern Shore. It was quiet over there, safe. Washington, DC, and its suburbs were going to be chaos for a while.

"I need to call my wife," he said.

The Secret Service man in front of him gave Luke a sharp jab in the stomach. It startled Luke into the present moment. He looked into the man's hard eyes.

"Are you hiding any weapons?" the man said again.

"I don't know. I was searched in the Oval Office. I think they got them all."

"Who are you?"

103

That was an easy one. "Agent Luke Stone, FBI Special Response Team."

"Where's your identification?"

"I don't know. Ask your buddies. They took everything. Listen, I really need to make a call, and I don't have my phone."

"You can make a call after you answer our questions."

Luke glanced around. It was bright and sunny, but his exhaustion, and the events of the day, conspired to give the sky a dark cast. Above their heads, the choppers made shadows on the ground like circling vultures. Over by the entrance to the facility, the President had turned around and was walking back this way. He was easy to spot among the crowd because he was so tall.

The Secret Service man snapped his fingers in front of Luke's face. "Are you listening to me?"

Luke shook his head. "Sorry. Listen, guys. I've had a long day. Just let me call my wife, and then I'll tell you whatever I know."

The man slapped him. It was a sharp, stinging slap, meant to get his attention. It did that and more. Luke struggled to get his arms free. A second later, he was on the ground, face down against the rough surface of the black tarmac. Two men held him. To his left, they had put Ed on the ground as well.

From his worm's-eye point of view, Luke watched the President approach, walking fast, surrounded on all sides, left, right, front, and back, by Secret Service agents. He stopped ten feet away.

"Gentlemen!" he said in a commanding tone. "Let those men up. They're with me."

Luke soon stood inside the entryway to the Mount Weather facility. A crowd of people, many of them military in formal blue uniforms, swirled around him. The entrance was literally a giant tunnel drilled into the granite face of the mountain. The ceiling was arched stone three stories above them. The President had disappeared.

Luke raised his phone again.

"Hi, this is Becca. I can't answer your call right now. Please leave a message after the tone, and I'll call you back as soon as I can."

Luke wanted to smash the phone on the cement floor.

"Damn it! Why doesn't she pick up?"

He already knew the reason, of course. The phone wasn't even ringing—it was going straight to voice mail. The cell towers were overwhelmed. All across the region, millions of people were trying to make calls at the same time.

Ed was standing nearby, also trying his phone.

"You get anything?" Luke said.

Ed shook his head.

Luke went into boss mode. "Listen, they're going to take me downstairs in a minute. I need you to get in contact with Trudy and Swann somehow. We need to get our hands on Ali Nassar. If the NYPD won't arrest him, we'll have to put our own guys on him. Detain him, disappear him, and take him to a safe house. Under no circumstances can we let him get out of the country. And we can't expect any help from Ron Begley."

Ed nodded. "All right. Should I contact Don?"

Luke shrugged. "Yeah, if you can get him."

"What should I tell him?"

Luke didn't know how to answer that question. Don was one of his mentors, but he was more than that. Don had been like a father to him. Yet Don had also suspended him today, and Don had recommended that Luke go for an in-patient psychiatric stay. And on both counts, Don had been wrong.

Two large doors slid open in the walls about twenty feet away. The group started moving for the doors, and Luke moved with them.

"Tell him we're alive, and so is the President."

"What then?" Ed said.

Luke shrugged. "If you get all that done, find yourself a bite to eat." He gestured at the elevator. "This shouldn't take long."

The freight elevator was large, and two stories high. Twenty people climbed aboard. The elevator moved slowly down and down, chiseled rock flowing smoothly upward just outside of its metal gates. A yellow sign on the gate read, in giant black letters: CAUTION—KEEP HANDS INSIDE. The elevator descended for several moments, sinking deeper and deeper into below the surface.

Luke glanced at the people around him. Men in suits. Men in uniform. Everyone was clean, everyone was smartly dressed, and everyone was electric with fear and determination. In comparison, Luke felt ragged, dirty, and worn out.

The elevator emptied them into a narrow hallway. They moved along it in a herd. It opened into a brightly lit situation room. Flat-panel video displays covered two walls. Each display could hold a dozen or more open windows, each with its own imagery or information. The displays were on, and a small team of technicians were at a touch pad console, loading images and video captures onto the screens. One video was of the White House burning, surrounded by fire trucks. Several were of mosques burning. A few were of scenes of riotous street celebrations, people chanting and bearded men firing AK-47s into the air.

One quick image caught Luke's eye. It was a few seconds of video at the front entrance to the West Wing. A dark, fast-moving blur appeared from the top right corner of the screen, and crashed through the doors of the lobby. An instant later, an explosion blew the front of the lobby out onto the lawn and the driveway turnaround. The video repeated itself again and again in slow motion. Even slowed down, it was impossible to tell what the blurry object was.

A young man in a tan suit took Luke by the elbow and guided him further into the room. Ahead, a dozen people sat in high-backed chairs at a long table. Another thirty or so people—assistants, staff people, strategists, God alone knew who all these people were—stood along the walls. The President stood at the head of the table. The Vice President, a head shorter, stood beside him.

"Here he is," President Thomas Hayes said, gesturing at Luke with a flat, open palm. His teeth were bright white and perfect. For a second, he reminded Luke of a game show host inviting the studio audience to take a look behind Door #3.

"What is your name again?" the President said.

Fifty faces turned to look at Luke. With all eyes on him, he felt even shabbier than before. "Stone," he said. "I'm Luke Stone, FBI Special Response Team."

The President nodded. "This is the man who saved our lives."

Luke sat at the conference table. He sank back into the soft leather of the chair. An assistant placed a plastic-wrapped apple Danish in front of him. Someone else brought him coffee in a Styrofoam cup. Luke poured a packet of non-dairy creamer into the coffee. The light from the overhead fluorescents made the coffee appear green.

The facility was designed to survive a nuclear war. The food they served was also designed for that purpose.

A lieutenant colonel in Army dress blues stood in front of the center display screen. He indicated images on the screen with a red laser pointer. "At approximately 10:54 a.m. Eastern time, the White House was attacked with multiple explosive devices, including at

106

least one radiological dispersion device, containing as of yet unknown radioactive agents. The West Wing, including the Oval Office, was almost completely destroyed. The Colonnade and the Presidential Residence suffered severe damage. The East Wing was not attacked, but has suffered ancillary damage from the force of the explosions, as well as from smoke and water."

"Any word about casualties?" the President said.

The lieutenant colonel nodded. "Seventeen confirmed deaths as of now. Forty-three injured, a few of those in critical condition. Eight people missing. In the initial response, at least two dozen firefighters and other emergency personnel were likely exposed to radiation. We won't know the extent of that for a few days. Since approximately 11:24 a.m., all fire and emergency personnel in the vicinity are required to wear Level One hazardous material protective suits. As you can imagine, this has considerably slowed the efforts to put out the fires and search for possible survivors."

There was almost no sound in the room. The man coughed quietly, then went on.

"The attack has created widespread panic. We've established a radiation containment zone with a half-mile radius, and the White House at its center. Only authorized personnel are permitted inside. Even though there is currently no measurable radiation at the borders of the zone, basically everyone in the city has tried to evacuate at the same time. Meanwhile, the Metro rail system throughout Washington, DC, and surrounding areas has been shut down. Main streets and larger arteries in the city are closed to all but emergency traffic, creating massive traffic jams on secondary roads.

"These effects have rippled outwards through the region. Amtrak service in the Washington to Boston corridor has been suspended, and all major airports in the region are closed pending thorough security screenings. Further, mosques have been attacked in more than a dozen cities, and new reports of mosque attacks come in by the minute. It seems that many Americans believe the attack was carried out by Muslims, so people are burning mosques and attacking Muslims in retaliation."

"It *was* Muslims," Luke said.

The man paused. "I'm sorry?"

Luke shrugged. "It was Muslims. The people who did it."

The speaker glanced at the President, who simply nodded.

"Can you clarify that statement, Agent Stone?"

"It's as clear as I can make it," Luke said. "My unit was brought in late last night to investigate the theft of radioactive material from a hospital in New York City. I'm sure you heard all about the theft on the news this morning. We were able to track it to a terrorist cell made up of at least two Americans and one Libyan, and organized by an Iranian diplomat attached to Iran's permanent United Nations mission in New York. Watch that short video on Screen C there, the one with the blurry object hitting the West Wing? That's either a fast-moving drone or a missile fired from a drone. The man in question has been using an anonymous bank account in Grand Cayman to buy millions of dollars in military drone technology from China."

Susan Hopkins sat across the table from Luke. She stared at him. Luke could see what people liked about her. She looked like exactly what she was—a fashion model pretending to be the Vice President of the United States. In person, she was even more beautiful than on TV.

"Is this fact or conjecture?" she said.

"Everything I've said is fact," Luke said. "My partner and I interviewed the diplomat this morning, but he was being protected by Homeland Security for reasons I know nothing about. We were forcibly removed from the scene before we could get much from him."

She smiled and shook her head. "Was that the torture incident? I was briefed about that on my flight in from Los Angeles this morning. If it weren't for everything else that's happened, you and your partner would probably be one of the biggest news stories in America right now."

It was either the hostility in her tone, or the coffee hitting his system, but whatever it was, Luke started to rouse from his fog. Less than an hour ago, he had saved this woman's life. Being fickle was one thing, but...

"We questioned him," he said. "He was a reluctant subject, and lives were at stake. Including, as it turns out, your life, the President's life, and the lives of all the people at the White House. Believe me when I say that given the circumstances, we went easy on him. If I'd had a crystal ball, I would have gone harder."

She nodded. "That's very brave of you to admit, considering how much torture is frowned upon these days. It's also quite courageous of you to decide that this was a Muslim attack, since we really don't know anything yet. In fact, given the current state of

108

international relations, to simply announce that the Iranians did it is more than just brave or courageous. It's dangerously premature."

"I said an Iranian organized it. He purchased drones. He paid the people involved. I stand by that."

"Do you recognize that we are on the verge of war with Iran, and that there are members of Congress who want to impeach the President if we don't go to war? Do you also recognize that a war with Iran likely leads to war with Russia?"

Luke shook his head. "That's not my department. I'm just telling you what I know."

The room erupted in background chatter.

The President raised his hands. "Okay, okay." He looked directly at Luke. "Tell us straight out. We don't have to act on your opinion, but I personally would like to have it. Do you believe the Iranian government is behind this attack?"

"I don't make leaps of faith like that," Luke said. "What I know is an Iranian organized the attack. I know that he's a diplomat attached to their U.N. mission. And the last I knew, he is alive and still on American soil."

The President looked around the room. "Again, we don't have to act on Agent Stone's information. But I would like him to continue gathering that information, and report his findings to this group, even if it results in some controversy."

"It might be difficult for me to do that," Luke said.

"Why?"

Now Luke shrugged. "I was suspended from duty this morning. I'm under investigation for alleged felonies I committed while investigating this case."

The lieutenant colonel stared at Luke. "Is that all?"

Luke shook his head. "There's also a warrant for my arrest in Baltimore."

"What's it for?"

"Murder."

The entire room went silent. All eyes were on Luke again.

"I've had a busy day," he said.

Chapter 25

"How'd it go down there?" Ed said.

They stood at the edge of the helicopter pad, watching a crowd of people climb off a just landed chopper and run for the safety of the Mount Weather entrance. Luke recognized the United States Representative from Vermont among them.

He shrugged. "I told them what I know. They told me thank you very much, we prefer to believe something else."

"Sounds about right," Ed said.

"They don't want to go to war with Iran," Luke said.

Ed shrugged. "Can't say I blame them. War is hell."

The signalman on the helipad waved to Luke and Ed with bright orange wands, giving them the green light. They ducked low and ran for the helicopter. There was only one active pad at this entrance, and they were moving the choppers in and out, two minutes or less.

No sooner were Luke and Ed inside the chopper than it took off again. Ed yanked the door shut twenty feet above the ground. Luke sank into the seat and clipped his safety belt. They were alone inside a machine built to carry eight passengers. A lot of people in civilian government were flying out of Washington, DC, to Mount Weather. Not too many were flying back into the city.

He glanced at his watch. It was 12:35. More than eleven hours since Don had called him. About thirty hours since he had awakened yesterday morning. Counting the couple of times he had dozed off, he probably hadn't slept thirty minutes since yesterday.

They rose above the sprawling bunker complex. It fell away behind them and soon the view was of green woods and low, rugged mountains. The sky was black with helicopters waiting for their turn to land. Looking east, there was an almost unbroken line of helicopters in the air, single file, all the way to the horizon. Luke glanced at the ground. There was a highway down there. The westbound lanes were bumper-to-bumper, choked with traffic. In the eastbound lanes, a handful of cars zoomed along.

"It'll be a good night for the motel business in West Virginia," Ed said.

"Pennsylvania, Maryland, North Carolina," Luke said. "There probably won't be an empty room for two hundred miles."

Ed nodded. "And a lot of people sleeping in cars."

Luke looked at Ed's face. He had washed up in the men's room, so at least he was clean. But the Secret Service had roughed him up, worse than they did Luke. Maybe it was payback for knocking out two of their agents at the Oval Office. Maybe it was because he was black. Hard to say. But his eye was mostly swollen shut now. He had a couple of darkish lumps on his jaw line that were going to bruise up nicely. And he looked tired. Drained.

"Man, you look like shit."

Ed shrugged. "You should see the other guy."

"You going to file a worker's comp claim?"

Ed shook his head. He smiled. "No, I'll probably just sue you for reckless endangerment. How's your malpractice insurance? Up to date?"

Luke laughed. "Good luck with that. By the way, we're not suspended anymore."

Ed raised an eyebrow. "Was I ever suspended?"

"I don't know. Maybe you were. Maybe you weren't. But you're not now. Also, you have a new boss."

"Oh yeah? Who's that?"

Luke stared down at the highway. The traffic jam went on as far as the eye could see. "The President of the United States of America," he said.

Chapter 26

Luke had never really looked at Don Morris's photos before. The walls in his office were covered in them. Then again, Luke had never really stood around in Don's office with nothing to do before, either. Don was usually here when Luke walked in.

The photos were amazing. In one photo, a much younger Don was standing with Arnold Schwarzenegger, demonstrating to the actor a big MK-19 grenade gun. In a newer one, Don was putting a jiu-jitsu move on Mark Wahlberg. Wahlberg was inverted, his legs in the air, his head on its way to a safety mat. Luke knew that Don sometimes consulted with Hollywood, helping to make their celluloid fakery seem vaguely realistic.

There was more. Here was Don, receiving what looked like a Bronze Star from Jimmy Carter. Here he was shaking hands with Ronald Reagan. Here was one with Bill Clinton. Here was one of Don with a paternal arm around Susan Hopkins. And another of Don standing near a river with the current Speaker of the House, both men wearing fly-fishing gear. Here was Don addressing a Congressional committee.

Luke sensed a presence behind him in the room.

"Hello, son," Don said.

"Hi, Don. Great pictures." Luke turned to face him. "You get around, eh?"

Don came all the way into the room. He wore a dress shirt and slacks. His body language was relaxed, but his eyes were sharp. He sat behind his big desk, and gestured to the chair facing it.

"Have a seat. Take a load off."

Luke did.

"Politics…" Don said, "…is war by other means. Networking is a big part of how I've kept this place going. Our people do a great job, but if the big-wigs don't know about it, then we're out of work. To the bean counters, we are a line item, about as important as the one marked Miscellaneous."

"Okay," Luke said.

"I see you got a shower," Don said. "Freshened up a bit?"

Luke nodded. The shower facilities here were first rate. And he kept two changes of clothes in his locker, even while he was on leave. He wasn't feeling a hundred percent, but he was a lot better than before.

"Close call today, huh?"

"I guess we've had closer ones," Luke said.

Don smiled. "Either way, I'm glad you're not dead."

Luke returned the smile. "Me too."

"We still partners?" Don said.

Luke wasn't sure how to answer that. They had been together a long time. Until today, there had never been a moment, not one, when Luke thought Don didn't have his back. Today there had been two such moments. And in both cases, Don's instincts had been wrong. Don had been skating in one direction, and the puck had been sliding off at full speed in the other direction. If Luke had listened to Don, then the President, the Vice President, and a lot of other people would have died.

It was a profound change, much like seeing an iceberg the size of Kentucky calve away from Antarctica and fall into the ocean. It was a huge thing to witness, but the implications of it were even bigger.

Maybe Don was getting old after all. Maybe he was seeing the Special Response Team collapse all around him, this organization he had built over ten years, and he was scared. Maybe its demise was giving him a whiff of his own mortality. Maybe it was clouding his judgment. Luke was willing to believe these things.

"We'll always be partners," Luke said.

"Good," Don said. "Now listen, you're still under suspension. I haven't been able to budge them at all. I think they'll rescind it, but it may be a day or two, so I'm going to send you home. You okay with that?"

"Don—"

"I wouldn't worry about it, son. You were on leave anyway. After everything you've done, you deserve a couple of days off. Hell, you look like something the cat dragged in here."

"I have new orders, Don."

Don's face was firm. "On whose authority?"

Luke looked him directly in the eyes. "The President's. He told me to continue pursuing the leads we had this morning, and then report back to his security team at Mount Weather. I'd like to

113

do that with the people here at SRT, but he told me if I had any trouble, they'd put Secret Service resources at my disposal."

Don smiled, but the smile didn't reach his eyes. Luke felt a small twinge about that. SRT was teetering on the brink, and now the President was taking Don's agents. Even so, Don needed to man up. This wasn't about egos or agency budgets. This was about getting a job done.

Don looked at the top of his desk. "Well, if the President ordered it, I don't see how I can say no. I don't see how the FBI Director can, either. Until I hear otherwise, you have whatever you need."

*

Trudy Wellington's disembodied head appeared on the flat-panel wall monitor.

Luke, Ed Newsam, Don Morris, and half a dozen members of the Special Response Team sat in the conference room. Real food was spread out on the long black table—sandwiches from the delicatessen less than a mile from headquarters. Luke's was corned beef and sauerkraut on pumpernickel bread.

He glanced at Ed. Ed had also showered and changed. He wore a black SRT jumpsuit now. He held a cold pack to his eye. He had devoured two sandwiches and had a large mug of coffee in front of him. The mug was black with red lettering: JET FUEL. Ed looked alert, immense, formidable—a different man from half an hour ago. Outside of the busted face and the swollen eye, he was very much the same man Luke had met that morning.

"Can you guys hear me okay?" Trudy said.

"We hear you fine," Don said.

"Video output look all right?"

"Looks good to me. Is Swann there with you?"

"He's right behind me. He established this uplink."

"Good," Don said. "What do you have for us?"

"Well, we've got chaos," Trudy said. "The National Guard has been mobilized. Every single vehicle, at every bridge and tunnel out of Manhattan, is being searched. The traffic is gridlock everywhere. Tow trucks are clearing out parked cars to open lanes for emergency vehicles. The police have the subways and commuter rails on lockdown. One entrance and exit at each subway station is open, and every person coming in searched. Every single bag is being opened. The lines are several blocks long. The crowds in Times Square became so large that the police closed the subway station there and cleared the square. At least ten thousand people are walking north toward Central Park. Reports of vandalism, mostly smashed shop windows, are widespread in that area."

"What else?" Don said.

"As we speak, hundreds of thousands of people are walking across the Brooklyn, Manhattan, Williamsburg, 59th Street, George Washington, and 138th Street bridges out of Manhattan. It looks like September eleventh all over again. Mostly, people are calm, but I hate to think what this place would be like if the attack had happened here."

"Any word on that laundry van?" Luke said. "We don't know what radioactive materials were used in the attack on the White House. With the van still at large, there's always the possibility of a second attack."

"We're on that," Trudy said. "Eldrick Thomas, remember him? He was found in a parking lot along Baltimore Harbor. That lot is right off an exit ramp from I-95. It's a hot-spot of drug trafficking and prostitution, so the Baltimore police have surveillance cameras at the top and bottom of the driveway leading to the lot. The camera at the bottom, which is right at the parking lot entrance, has been disabled, probably by the very people it's meant to monitor. The camera at the top is still functional. Swann, can you load those videos?"

The display monitor went to split-screen. On the left side, Trudy was looking back at something out of sight of the camera. On the right side, grainy video footage appeared. It showed a four-lane road at a stoplight. The road was empty.

"We just got this half an hour ago," Trudy said. "For whatever reason, Baltimore PD was reluctant to give it up. There was a moment when I thought we were going to have to go to a federal judge."

As they watched, a white delivery van came onto the screen. The logo on the side of the van was clear. *Dun-Rite Laundry Services.* The van turned right, which made it face the camera directly.

"Okay, Swann, stop it right there," Trudy said. "You can see the license plate. It's grainy, but we made it out. New York commercial plate, AN1-2NL. The same plates that were on the van

115

when we first caught it on camera near Center Medical Center. Now watch when it leaves."

The video skipped, and the van disappeared. In a moment, it was back, this time facing away from the camera. Luke could make out an orange blur where the license plate would be.

"This is twenty minutes later," Trudy said. "See the plate? It's a New York residential plate, 10G-4PQ. Now watch as the van turns left to get back on the highway. See that? The laundry logo is gone. Very clever."

"So what are we doing about it?" Luke said.

"There are APBs with every municipal police force in a three hundred mile radius. Maryland and Virginia State Police helicopters are in the air with still images from these videos, scanning every white van on the roads."

"What if they garaged it?" Ed said.

Trudy shook her head. "It won't matter. The past eight hours of footage from every single traffic camera in Maryland and Virginia has been outsourced to a company in India. Right now, four hundred people in Delhi are watching videotaped traffic with one task: look at every white van, and find the one with orange New York license plates that say 10G-4PQ. Bonuses for the workers, and the company, are triggered by how fast they find it, and not by how many hours they put in. Someone is going to spot that van very soon, and once they do, it'll be a simple matter to track every single street light it passes until it stops."

"Whoever is in that van is going to be desperate," Luke said. "They've already lost two of their guys. If they get the sense we're closing in, they're likely to blow themselves up. When someone finds that van, I want us, meaning SRT, on the scene. We need to take those people alive."

"We're going to do the best we can," Trudy said. "But we had to open it up. There are fifty police forces with this information, and a dozen intelligence agencies. If we kept it to ourselves, the danger is we would never find it."

"I understand that," Luke said. "But if we take the Little Bird, we can be anywhere and land almost anywhere pretty quickly. Just give us some warning."

"Will do," she said.

"Now what about Ali Nassar?"

"For that, you need to talk to Swann."

116

Trudy disappeared and Mark Swann's face appeared. "Luke, we sent a three-man team up to extract Nassar from his apartment. Unfortunately, they got there a few minutes late. When they arrived Nassar was already leaving with a security contingent from the Iranian mission. They were armed, showing their weapons. We didn't want to risk a shoot-out on the street, and frankly, our guys were out-numbered and out-gunned."

"Where did they go?"

"This was before the White House was attacked, so street traffic was pretty open. They came downtown and brought Nassar inside the Iranian mission on Third Avenue. The place is locked up tight. It would take an army, plus some casualties, to get in there and bring him out. Short of a declaration of war, we're not going to do it, and even if we did, we'd probably find him dead."

"Shit," Luke said.

"Never fret," Swann said. "CIA has managed to plant more than two hundred listening devices in that building over the years. Eleven of them are still active. It's a big building, but Nassar's voice was captured on at least two of the devices. There was a lot of arguing going on when they brought him in. It's all in Farsi, so it doesn't do us much good, but CIA has translators, and my Langley connection, gave me the scoop on what was being said. They're going to smuggle him out of the country, possibly as early as today."

"How are they going to do that? All the flights are grounded."

Swann raised a finger. "All the *commercial* flights are grounded. Private flights are still taking off. There's a private jet at Kennedy airport gassed up and ready to go. The Iranian mission is a few blocks from the Midtown Tunnel. If and when the traffic clears up, it's a straight shot through the tunnel, out to the Van Wyck Expressway and down to Kennedy."

"Can we have him arrested if he comes out?"

Swann shrugged. "The NYPD and Homeland aren't cooperating. I think Begley is pissed that you were right, and he's going to bite his own nose off on this. We could detain Nassar ourselves, if we're willing to fight for him, and if he doesn't come out in some kind of disguise, or packed away in the trunk of a car."

"I want every exit from that mission watched," Luke said. "We can't let him get away, even if it means we—"

"Luke? Luke?" Trudy's voice was back, but not her face. "Luke, we're just getting some intel on that van. It's been spotted.

They tracked it to a junkyard in Northeast DC. It's parked. We're going to have satellite imagery of it in about thirty seconds."

Luke was already standing. He glanced at Ed Newsam's chair. Newsam wasn't in it. Luke looked at the door of the conference room. Ed was at the door, holding it open.

"I'm waiting for you," Ed said.

Luke looked around the conference room. Don was sitting up in his chair, staring straight head.

"Don?"

He nodded.

"Go."

Chapter 27

1:45 p.m.
Ivy City - Northeast Washington, DC

The man was a ghost.

He had no name. He had no family. He carried no identification. If he were fingerprinted, his prints would turn up in no criminal or military database that existed. He had a past, of course he did, but that hardly mattered now. He had broken from that past life, and then he had broken from the man who once led that life. Now he lived in a sort of eternal present. The present had its rewards.

He lay on his stomach on the roof of an abandoned three-story building, he and his long-range rifle, the THOR M408. He thought of it as the Mighty THOR, and he and the rifle acted as one. He was its life-support system. It was the source of his creative expression.

All around them, the roof was piled up with discarded junk. Clothes, boxes, an old microwave oven, a shattered black and white television. There was a rusty shopping cart up here, as well as the entire drive train from what had probably once been a pickup truck. How or why someone had carried that thing up here...

It wasn't worth thinking about.

The building, as dilapidated as it was, had been only recently abandoned. Forcibly so. Until this morning, it was the home of eight heroin addicts who took shelter there every night. Their stained mattresses, their discarded clothes, their dirty needles, and their pathetic keepsakes were spread throughout the various rooms. Their mindless graffiti ramblings were all over the walls and in the stairwells. The man had walked through it all on his way to this roof. It was quite a spectacle.

The addicts had been quietly rounded up and removed before first light. The man had no idea what their fate was, nor did he care. They were in the way, so remove them. It would probably be a favor to everyone, including themselves, if they were killed.

The man took a deep breath and closed his eyes for a few seconds. When he opened them again, he re-sighted on the target. He lay under a remnant of an old green awning, the kind that people used to cover their side yards with to keep out the rain. The giant sound suppressor from his rifle was the only part of him that was visible from the outside. Yes, he was very confident that no one could see him here. And no one would hear the shot when he fired it.

His scope was zeroed in on the front passenger door of a white van parked in a junkyard across two alleys from here. The powerful scope made the van door seem bare inches away. The man would prefer to take the shot now, but the glare from the sun made it hard to see through the window. Anyway, the instructions were to wait until the door opened and the subject stepped out.

That was the entire job. Wait until the door opens and a man steps out. Fire one shot into the man's head. Break down the Mighty THOR. Slide out from under the awning and walk downstairs to the street. A nondescript car would be waiting for him in front of the building. Get in the passenger seat and let someone he had never met drive him away.

There was more to it, something about a drunken hobo who would then wander into the junkyard to relieve himself, and remove any telephones and other traceable communications devices. But that wasn't the man's business, and he knew nothing more about the hobo. The streets around here were overcrowded with ragged hobos drunk on wine and beer. It could be any one of them.

The man on the roof wasn't a hobo. He was wearing a brown maintenance man's uniform and when he left the building, he would be carrying a toolbox. No one would look at him twice. He was probably a representative of the absentee landlord, and had come to fix some minor problem with the building.

Until then he waited. And he watched that van door.

*

Nothing made sense anymore.

Ezatullah Sadeh sat in the front passenger seat of the white van. He had just awakened from a feverish sleep filled with nightmare visions. His body and his clothes were soaking wet with perspiration.

He shivered, though he knew it must be a warm day. He had been vomiting earlier in the day, but it seemed to have stopped. He glanced at his phone and saw that it was already well into the afternoon. He also saw that there were no messages for him.

The confidence he had felt this morning had long since evaporated. It had been replaced by confusion. They were parked in

120

a dirt lot overgrown with weeds and filled with junked cars and garbage. Outside of the gates to the junkyard was a slum. It was a typical American concrete wasteland, dismal shops all crammed together, crowds of women carrying plastic bags and waiting at bus kiosks, drunken men on street corners holding beer cans in brown paper bags. He could hear the sounds of the neighborhood from here: automobile traffic, music, shouts and laughter.

The last instructions he had received were to come here to this lot. That was early this morning, in Baltimore, just before they lost the one called Eldrick. Ezatullah had never completely believed in Eldrick's submission to Allah, and could never bring himself to call the man by his Islamic name, Malik. At the time, it seemed a shame that Eldrick had panicked and run when he did, just steps from glory. But now…

Now Ezatullah wasn't sure.

When they arrived here, the gate was locked. No one told him that would happen. They had to cut the heavy chain with bolt cutters. Both he and Mohammar were so weak by then they could barely get the job done. They drove in here, parked the van between two wrecked cars, and waited. They were still waiting all these hours later.

Well, technically, "they" weren't waiting. Mohammar had died sometime this morning. Ezatullah lost track of time, but at one point after sunrise, he had turned to say something to Mohammar. Except that Mohammar wasn't listening anymore. He was dead, sitting up straight in the driver's seat. He was the last of them. Assuming Eldrick had died in the weeds, all of Ezatullah's men, his entire cell, were dead.

Ezatullah had texted the news of Mohammar's death to their handlers, but of course there was no response. He sighed at the thought of it. He hoped Mohammar's sacrifice had been pleasing to Allah. Mohammar was not yet twenty years old, and while he was very intelligent, in many ways he was much like a child.

Ezatullah punched the dashboard in his frustration. The punch was weak. His name meant "Praise Be to God," and he had intended for this operation to be his great testament, his public display of faith. Now it would never happen.

The attack had gone on without them. He had seen news of the White House explosion on his telephone. This suggested that he and his group had been decoys all along. No one ever intended for them to carry out an attack. They had been led here to this dead end, and then abandoned. It was hard to think about. Ezatullah had considered himself a valuable operative. Instead, he had learned that he was a mere pawn to be used and discarded.

And the attack, while spectacular, had mostly been a failure. A relative handful of unimportant people had died, and the President had escaped unscathed. They should have trusted Ezatullah. He would have done the job the way it was meant to be done. He shook his head at the stupidity of it.

Suddenly, a text came through on his phone.

We are proud. You have done well and all will become clear to you in time. Green car waiting for you on street. Come now, Mujahideen.

Ezatullah stared at the message. It was almost impossible to believe, after these many hours. If this were true, then they hadn't betrayed him. Now, after the operation was over, they had sent someone to rescue him and bring him home.

But he hesitated. Did he dare trust it?

It was possible, he realized. Of course his handlers wouldn't tell him every facet of the attack. He couldn't be allowed to see the big picture. It was a dangerous and difficult operation, one which must have many people involved. The others must be protected. If Ezatullah had been captured, even under CIA torture, all he could tell was what he knew. He had received money, he did not know from whom. He had received instructions, he did not know from where. He had an objective, but it had changed several times, and he didn't know why.

"Get up," he said to himself. "Get up and walk to them."

He could escape from this. He just needed to open the door and stumble out to the street. He was sick, yes, but they could heal him. This was the United States. A secret back alley medical clinic, with a blacklisted doctor, would be an outpost of dazzling modernity compared to what was available in many other countries.

Okay. Then it was settled. He would live to fight another day. His great statement would come at another time on a different battlefield.

He unlocked his door and pushed it open. He was surprised that the door swung easily. Perhaps he had more strength than he thought. He gave young Mohammar one last glance.

"Goodbye, my friend," he said. "You were brave."

Somewhere in the near distance, sirens raged. They were coming closer. Perhaps there had been another attack, or perhaps it was just a normal day in a bad neighborhood. Ezatullah swung his body around and slid out of the van. His feet hit the dirt of the parking lot and he found that his legs were unsteady, but he could stand. He took a tentative step, then another. Praise Allah, he could still walk.

He slammed the van door closed behind him and took a deep breath. The last thing he saw was the blue sky and bright sunlight of a warm June day.

Chapter 28

They called it the Little Bird. Sometimes they called it the Flying Egg.

It was the MH-6 helicopter—fast and light, highly maneuverable, the kind of chopper that didn't need room to land. It could come down on small rooftops, and on narrow roadways in crowded neighborhoods. The chopper was beloved by special operations forces, and Don had procured one when he launched the Special Response Team.

It came in low over the streets, just above the tangle of electrical wires. Luke and Ed rode in on the wooden side-mounted bench seats, their legs dangling in the air. Next to the junkyard lot, the pilot found a two-story cinderblock building with a fire escape. He touched down and both men slid out onto the roof. Three seconds later, the chopper was back in the air.

A minute after that, Luke and Ed walked across the dusty lot toward the van. The place was full of cops. Seven or eight DC police patrol cars were parked out on the street and sidewalk, lights flashing. Two fire engines were out there as well. A hazmat truck and a bomb squad truck had pulled inside the lot, and yellow police tape was suspended across the entrance.

In a far corner of the lot, men in full hazmat suits were searching inside the van. All the doors were open. A body lay on the ground by the front passenger door, blood pooled nearby. Another body was in the driver's seat.

Fifty yards from the van, a cop stepped in front of them.

"Far enough, guys."

Luke showed him the badge. "Agent Stone, FBI Special Response Team." He said it even though he wasn't quite sure who he worked for anymore. Anyway, he still had the badge. That was good enough.

The cop nodded. "I figured you were somebody. Most people don't show up by landing helicopters on rooftops. Past this point is considered a radiation contamination area. You want to go further, you need to put on a hazmat suit."

Luke didn't want to spend twenty minutes putting on a hazmat suit. He gestured at the men with the van. "You know anything about what happened here?"

The cop smiled. "I might have heard a couple things."

"How did they die?"

The cop pointed. "The one on the ground was shot in the head. Large-caliber weapon, hit from a distance. The bullet took a big chunk of his brains and skull when it exited. The guy was lucky— he probably never knew what hit him."

"Someone *shot* him?" Ed said.

"If you got a little closer, you wouldn't ask me that question. There's brain salad all over the ground. It looks like somebody dropped a plate of guacamole."

"He didn't shoot himself?"

The cop shrugged. "All I know is what the ballistics people are saying. They took some measurements and they're going to computer model it, but at first blush they think it was a shooter on one of the surrounding rooftops."

Luke glanced around the neighborhood. It was an area of two- and three-story apartment buildings, machine shops, warehouses. There were liquor stores, check cashing, and WE BUY GOLD places on street level. He turned and stared at the man.

"You're saying he was shot by a sniper? Who would put a sniper on one of these buildings besides the police?"

The cop raised his hands. "Look, I just work here. But I can tell you it wasn't us. Our orders were to take these guys alive, if possible, and the guy on the ground was already dead when the first coppers got here."

"What about the other one?"

"The driver? It looks like it might be radiation sickness, or maybe he took some pills. There aren't any obvious gunshot or stab wounds. No blood. He's just sitting there at the steering wheel, like he parked the van and died. They'll have to do a toxicology work-up on him, but it'll take a while. With all the radiation, it's going to be another couple of hours before they even get the bodies out of here."

"They have any tech on them?" Ed said. "Phones, tablets, laptops?"

The cop shook his head. "Not that anybody has found. Sounds funny though, right? Two guys out on a mission with no way to call the mother ship?"

"Did they fingerprint them?" Luke said.

The cop nodded. "That and DNA. It's one of the first things they did when the hazmat guys got here."

"Thanks."

Luke and Ed walked back toward the building where the chopper landed. "I was afraid of that," Luke said. "Outside of Ali Nassar, those guys were the last links to whoever attacked the White House. Clearly, it wasn't them."

"What are you thinking?" Ed said. "The whole radiation thing was a distraction?"

"Maybe. Or maybe it was a backup plan that went bad. I don't know."

Luke pulled out his satellite phone. He and Trudy had switched to sat phones now. Bad weather could take them out, but they were unaffected by communications meltdowns like the one that had hit the East Coast.

He waited for the phone to shake hands with the satellite, then for the bounce down to her location. Beep... Beep... Beep... Satellite phones always made him a little leery. He knew it was silly. It was a holdover from the days when drones could use the satellite uplink signal to lock on ground targets. In those days, a man with a satellite phone was holding a big red bull's-eye. But now, it hardly mattered. The newest drones could lock on to cell phones, laptops, GPS units, almost anything.

"Hello?" a voice said. It was Trudy. She sounded like she was speaking from the bottom of a tin can. "Luke?"

"Trudy. Look. We're at the site of the van. There are two suspects here, both dead. A cop told me they've taken DNA and fingerprints from them. Connect with whoever can get you inside the loop on that. When those identifications come through, I want them."

"Will do, Luke. But listen. Swann is getting almost real-time information from inside the Iranian mission. They're bringing Ali Nassar to the airport today. They want him out of the country. All indications are that the jet waiting for him has clearance to take off at 3:30 p.m."

Luke looked at his watch. It was 2:05.

"Jesus. Can we stop him?"

"I talked with Ron Begley about this," she said. "He laughed. He said Homeland Security won't touch it. As far as they're concerned, the man is a diplomat and had nothing to do with the attacks. There's no evidence it was Iran, and they don't want to risk another international incident today."

"Dammit!" Luke said. Nassar was the one remaining link to the attack and Ron Begley was going to let him walk away. "What the… what about the local cops?"

"No dice," she said. "They've already said that if Homeland doesn't want him, they don't have jurisdiction. And they're overstretched as it is. Practically the entire police force has been mobilized, guarding every train station and every public place. Ali Nassar is your obsession, Luke. No one else cares."

"So be it," Luke said. "I'll stop him myself."

"From there?" she said.

Luke shook his head, then realized she couldn't see him. "No. We're on our way back to New York. If we gun it, we should get there just in time. I want people outside the Iranian mission, reporting in as soon as Nassar leaves."

"Well, there are a couple more things you should know," Trudy said. "They're planning to go to the airport in an armed convoy of SUVs."

"I wouldn't have it any other way," Luke said. "Make sure our people have Nassar's image. If more than one convoy leaves, I want to know that, and I want best guesses as to which convoy he's in. If they need to think up a ruse to stop the trucks and see who's inside, do it. A fake checkpoint will work, it doesn't matter to me. Tell Swann to put some of his toy drones in the air, and get ready to follow multiple convoys. See how close he can get with his cameras."

"Luke, there's also this. Nassar has a five-year-old daughter. The mother is Lebanese and lives here in New York. Both of them are leaving the country with him. They will probably be in his car."

Luke didn't say anything. He had a pit in his stomach at the thought of that girl in the car. Why did there always have to be something? Why couldn't anything ever be clean?

Next to him, Ed was calling the chopper back in. A moment later, Luke could already see it, a black insect in the distance, coming in fast, growing bigger by the second. He and Ed started walking toward the fire escape they had climbed down.

"Don't go in with guns blazing," Trudy said. "That's what I'm telling you."

"I never go in with guns blazing."

"No?"

Luke smiled. "No. I leave that kind of thing to Ed."

Chapter 29

2:35 p.m.
Mount Weather Emergency Operations Center -
Bluemont, Virginia

The meeting was chaos. It had dragged out for well over an hour now.

Thomas Hayes was trying to preside over an unruly mob of frightened people. It wasn't working. These were smart, clever, inventive people for the most part, normally the best and brightest. But fear had shut down their creativity, and it was choking off their initiative. They couldn't even figure out where everybody was. Hayes could barely believe how disorganized the evacuations were.

An aide was making a report. "Sir, at approximately 12:30 p.m., the Airborne Communications Command aircraft, codename Nightwatch, took off from Joint Base Andrews and flew west. It is currently over eastern Missouri, cruising at forty thousand feet."

Hayes looked across the conference table at a line of blank faces.

"Who authorized that?"

No one said a word. Nightwatch was only supposed to take off in the event of a nuclear war. The missile codes were on that thing.

Hayes glanced around the room. A Secret Service agent was standing near the door with a leather satchel in his hand. The bag was strapped to the man's wrist with a steel cord. Hayes knew that inside the bag was an aluminum ZERO Halliburton case. He grunted in something like mirth. ZERO Halliburton, long the manufacturer of the President's nuclear football, was now the wholly owned subsidiary of a Japanese luggage company. Traditions were a funny thing.

Hayes looked at the aide. "Son, are we at war that we know of?"

"No sir."

"Well, who's on board the goddamned plane?"

"Sir, Senator Edward Graves of Kansas is on board the plane, along with a handful of Pentagon officials."

Thomas Hayes felt his shoulders slump. Ed Graves was Chairman of the Armed Forces Committee, and among the dumbest members of either Congressional body. The man had all the brainpower of a tree stump. He never met a war, or even a border

128

skirmish, that he didn't like. And considering that the Nightwatch plane was designed as a place where the President could order retaliatory nuclear strikes, that made Ed Graves dangerous. Hell, he probably thought being in the plane made him President.

Hayes spoke to the room at large. "Can someone do me a favor and get him down? Please? St. Louis, Kansas City, whatever's closest. Tell him I said so."

Hayes rubbed his forehead. He was tired, and he had a headache.

David Halstram was in the corner of the room. He moved in when he saw the state Hayes was in.

"Okay, everybody. Let's do this. Let's break this up for half an hour, use the restrooms, get some coffee, relax, whatever you like." He looked at his watch. "That would mean coming back at ten to three. You know what? Let's make it forty minutes and come back at exactly three o'clock. These are serious problems, I understand that, but they're not going anywhere. They'll all still be waiting for us forty minutes from now."

"Thank you, David," Hayes said. "That's a good idea."

Susan Hopkins raised an open palm. It looked like a STOP sign. "Thomas, can I say something?"

"Susan, I wish you wouldn't."

"Thomas, I think this is important, and I'm not sure it can wait until three o'clock."

Hayes was out of patience. He might have snapped at anyone who spoke right now. But it was the Vice President, and the sheer absurdity of their relationship made it worse than it otherwise might have been. The words were out of his mouth before he could catch them.

"This isn't a bake-off, Susan. And we're not organizing a fashion show. What's so important that it can't possibly wait?"

She didn't speak. Her face flushed a deep crimson. Without another word, she stood and walked out of the room.

Chapter 30

3:15 p.m.
In the Sky - The Borough of Queens, New York

The helicopter had come in over Staten Island, across the Verrazano-Narrows, and into Brooklyn. Now they were moving east along the ocean beaches, flying low and fast. Soon they would hook left and move north along the Van Wyck Expressway.

Luke and Ed were hunched in the small cargo hold. Back in New Jersey, they had both dropped another Dexedrine. The effects were starting to kick in.

It had been a long and brutal day. Luke had been awake far too long. He had been choked, shot at, tackled, stepped on, punched, kicked, and oh yes, almost blown to bits. He had been suspended from his job and accused of murder. But as the Dexie hit him, he began to feel a surge of guarded optimism. Hell, they had saved the President of the United States today. That had to count for something.

The helicopter was tiny. He could reach out and touch both the pilots. He poked his head between them. It was Jacob and Rachel, the same pilots from this morning.

"You kids ready to fly this thing?" he shouted.

Behind him, Ed was sitting near the open cargo door, loading thirty-round box magazines for an M4 assault rifle. He had a little stack of them going.

"Isn't that what we're doing right now?" Rachel said.

Luke liked Rachel. She had dark auburn hair. She was brawny like the old Rosie the Riveter posters. Of course, she was. She was a mixed martial arts fighter, after all. Big arms, big legs, she must be hell inside a steel cage.

"Ed could do what you're doing," Luke said. "But I'm going to need him on that M4. I mean, are you ready to fly this thing like they taught you in the United States Army? We might have to go in a little hard here."

"We're ready, Luke," Jacob said. Jacob was nearly the opposite of Rachel. He was thin and reedy. He looked nothing like your typical elite soldier. Special ops could be as hung up on looks as anybody else. Probably no one would have accepted him, not Delta, not SOAR, not the Rangers, or the SEALS. The only thing he had going for him, besides his profound sense of calm, was that he was probably one of the ten best helicopter pilots alive on Earth.

Rachel nodded. "You know we're ready."

"Good. There's a convoy of SUVs on its way to Kennedy Airport. It's not going to get there. That's because we're going to stop it."

"What kind of support do we have?" Jacob said.

"Swann is operating some small drones that are spotting for us. He'll probably have a couple of our cars as well. Other than that, you've got me, and you've got that big man with that big gun back there."

"What are you going to do?"

Luke smiled. "I'm the head cheerleader. Keep the intercom wide open and listen for my screams."

"Hey, Luke," Rachel shouted. "When I was leaving SOAR, my C.O. asked me what I was going to do with the rest of my life. You know what I said? I told him I was gonna go work for the SRT. You know why? Because Luke Stone was there. All these years of flying choppers, and I never got the chance to die in one. I'm hoping Luke can fix that for me."

"You're my kind of girl," Luke said.

"By the way," Jacob said. "This is an area full of civilians."

Luke nodded. "And that's why we're going to get this done without firing a shot."

A moment later, Luke's satellite phone started beeping. He answered, and held the phone tight to his ear.

"Swann? What's the story?"

"We're watching them. They left the mission about fifteen minutes ago."

"And?"

"They must not know we were listening," Swann said. "That's as near as I can figure. They went out with one convoy. It's two Range Rovers sandwiching a big black Lincoln Navigator. Nine out of ten Nassar's going to be in the Lincoln. They went straight across to the Midtown Tunnel and stopped at the checkpoint there. The cops checked identification and waved them through. I picked them up with the drones on the other side. I'm watching them now. They just got on the Van Wyck, headed south to the airport. We've got two of our SUVs following about a mile behind them."

"Nobody else came out of the mission?" Luke shouted into the phone.

131

"We've still got two agents there," Swann said. "Nobody else has come out so far. I really think this is it. They don't know we heard them and they don't know we're coming. They didn't try to misdirect at all."

"Good enough," Luke said. He scanned the roadway below them. The chopper was flying north, just west of the highway. The convoy was coming south. They should pass each other any moment. Traffic was remarkably light now, and cars were moving along at a nice clip. Everybody still on the roads was trying to speed home before the world ended.

"What are you going to do?" Swann said.

"We're going to pull them over," Luke said. "Just like the cops do to speeders. When I give the word, have our SUVS come up with the lights and sirens going. We'll hover close and put our gun on the bad guys. I think that should do it."

"Okay," Swann said. "Standing by."

As Luke watched, a white Range Rover went by, followed closely by a black Navigator. Another white Range Rover brought up the rear. They were moving fast. The chopper blew past them. Luke tapped Rachel on the helmet.

"You guys see that?"

"We saw it," Rachel said.

"Those are our subjects," Luke said. "Let's swing this thing around."

The chopper made a looping, banking turn and headed south.

"Swann, give me those SUVs."

"Coming right up," Swann said.

Below them, two black SUVs about a quarter mile apart suddenly came to life. Red and blue lights began to flash in their front windshields. The drivers gunned the accelerators, and within seconds, both cars were going close to a hundred miles per hour.

The chopper was faster.

Luke looked at Newsam. "You ready with that gun?"

Ed showed a ghost of a smile. He patted the barrel. "This old thing? We go way back." He wore yellow-tinted shooting glasses. A pair of ear muffs were perched on top of his head. He slid out the cargo door until he was perched on the outboard bench. He strapped himself in.

They watched as the SUVs caught up to the convoy. It all happened within a few miles. The Range Rovers and the big Navigator saw the dashboard lights coming up and moved over to the soft shoulder of the highway. The SRT vehicles pulled in behind them. Civilian traffic roared by three feet to their right.

"That was easy," Newsam shouted from outside.

"Yeah," Luke said. "Too easy."

The chopper came down. Soon, it was fifty feet in the air, hovering thirty yards ahead of the lead car.

"Swann, we don't want anybody but Nassar. If he's in that Navigator, just have your guys extract him and drive away."

"Got it, Luke."

Two SRT men walked up the line of cars on either side. They moved fast with sidearms drawn. They moved to the middle car, the black Lincoln. The man on the shoulder side banged on the door. There was a delay. No one came out.

Luke tapped Ed. "Put your weapon on that! I don't like it. Two men aren't enough."

Newsam lifted the gun and sighted. "Got it."

"Swann! Give me two more men on that car."

Without warning, the rear door of the lead Range Rover swung open. A man popped out, machine gun firing. Luke could hear the ugly blat of the Uzi from all that way. The first SRT man went down in a hail of gunfire. The second SRT agent ducked and ran back toward the agency cars.

"Man down!" Swann shouted. "Man down! Jesus. Trudy, call 911. We need an ambulance out there. Holy shit."

The man from the Range Rover walked calmly toward the injured agent. He pushed his Uzi aside. It hung on his back from its shoulder strap. He pulled a handgun from inside his light jacket and pointed it at the agent's head.

"Ed!" Luke said. "Don't let that happen."

The sudden roar of the M4 was earth shattering next to Luke's head. He ducked away, ears ringing instantly. Newsam rode the recoil, muscles bulging, his face a blank mask.

He was dialed in. A line of bullets strafed the Range Rover. The front left tire exploded and the windshield shattered. The man with the gun jittered for no more than a second, then collapsed to the ground next to the man he was about to kill. The agent, wounded but alive, began to crawl away downhill into a drainage ditch.

"Your man's moving, Swann. He's alive. Get somebody out there to cover him."

133

The first Range Rover was disabled. It started to roll out, but a dense burst of steam blew out from its radiator. Behind it, the Navigator pulled sharply into the roadway, the second Range Rover right behind it. Both cars peeled off down the highway. They were making a run for it. One SUV pulled out and followed them.

The Navigator zoomed by just below them. The helicopter was broadside to the road, the cargo door wide open. Ed was out on the bench. The Range Rover was coming. Too late, Luke saw machine gun snouts poking from both of the rear windows.

"Watch it! Incoming fire!"

Gunfire erupted all around them, like a swarm of angry wasps. Luke dove to the floor. Something cut a sharp path across his right shoulder. There was a slice, then stinging pain. Metal shredded. Glass shattered. Ed Newsam screamed.

Luke crawled to him. He grabbed Ed under the shoulders, and dragged him back into the chopper.

Ed's teeth were gritted in pain. His eyes were wild and mad. His breathing was fast. "I got hit," he said. "Dammit, that hurts."

"Where is it?"

"I don't know. Everywhere."

A voice came over the intercom. It was Jacob. "Luke, we lost the right side of our windshield up here. The gunfire just about stove it in." He sounded relaxed, like he was describing a quiet weekend at home.

"Is anyone hurt?" Luke shouted.

"Uh, we've got glass all over us, but we seem okay. The windshield's probably not going to hold though, not if we get up to speed."

"Ed's hit," Luke said.

"Sorry. How bad?"

"I don't know." Luke pulled his knife and began to cut away Ed's jumpsuit. There was a black padded garment beneath it. A flak vest. That was a surprise. Luke hadn't thought to put one on. He touched it.

"Aren't you hot in this thing?"

Ed shrugged. His eyes watered from the pain.

"Stylish," he managed to say.

"Yeah. More like out of stylish. Probably saved your life, though."

Luke felt beneath the vest. Nothing had penetrated it. His hands moved along Ed's body. Ed's right arm and shoulder were cut to ribbons. A big chunk of his right thigh was ripped up. The right edge of his pelvis had been hit. His jumpsuit was ripped and bloody at that spot. When Luke touched there, Ed screamed again.

"Okay," Luke said. "Something's broken."

"Did you hear me just now?" Ed said through clenched teeth. "I sounded like a girl."

"I know," Luke said. "I'm embarrassed for you. Especially since you're gonna live, and I'm going to tell people about that scream until the end of my days."

The chopper spun and headed south again, following the cars. Luke stood and pulled the first aid kit off the wall. He dropped down to Ed and immediately started to disinfect his wounds. Ed's entire body clenched as the disinfectant hit his skin.

"It hurts," Ed said. "A lot."

Luke didn't want to think about the kind of pain that would make a man like Ed Newsam say it hurt a lot. "I know it," he said. "I'm going to give you a pill. It's going to take the edge off that pain, but it's also going to take you out of the game."

Ed shook his head.

"Just help me get out there. I can still man the gun. I'll strap myself at the edge of the doorway. It'll be okay. I won't fall out."

"Ed..." Luke glanced out the door. They were flying fast and low. The highway was just below them. From this vantage point on the floor, he couldn't see where the cars were. He poked his head out the side of the doorway and looked at the road ahead.

A man's upper body leaned from the passenger window of the Range Rover, pointing a machine gun back at them.

"Jesus."

Luke ducked back in as more bullets ripped up metal. He and Ed were eye to eye on the floor. Luke clambered back up to his knees. "I'm not going to argue with you, Ed. I don't have time right now."

Ed shook his head violently. "Then don't argue."

Another burst of machine gun fire hit the chopper. More glass shattered up front.

"Luke, we've got instruments down. We can't keep taking hits like this. We're going to lose this bird in a minute."

"Take evasive action," Luke shouted.

The chopper pulled up abruptly. It made a steep climb and banked hard to the left. Luke fell over sideways. He clung to the floor, his fingers gripping metal slats. Another burst of gunfire came, but this one sounded further away.

An alarm in the cockpit began to sound.

BEEP, BEEP, BEEP...

Jacob's disembodied voice said: "Luke, we've got mayday. A rotor's been hit. It's wobbling. I've seen it before. It's not going to hold. We either land or we crash, but we're going down."

"How long do we have?"

"Ninety seconds. Maybe. The longer we hold out, the harder we hit."

Luke's shoulders slumped. Was this really happening? The Iranians were really going to run like this? What did they think, they were just going to shoot their way to the airport, jump on the plane, and fly away?

Luke clambered to his feet again. He looked through the cockpit. The windshield was gone. A matted blanket of glass had caved in. As he watched, Rachel grabbed it with her gloved hands, pulled it into the cockpit and shoved it aside. The cyclic control was shuddering in Jacob's hand.

He tapped Jacob on the helmet.

"Drop this thing right on top of that Navigator!" he shouted. "Give me two seconds to get out, then go land somewhere."

BEEP, BEEP, BEEP...

Luke propped Ed up on the outboard bench after all. He had no choice.

"You know what you're doing?"

Ed nodded. Much of the color had drained from his face. He suddenly seemed very tired. "I think you're crazy, but yeah, I know."

"Tell me."

"As soon as you land, we pull up and ahead, and I blow the windshield out."

"Great," Luke said. "But don't kill the driver."

"I'll do my best."

They were five hundred feet in the air and a quarter mile to the west, out of range of the Range Rover's guns. The dangerous moment would be arcing back down and into range. In the distance and well below them, Luke followed the progress of the cars. As he watched, a police car entered the highway, light blazing. A mile back, two more were gaining.

He yelled to Jacob. "Ready when you are!"

136

Instantly, the chopper banked hard left and down. They got out ahead of the cars. They dropped a hundred feet in a few seconds. They were coming in fast. Three hundred feet. Two hundred. A gunman poked out of the rear window of the Range Rover. He aimed his gun at the chopper.

"Put the smack on that bastard!" Luke shouted.

Ed let him have it, the gun roaring again. The door to the Range Rover collapsed in, like a beer can crunched by an invisible hand. The man's head blew up in a spray of blood. He dropped his gun, slumped, and fell back. The gun clattered along the roadway.

"Bull's-eye. Now put me in there."

The chopper dropped in fast, moving sideways along the road. It turned, the doorway facing the Navigator. Luke climbed past Ed onto the running board. The chopper came all the way down and bounced off the roof of the Navigator. It went three feet in the air, then came back down again.

The time had come.

Luke jumped.

Chapter 31

Luke fell to his hands and knees, and clung to the car's roof rack.

The driver must have heard Luke hit the roof. The Lincoln started veering back and forth across lanes, swaying crazily, trying to shake Luke off. Luke gripped the rack with all of his strength, his lower body rolling from side to side.

The chopper raced out ahead and banked around to the left. It hooked sharply and zoomed directly across their path. Ed was in the doorway, broadside to them. Luke ducked his head just as the muzzle flashes erupted from Ed's gun.

A hail of bullets sprayed the front of the car. Luke crawled to the front. The right side of the windshield had collapsed inward. He leaned over and punched at the remnants of the glass, pushing it, forcing it down into the car. Somewhere inside, a woman screamed. A child was crying.

Half the windshield fell into the car. Luke spun his body around, pushed his legs through, and slid into the front passenger seat. He landed on the lap of a dead man. The driver fumbled for his gun. He pointed it in Luke's direction. Luke grabbed his wrist and banged it against the dashboard.

The man dropped the gun without firing. It fell between his legs and down to the floorboards on the driver's side. The man looked away from the road and reached around down there. Luke pulled his own gun.

Suddenly, a shot fired from the back seat. The sound was enormous in the close confines of the car.

BOOM.

People screamed back there. Luke ducked and the dead man's head exploded.

Luke's ears were ringing. He looked behind him, peeking between the seats. Ali Nassar was there with a woman and a little girl. They all had wide eyes, terrified, stricken. The little girl sat in the middle. Behind them, in the third row, was a big man with a gun.

The man crouched down behind the little girl's head. His gun poked out over her shoulder. It was right next to the girl's face.

This was his chance to end this. To save his life. To get Nassar.

But Luke couldn't bring himself to take a shot. He couldn't risk it. Not with the girl there.

"Ali!" Luke shouted. "Get that gun! Stop him!"

Ali Nassar stared at Luke with dull eyes.

BOOM. The man fired again.

The girl screamed, shrieking now. Everyone in the back seat screamed.

The bullet hit the center mass of the dead man. In a moment, those bullets were going to start breaking through the dead man's seat and his body.

The driver had found his gun.

There was nothing left to do. Luke flipped his own gun around. He held the barrel in his hand and brandished the hand grip. He hammered the driver's head with it.

Once. Twice. Three times.

He ducked as another gunshot rent through the car.

BOOM.

The plastic dashboard shattered, shards flying everywhere. Luke felt them bite into his flesh.

The car floated to the left, off the highway, up and over the shoulder. The driver had gone unconscious at the wheel. The car went down a grassy embankment. It leaned way over to the left, tilting, tilting… up on two wheels. Luke reached for the steering wheel.

Too late. The car rolled. Luke banged his head against the dashboard. Then the car was upside down. He crashed into the ceiling hard, and with sickening speed. He landed on his back. His breath rushed out of him with the force of it.

Airbags blew all around him.

The car rolled again. He was thrown like a doll. He dropped down off the ceiling. The last thing he felt was his head hitting the steering wheel. Then all he saw was darkness.

Chapter 32

Ed Newsam watched the whole thing from the Little Bird.

The Navigator had rolled twice and landed right side up on some hard-packed dirt along the side of the highway. Its tires were all blown out. Its windshield was gone. The car was smoking from several places.

The second Range Rover pulled up on the soft shoulder. Three men jumped out and ran down the grassy embankment, guns out, charging toward the ruined Navigator.

The chopper was moving fast, sideways and to the left. Ed tried to get a bead on the men, but it was no use. The chopper was shuddering. He let off a burst of gunfire anyway. Two of the men dove into the grass. The third kept running.

"Mayday, mayday," Jacob's voice said. "Assume crash positions."

Ed was tied to the bench with leather straps. The setup was not secure. Grinding pain dug at his right hip. Sharp pains, rips, and slices were everywhere else across his body. He stared back through the doorway at the cargo hold, with its safety straps dangling. There was no way he could make it in there and tie himself down in time. He slid his gun inside the door, then reached down and hugged the bench as hard as he could. This was his crash position.

In front of him, the ground was coming fast. If the chopper rolled, he was going airborne. He could never hold on. He'd be out there, moving through the same space as the spinning rotor blades. He shook his head. Not good.

The world zoomed by with dizzying speed. They were twenty feet from the ground.

Jacob's voice, like a man ordering a pizza: "Impact in three, two…"

Ed gripped the bench tighter than ever. He closed his eyes. *Please don't roll it. Please don't roll it. Please don't.*

*

It took a few seconds for Luke's eyes to focus.

He was still in the front row. He had hit hard, forehead to the steering wheel, and he was almost blind from the pain. The air bags had deflated, but the white dust hung in the air. His head rested on the driver's legs. His own legs lay across the dead man in the passenger seat. Both men had been wearing their seatbelts. Luke had flown through the air. They had hardly moved at all.

Luke reached below the driver's seat and felt around near the man's feet. He found the man's gun and brought it up. A Glock nine-millimeter. That was fine. It felt good in his hand. He clawed his way to a seated position. Shattered safety glass from the windshield was all over the front row. The driver was still unconscious, his head hanging against his seat belt.

Outside the car, two men approached warily, in crouches, Uzis drawn.

Luke glanced in the back seat. Ali Nassar and his little family were alive and awake, if a little dazed. Nassar had a big white cast on his right hand.

The little girl was cute, with a bright green ribbon in her black hair. She had big brown doe eyes. The woman was reed-thin and ethereal. To Luke, she had the air of a woman who spent her days reading about the latest fashions in Paris and Milan, and what the British royalty were up to. She had probably awakened this morning thinking she had seen and done it all.

Not anymore. Now she stared straight ahead. Luke had seen people in that state before, many times. The woman was in shock.

Luke forced the driver's seat up and climbed into the back with them. He crouched low, in case one of those gunmen out there lost their discipline. He wedged himself deep at the feet of the little girl.

"You are a madman," Nassar said.

Luke ignored him. He looked at the little girl instead, and past her.

The man in the back had hit hard. He was either unconscious, or dead.

"What is your name?" Luke said.

The girl was terrified, but still she spoke. "Sofia."

"Hush, child! Do not speak to him!"

"Sofia, what a pretty name for a pretty girl. Okay, Sofia, I want you to do something for me. It's really very easy. I want you to unclip your seat belt and come to me."

Nassar moved to unclip his own seat belt. "Don't you dare..."

Luke pointed the gun at his head. "Say another word."

"Please don't hurt him," Sofia said. Tears began to roll down her cheeks.

"I won't hurt him, Sofia, but I need you to come to me."

141

The girl did exactly as she was told. She undid her seat belt and moved to Luke gracefully, like a tiny animal. He wrapped a gentle arm around her as if she was his own child.

Outside the car, the gunmen had arrived. They were both on the same side of the car, the left. They pointed their guns through the windows. The rear window was shattered. All it would take was for one of them to lose his cool. There would be a bloodbath in this car.

"That's far enough!" he shouted to the men. "We've got a woman and a child in here. If you fire those guns, you're going to kill us all."

They didn't care. Outside the car, one of the men slid his Uzi behind his back. He pulled a handgun and pointed it through the hole where the window once was.

BOOM!

The glass shattered as one of them fired into it.

The girl screamed as Luke held her, and he saw the bullet mark in the leather seat, just an inch from her head. Luckily, they'd missed. She might not be so lucky next time, he knew. Strangely, Luke found himself worrying more about the girl than he did himself.

So when one of them raised their gun again and approached, blinking into the darkness, it was the girl Luke thought of first. He could have had his shot. He could have killed them both. But he couldn't risk it. Not with her in harm's way.

BOOM!

Luke grabbed her and spun her around and fell on top of her a split second before the gun fired.

He felt excruciating pain as he felt the bullet graze his arm. Blood squirted everywhere. But he knew from experience it was a flesh wound. It was a small price to pay for saving her life.

Her mother shrieked, and Nassar yelled: "STOP FIRING, YOU MADMEN!"

Luke heard the men raising their guns, and sensed them finally locking him in their sights. He knew this was his last chance.

He spun, took a knee, and fired two shots. He knew they had better be perfect shots, or else he was dead. He wouldn't have time to take a third.

BOOM. BOOM.

Luke saw no movement, as all became still. Finally, there was silence. He looked outside and saw the two men, both dead, both with perfect head shots.

He breathed a long breath of relief.

"You are a madman!" Nassar repeated again, his voice tremulous, shaking.

Luke turned to him and scowled as he leaned in and grabbed his shirt.

"I want them out," he said. "Both the girl and your wife. Far from here. More people are coming and they might get hurt. And this is between you and me now."

Nassar nodded to his wife, but she made a deep moan in the back of her throat.

"ALI!" Luke shouted, and raised his gun to his head. "NOW!"

The woman started to howl, and now the girl was crying, too.

Nassar leaned across, took the woman by both shoulders, and shook her violently. "Irina! Get hold of yourself. Take Sofia and leave."

The woman unclipped herself. She climbed out and took the girl. The woman and girl were thirty yards away and running. Now fifty. For a second, Luke watched them go. He took a deep breath. If he'd ever had a daughter, he wondered if she would be like her.

Nassar made a move to leave the car. Too late. Luke grabbed him by the shirt and pulled him back. He slammed the door and put his gun to Nassar's head.

Nassar stared at Luke with fierce eyes.

"Now you listen to me," Luke said. "I want to know everything. Who you're working for. How you did it. When it started. What happens next. Everything, you got me? If I even smell a lie, I swear to God I'll kill you."

"If you shoot me, I promise it will be the last thing you ever do."

"Talk! I'm going to count to three. Just like last time. Remember how that went? But this time, on three I blow your brains out."

"You're insane! Do you know that? You're insane! You're…"

"One," Luke said.

Outside the windows, men in uniforms were sprinting down the hill. Cops. New York City cops, state troopers, a flowing river of policemen. Men in suits were with them, probably the SRT guys. Things were about to wrap up out there.

143

He was running out of time.

"Two…"

Nassar couldn't bear it. "Stop! I'll tell you what you want to know."

"Who did this?" Luke said. "Who do you work for? Iran?"

Nassar's shoulders slumped. The strength, the very life, seemed to flow out of him. He shrugged.

"I work for you."

Chapter 33

It took over an hour to process Ali Nassar and bring him downstairs.

While he was waiting, Luke talked to Becca on the phone.

"You're a wonderful man."

Luke pressed his forehead against the grimy wall in the basement of the precinct house, and listened to the musical sound of his wife's voice in his ear. The police station was a harsh environment. The overhead fluorescents were too bright. Voices and footsteps echoed around him. Someone down the hallway laughed, a deranged cackle.

"I don't feel very wonderful," he said.

"But you are. You saved the President today. It's incredible. It's a miracle."

Luke sighed. He didn't feel like a hero. And it didn't feel like a miracle—it felt like a nightmare, still unfolding.

"You're just tired, Luke. That's why you feel down. When was the last time you slept, over thirty hours ago? Listen, Gunner and I are both really proud of you. When you get back to DC, why don't you go back to the house, get a good night's sleep, and then come out here. It's beautiful here right now. We'll just take a few days, we'll turn the clocks off, we'll all be together. How does that sound?"

"It sounds really good."

"I love you so much," she said.

Luke loved Becca too, and he wanted to see her. He wanted to spend a few quiet days at the country house with both her and Gunner. But as much as he wanted it, he didn't see how it could happen.

He couldn't tell her anything. All he told her was that, after the briefing with the President, he had flown back to New York to track down another lead. He didn't tell her about the helicopter attack. He didn't tell her about leaping onto the roof of a moving car at a hundred miles per hour. He didn't tell her about killing two men. He didn't tell her that this case seemed nowhere near over.

145

A young detective with thinning hair, his tie pulled askew and his sleeves rolled up, came down the hall toward Luke.

"Agent Stone?"

Luke nodded.

"They're about to start the questioning."

Luke signed off with Becca and followed the detective to the observation room. The room was dim, with half a dozen men in it. Luke welcomed the half-darkness after the harsh light of the hallway.

The detective introduced Luke to three men in dark suits and ties.

"You probably want to meet these guys. This is Agent Stone with the FBI, these are Agents Stern, Smith, and Wallace."

"We're with Homeland," one of the men said, while shaking Luke's hand.

"Begley send you here?" Luke said.

The man's smile faltered, just a touch. "Begley?"

"Yeah. Ron Begley." Luke made the shape of a basketball with his hands. "Round guy? He runs a unit over there, don't ask me what. He and I had a little misunderstanding this morning about whether or not Ali Nassar was worth pursuing. I guess he changed his mind."

The three men laughed. "We don't work for Ron Begley."

"Good for you. You're probably happier that way."

On the other side of a large false window, Ali Nassar sat a metal table. He sipped from a white coffee mug. His ankle was cuffed to the table leg, which itself was bolted to the floor. It didn't matter. Ali Nassar didn't look like he was going anywhere.

He was utterly and completely disheveled. His dress shirt was torn and rumpled, and unbuttoned halfway to his stomach. His hair stood on end. There were black half-moons under each eye. His jaw hung open. His hand trembled whenever he lifted his coffee mug.

An NYPD detective loomed over him, a big, brawny, red-haired Irishman. Everything in the observation room went quiet when Nassar started to talk.

"Where is my daughter, and her mother?" he said.

The cop shook his head. "They're fine. You don't need to worry about them. We brought them back to the Iranian mission. They didn't do anything. They have no idea what's going on. Nobody's even interested in them."

Nassar nodded. "Good."

"Right," the cop said. "It is good. They're safe. Now let's put them out of our minds for a minute. I want to talk about you."

Now Nassar shook his head. "You have no right to hold me here. I want to speak to a lawyer."

The cop smiled. He was relaxed. Luke recognized a guy who heard that lawyer demand every single day, and then found a way around it.

"Why do you want to do that?" the cop said. "You have something left to hide? You already talked to the FBI agent in the car."

"He put a gun to my head."

The cop shrugged. "Maybe he did, maybe he didn't. That's the first I heard of it. I wasn't there, so what do I know?"

"It's illegal for you to hold me here," Nassar said.

"Ali, let me tell you something. We're not actually holding you here. That's the thing. You're not under arrest. We couldn't arrest you if we wanted to, you know that. We've got that leg iron on you for your own safety. These halls out here are crawling with violent criminals. Sometimes they get loose. Believe me, you're safer in this room. But if you want to leave, you're free to go at any time."

Nassar seemed about to speak. He hesitated, maybe expecting a trick.

The cop raised a meaty hand. "Now let me tell you why leaving is a bad idea," he said. "You've been involved in something. It's something bad. You know that and I know that, so there's no sense pretending. People tell me you blew up the White House. I don't know if I believe that."

"I didn't do it," Nassar said.

The cop pointed at him. "Right. That's what I believe. I believe you didn't do it. But it seems like maybe you know the people who did do it. And if I were those people right now, you know what I'd be looking to do? Clean up loose ends. A guy like you walks out that door, how long do you really think you're going to live? Twelve hours, if you're lucky? Personally, I doubt you'll make it that long."

Nassar stared at him.

"Your friends from the Iranian mission?" the cop said. He shook his head. "I don't think they're coming back for you. They lost four men today trying to get you to the airport. You're a

147

liability for them. You're an embarrassment. If they do come back, I think it's to put a bullet right here."

The cop tapped Nassar on the forehead.

Nassar shook his head. "They weren't involved. They have no reason to kill me."

"Yeah. That's what you told the guy from the FBI." The cop referred to some notes on a clipboard. "You told him you were working for an agency of the U.S. government, something called Red Box. You don't think the Iranian government would kill you if they knew you were working for the Americans? Come on, I think you're a little smarter than that."

Nassar's eyes briefly widened.

The cop nodded. "Yep. You're smart enough. You see it. You don't have too many friends left, Ali."

Luke thought back to that moment in the car. Cops were all around them. "I work for you," Nassar said. Then he did say Red Box. Luke barely remembered it. He had jumped out of a helicopter. He had crashed the car. He had shot two men in the head only seconds before. He was as shaken up as anyone. At that moment, he almost couldn't process what Nassar was telling him.

Now, as he watched, Nassar and the cop stared at each other for a long moment.

"I want to share something with you," the cop said. "I know exactly what you're going through. I have a younger brother. Maybe fifteen years ago, he gets involved in something, like you did. It was a mistake, like you made a mistake, and he got in over his head. Turns out he's smuggling guns to the Irish Republican Army out of a bar up in the Bronx. I tell him Mikey, you're stupid. You're not Irish. You're American. But by then, everybody's on to him. He's wanted by the American government. He's wanted by the English government. And if his buddies in the IRA find him, they're going to drop him in the river. They have to. What else are they gonna do, let him talk?"

A couple of cops in the observation room laughed. Luke glanced at them.

"This guy and his younger brothers," one of the cops said. "My brother the rapist. My brother the arsonist. My brother the terrorist. You want to know the truth? He has three sisters, and they're all older than he is."

Inside the interrogation room, Ali Nassar said, "I think I'm in a bad position."

148

The cop nodded. "I'd say you're in a very bad position. But I can help you. You just have to tell me what's going on."

Nassar seemed to have come to a decision. He shook his head. "Red Box is not an agency. It's a program, an operation. Operation Red Box. I didn't know what it was for. I knew what they wanted me to do, and that was it. They wanted me to buy some drones from China. They told me to pay some jihadis, men who wanted to commit suicide for God. I made the payments from an offshore account they themselves set up for me. It wasn't my account. I didn't hire these men. I didn't even know what they were going to do until two days ago."

"You keep saying they, they, they," the cop said. "Can you be a little more specific? Who are they?"

Ali Nassar sighed. "The Central Intelligence Agency. That's who hired me. A man I know from your CIA."

An almost silent gasp went through the room, and Luke felt a sharp jolt in his midsection. It felt like his body was impaled by a spike. He looked around at the men in the room with him. Everyone—cops, Homeland agents—*everyone* seemed puzzled. There was a low level buzz of muted conversation. The CIA hired Nassar to help attack the White House? The CIA?

Luke's entire world spun beneath him. It felt true; Luke could always tell if someone was lying, and Nassar wasn't. Either the CIA hired him, or he genuinely believed that they did. Luke, reeling, wondered if it could be true. If so, he would have to look at everyone around him differently. Who would he be able to trust?

"It was a year ago," Nassar said. "He visited me at my hotel room in London. At first, he called it Operation Red Box. Then, a month later he came to me and told me he made an error, it wasn't Operation Red Box. We must never speak of Operation Red Box again. We must never even say the words. But I remembered it. I'm sure that is the name, but I don't know what it means. So if you want to learn about Operation Red Box, don't ask me anything. Ask your CIA Director instead."

"Who's got this guy?" Luke said. "Is someone taking custody?"

One of the men from Homeland Security raised his hand. "When the NYPD is done with him, they're going to release him to us."

Luke nodded. "Good. Hang on to him."

He started walking toward the door.

149

"Where are you going?" one of the men said.

Luke didn't even turn around.

"I'm going back to Washington. I need to talk to someone."

Chapter 34

The man wouldn't meet him until nightfall.

Luke waited alone on a wooded path by the shore of the Potomac River. The sun had just set, but no light was visible. A thick, cold fog had rolled in off the water sometime earlier. It swirled around him. No one could see him. He could be anyone in here. He could be a dead man. He could have ceased to exist. He could be the last person left on Earth. It was a good feeling.

He had raced back here to Washington, only to end up waiting. He was past exhausted, and with so much at stake, the waiting bothered him. The man always made him wait. Always had, always would.

Luke had talked to Ed Newsam on the phone ten minutes before. Newsam was in the hospital. Jacob and Rachel had managed to crash land the chopper in the middle of an empty Little League baseball field. Newsam's hip was cracked, and he had been strafed pretty good with bullets, but he was going to be fine. It would take more than an Uzi to kill a man like Newsam. Still, he was out of commission, and the thought of that worried Luke just a bit.

There was a lot more to do.

"Quite a day you've had," a voice said.

Luke looked up. A tall elderly man in a long leather coat stood nearby, walking a small gray and brown dog. The man's hair was so white it almost seemed to glow in the just settled darkness. He didn't face Luke directly, but came closer and sat at the far end of the bench. He lowered himself to the bench slowly and with some difficulty. Then he patted the little dog with thin hands. A biscuit appeared in one of those hands like a magic trick, and the man fed it to the dog. He smiled at his own sleight of hand.

"Nice dog," Luke said. "What breed would you call that?"

"Mutt," the man said. "I think he must be half rat. I got him from the shelter. He was twenty-four hours from the gas chamber. How could I go to a breeder when there are so many lost souls on death row? It's unconscionable."

"What can I call you?" Luke said.

"Paul is good," the man said.

151

That was funny. Paul, Wes, Steve, the man always went by some nondescript name. When Luke was young, the name had been Henry, or Hank. He was the man without a name, the man without a country. What could you say about someone who was a Cold War spy, who sold his own country's secrets to the Soviets, then turned around and sold the Soviets' secrets to the British and the Israelis? And that was the little Luke knew about. There was probably a lot more.

One thing you might say is he was lucky to be alive. Another thing is that it was amazing he could choose to live in Washington, DC, now, right under the very noses of people who would be happy to kill him or put him away forever. But perhaps betrayal had an expiration date. After a certain amount of time had passed, maybe no one cared anymore. Maybe all the people who once cared were dead.

Luke nodded. "Okay, Paul. Thanks for coming. I want to tell you that I met with a man this afternoon. Up in New York."

The old man laughed. "Oh my, yes. I heard all about it. I gather you dropped in on him somewhat uninvited. Dropped out of the sky, in fact."

Luke stared into the fog. It was as thick as soup.

"He said some things I don't understand."

"Being smart is not the same as being quick-witted," the man said. "Some people, as clever as they may be, are still slow in the uptake."

"Or maybe I understand what he said, I just don't believe it."

"What was it?"

"Operation Red Box," Luke said. "That's what he told me."

The old man said nothing. He looked straight ahead. A moment ago, his hands had been stroking the dog. Now they had stopped.

Luke went on. "He said to ask the CIA Director about it. Well, I don't have access to the CIA Director. But I do have access to you."

The man's mouth opened, then closed again.

"Tell me," Luke said.

The man looked straight at Luke for the first time. His face was like wrinkled parchment. His eyes were deep set and pale blue. They were eyes that still knew secrets. They were eyes without pity.

"I haven't heard those words in a long while," he said. "I wouldn't recommend you say them again. Never know who's listening, even in a place like this."

"All right."

"I imagine you asked him a question to elicit that phrase. What was the question?"

"I asked him," Luke said, "who he was working for."

A long sigh came from the old man. It sounded like the air going slowly out of a tire, all the way, until there was nothing left. Abruptly, the man stood up. He moved quickly, and without the apparent frailty of a few moments before.

"It's been interesting talking with you," the man said. "Perhaps we'll meet again."

The gun appeared in Luke's hand as if by magic, a better trick than the dog biscuit. It was a different gun from the one he had held earlier that day. This one had an eight-inch silencer attached to the end of the barrel. It was longer than the gun itself. Luke casually pointed the gun at the man's belly.

"You know this silencer?" he said. "It's called the Illusion. It's new, and you've been out of the game for a while, so maybe you don't. Suffice to say that it works really, really well. A night like this one, with all this fog? The gun will go off, and it'll sound like somebody sneezed. Not a loud sneeze. A quiet sneeze, like someone might do at the ballet." He smiled. "We get all the best toys at SRT."

A ghost of a smile passed over the man's lips. "I always enjoy our meetings."

"Tell me," Luke said again.

The man shrugged. "You should go home to your lovely wife and handsome young son. This is a situation that doesn't concern you. Even if it did, there wouldn't be a thing you could do about it."

"What is Operation Red Box?"

The old man seemed to wince at the name.

Luke waited a few seconds, but the man didn't seem ready to speak. "Give me one reason not to pull this trigger."

The man blinked. "Kill me," he said slowly, "and you won't have me as the source you need on future cases."

Luke shook his head. "There are no future cases," he said. "If this one isn't solved, there is no future for any of us."

Luke scowled. "What is Operation Red Box?"

The man shook his head. "You're in way too deep. You've become a danger to yourself and others, and the worst part is you don't even know it. I won't say the words. But the operation you mention is one designed for expedited Presidential succession. It's for when a President has to be removed from office, but there's no time to wait for the next election cycle."

"They were threatening to impeach the President this morning," Luke said. "It was on the radio." The statement felt odd as soon as he said it. Impeaching the President and terrorists blowing up the White House… the two items didn't fit together. Luke was beyond tired. It was hard to make sense of things.

"Faster than impeachment," Paul said. "And more certain. Think abrupt change. Think 1963. It's an operation reserved for when the President's loyalty is no longer unquestioned. It's also for when events are too large, or too sensitive, for the man in office. It's for times that demand action."

"Who decides this?" Luke said.

Paul shrugged. He smiled again. "The people in charge decide."

Luke stared at him.

"Tell me you don't know who's really in charge," Paul said, "and I will start to wonder about your mother's relationship to the milkman."

The old man stared at him. There was a wild sort of light in the man's eyes. To Luke, he looked like a carnival barker, or a conman with the traveling medicine show. The man smiled. There was no humor in it.

"You saw the White House blow up today, did you not?"

Luke nodded. "I was there."

"Of course you were. Where else would you be at a time like that? Did it look like a drone strike to you? Or did it look like something clsc? Think back. Perhaps it looked more like a series of detonations, bombs that were planted inside the building, maybe days or weeks ago?"

In his mind's eye, Luke saw the explosions again, an entire line of them, moving from the West Wing, along the Colonnade, to the Residence. A huge explosion tore the Residence to pieces, throwing a massive chunk of it high into the air. He felt the shockwave again, the one that had threatened to knock their helicopter out of the sky.

But how could someone put bombs inside the White House?

154

Everyone who worked there had high-level security clearance, from the maids and the maintenance men, to the dishwashers and onion peelers, to the press secretary and the President's chief-of-staff. Everyone was vetted. If bombs had been planted, then that meant...

An inside job. All the way inside, inside the security apparatus, inside the intelligence community, far enough inside to take a group of explosives experts, erase their pasts, give them new identities, and get them jobs at the White House. Jobs without close supervision, jobs that gave them wide latitude to roam the hallways, especially at night when no one else was around.

In Luke's mind, a whole series of assumptions began to give way. All day, he had been focused on a ragtag group of terrorists. They were minimally trained, but they were violent and they were clever. They were hiding, they were running, they were employing asymmetrical tactics, using their smallness as a weapon against a vastly superior enemy. Maybe those men even believed that's what they were doing. They may have stolen the nuclear material. They may have flown the drone, and even blown up a part of the White House. Yet, still, they were but a small cog in a machine. They were being used by something much larger, something much more sophisticated.

What Ali Nassar said was true. It was the American government all along.

A strange feeling of heat began to radiate along Luke's spine. It went to the top of his head and down along his shoulders and arms. He looked at his hands, half expecting them to burst into flames. A wave of nausea passed through him. For a second, he thought he might vomit. He didn't want to do that, not here, not in front of Paul.

"How can I stop it?" Luke said.

Paul shook his head. "My friend, you don't stop Operation Red Box. You get the hell out of the way. This isn't your fight, Luke. If you try to make it yours, you will fail. You will fail in a way that will probably feel spectacular while it's happening, but in the end will be much closer to pathetic."

"Then give me enough to do that."

Paul grunted, and then laughed. "You're a fool. You have no knack for self-preservation. You're like one of these Japanese kamikaze pilots from World War II, flying an airplane full of

155

bombs into the side of an aircraft carrier. Except in this case, the plane you're flying is a bathtub toy."

The old man paused, thinking for a moment, seeing Luke would not back down.

"Okay. You're looking for a way to die? Get in touch with a man named David Delliger. He's the Secretary of Defense, in case you don't know. He was roommates with the President at Yale. There's no way he'll be in on the plot, but he will be very, very close to it, probably without knowing. The pieces will only become clear to him after the fact, but he'll see them. Maybe he has no knack for self-preservation either. If so, the two of you will make quite a pair."

"What about the President?" Luke said.

Paul shrugged. "What about him?"

"He's safe now, isn't he?" Luke pressed. "He's ten stories underground."

Paul smiled. "I need to be going. It's getting late for an old man to be out and about. These parks can be dangerous at night."

"The President is safe," Luke insisted, grabbing his arm, frantic, needing to hear him say it.

Paul slowly shook his head and removed Luke's hand.

"You don't understand," Paul replied, his voice hoarse, before turning around, drifting back into the silver and gray fog. "If this is truly Operation Red Box, then the President is already dead."

Chapter 35

8:53 p.m.
Mount Weather Emergency Operations Center –
Bluemont, Virginia

An earnest young man poked his head into the room.

"Mr. President? We are going live in seven minutes. We'd like to have you on the set two minutes early."

Thomas Hayes sat in a leather barbershop chair in what amounted to his dressing room. The room was shaped like an oval. The walls were bare, except for the mirror in front of him and a long dressing table. In the mirror, he could see his Chief of Staff, David Halstram, trying to relax on the couch.

David seemed to have two speeds—Go, and Go Faster. He couldn't relax in the calmest of circumstances. Today had been anything but calm. He was fidgeting a lot. One of his shoes was tapping out a machine gun rhythm on the cement floor.

The President held the final draft of his speech in his hand. Old-fashioned paper for President Hayes—he had never fully adapted to the digital revolution. David had the same speech on an iPad.

Two young women were putting the final touches on Hayes. One was smoothing his makeup in such a way that it would look like he wasn't wearing makeup. The other was fluffing his hair so that it was neat and presentable, almost but not perfect. He had nearly been killed today. He should seem at least a little bit windblown.

"What does that mean?" he said to the young man who had spoken. "Is it a math problem?"

"It means five more minutes, sir."

"Okay. We'll be there."

When the man left, President Hayes looked at David again through the mirror. "What do you think of this phrase he uses toward the end, *greatness awaits us*? He's got it in there three times. It sounds like the advertising tag line for a no-fee checking account. I mean, what am I supposed to do with that?"

Hayes was nervous, as he should be. In a moment, he was going to go on air and talk to the American people about the crisis they were facing. He could only assume that nearly every single

157

adult in the country, and hundreds of millions more abroad, would see him or hear his voice. Every TV network was pre-empting their broadcasting. Nearly every radio network was. YouTube was streaming it live.

It was the biggest single speech he was ever likely to give, and it had been whipped together this afternoon and evening by a lead speech writer that Hayes probably would have let go weeks before, if only he didn't have so many other things on his mind.

"Thomas," David said, "you are the best public speaker I've heard in my lifetime. No, I wasn't around for John F. Kennedy or Martin Luther King, but that doesn't matter. No one alive right now even comes close to you. Someone tried to murder you today. They destroyed the White House, and killed nearly two dozen people. The American people want to hear from you. I say speak to them. Speak from your heart. Move them, and lead them. Use this speech as a guide if you want, or throw the whole thing out and wing it. I've seen you speak off the cuff and bring entire rooms to tears."

Hayes nodded. He liked the idea of winging it. He liked the idea of taking leadership. And when he thought about leading, he realized what was missing now. That sense of dread, of trepidation, of being pulled apart like a piece of saltwater taffy. It was gone. The attack today had focused his mind. He felt confident. He felt that he could be a leader again. He no longer cared what the House of Representatives thought, or what people like Bill Ryan did.

Thomas Hayes had been elected to lead by the people of the United States of America. Lead was what he intended to do.

"Do you suppose Susan will show up for this?"

David nodded. "I know she will. I talked to her late this afternoon. She doesn't like you very much right now, but that's neither here nor there. We'll get that patched up later. In the meantime, she's going to do her job. When your speech ends, and you are greeting and chatting with the most powerful people in America, and everyone gathers together for a show of unity in front of the cameras, she will be right out in front and very, very visible."

"Okay, David. I feel badly about today. I do want to patch it up."

David nodded. "You will."

When the time came, Hayes rose from the chair, shrugged into his suit jacket, and marched out of the room. David was with him, a half step behind. Hayes entered the underground TV studio. His

158

podium, with the seal of the President, was on a raised stage a foot high, with blue carpeting. It was surrounded by cameras and lights.

Hayes felt good, he felt energetic, and he felt powerful. He felt that surge of electricity he used to get before a race, back when he was the captain of a nationally ranked rowing team.

He resisted the urge to run up onto the stage like a game show host.

Behind him, David's phone started to ring. He glanced back at his Chief of Staff. David was looking at the caller ID. He glanced up.

"It's Luke Stone."

The President shrugged. "Take it. We have a couple of minutes. And anyway, I can handle this. I've done it before a million times."

He stepped up to the podium and looked out at all the bright lights.

*

Luke stood by the water's edge. He had taken exactly five steps from the bench where his father had left him sitting. He could barely see a thing. The fog was so dense he was lucky this call had gone through.

The phone rang and rang.

"Halstram," a voice said.

"David, I need to talk to President Hayes."

"Luke, I'm sorry. You and your partner did an amazing thing today. But the President is going live on the air in two minutes. If you want, you can leave a message with me, and I'll get it to him as soon as this is over, probably an hour from now. Listen, you should go somewhere with a TV set and watch the show. I'm expecting dynamite from him. They tagged us one, but we're not out of the fight, not by a long shot."

"David, we've got big trouble."

"I know. I was there today, remember? We're going to work hard and we're going to dig our way out of it. And you're going to be a big part of that, believe me."

Luke didn't know how to handle people like David Halstram, at least, not over the phone. David tended to talk a blue streak, pause for breath, then start talking again. He was energetic, hyperkinetic, and probably very smart. He was certainly convinced

159

of his own abilities, and he was convinced that people should listen to him and do what he said. It was hard to slow him down long enough to listen.

If Luke were there in person right now, he might put the business end of his gun against David's forehead, and grab him by his thinning hair. Or, if he were feeling relaxed, he might just give David a karate chop to the collarbone. Either thing would likely focus David's attention. But over the phone? It was hard.

He spoke slowly, as if to an imbecile. "David, you have to listen to me. The President's life is in danger."

"That's why we're underground right now."

"David..."

"Luke, listen, I need to be available here. If you don't have a specific message you want to leave, I need you to call me back in... let's say ninety minutes, okay? If you don't get me, try me a half hour after that."

"You have to get out of there."

"Okay, Luke, we'll talk about it. He's coming on right now. I have to go."

The line went dead. Luke stared at the telephone. He fought the urge to throw it into the river. Instead, he started to walk to his car. A minute later, he started to run.

Was he really going to drive out to Mount Weather, now, after almost forty hours without sleep?

Yes.

Chapter 36

How she would love to be almost anywhere but here.

She stood outside the gaping maw of the Mount Weather facility's entrance, smoking a cigarette and holding her smartphone to her ear.

The smoking was one of those secret things that the American people were never supposed to know. Susan Hopkins enjoyed a cigarette now and then, and she had done so ever since she was a teenage supermodel. Especially in times of stress, nothing could beat it, and this was probably the most stressful day of her life. No one had ever tried to murder her before.

She wore a red skater dress, one that was maybe a tad sexy for the occasion. They had choppered it in from the Nordstrom store in the mall near the Pentagon, along with a seamstress to do the fitting. It was David Halstram's idea. It was for the people watching on TV, so they could easily spot her. That way, after Thomas's speech, no one in the world could miss the fact that Susan Hopkins was in a tunnel deep underground, hanging on the President's every word. It was a good idea. But it was also a cool night, and the mountain air went right through the dress's material.

She shivered. Three very big Secret Service men stood right nearby. They loomed over her. She hoped that none of them offered her their jacket. That kind of chivalry made her want to puke.

Pierre was talking at the other end of the phone.

"Honey," he said, "I would really like to see you get out of there. It's making me nervous. I can send a plane to whatever municipal airport is closest to you. You could be on the way back out here an hour from now. I've doubled security. The electric fence is on. It would take a small army to get through. You can just tell everyone that you need a couple of weeks off to regroup. Relax by the pool. Get a massage."

Susan smiled at the thought of Pierre holed up in his thirty-room mansion, safely behind his electric fence. Who did he think he was trying to keep out, fraternity pranksters? His fence and his entry gate, and his eight (instead of four) retired detectives wouldn't even slow down the people who had almost killed her.

Good Lord.

"Pierre…"

He kept talking. "Just let me finish," he said.

She thought of the early times with him. She had already done *Vogue*, *Cosmo*, *Mademoiselle*, *Victoria's Secret*, even the *Sports Illustrated* young masturbators issue. But she was starting to age out. She could feel it, and her agent told her as much. The covers had stopped coming. She was twenty-four years old.

Then she met Pierre. He was twenty-nine, and his start-up company's initial public offering had just turned him into an instant billionaire. He had grown up in San Francisco, but his family was from France. He was beautiful, with a skinny body and big brown eyes. He looked like a deer in the headlights. His dark hair always flopped down in front of his face. He was hiding in there. It was unbearably cute.

She had made a lot of money in her career, several million dollars. Financially, she had been very, very comfortable. But suddenly money was no object at all. They traveled the world together. Paris, Madrid, Hong Kong, London... They always stayed in five-star hotels, and always in the most expensive suite. Astonishing views became the backdrop to her life, even more so than before. They skied in the Alps, and in Aspen. They sunned themselves on the beaches of the Greek islands, but also in Bali and Barbados. They married, and they had children, two wonderful twin girls. Then the years began to pass, and slowly they grew apart.

Susan became bored. She looked for something to do. She got into politics. Eventually, she ran for United States Senator from California. It was a crazy idea, and she surprised everyone (including herself) by winning in a landslide. After that, she spent much of her time in Washington, sometimes with the girls, sometimes not. Pierre managed his businesses, and increasingly, his charitable efforts in the Third World. Sometimes they didn't see each other for months.

About seven years ago, Pierre called her late one night and confessed something she supposed she already knew. He was gay, and he was in a relationship.

They stayed married anyway. It was mostly for the girls, but for other reasons as well. For one thing, they were best friends. For another, it was better for both of them if the world thought they were still a couple. They cut a media friendly image together. And it was comfortable.

She sighed. It was just another one of those secrets the American people couldn't know about.

She looked at her watch. It was almost nine o'clock.

"Pierre," she said again.

"Yes," he said finally.

"I love you every much."

"I love you, too."

"Good. I will take everything you said under advisement. And I will get out of here as soon as I can. But right now I have to go watch the President make his speech."

"The President is a jerk."

She nodded. "I know. But he's our jerk and we have to support him. Okay?"

"Okay."

She hung up the phone and flicked the remains of her cigarette. She looked at the three lumbering giants that surrounded her. "Let's go guys," she said. A minute later, they were all on the elevator, dropping down into the bowels of the earth.

*

"Forty seconds, Mr. President," a voice from the control booth said. "When my light goes green, you are live."

"Am I facing green?" Hayes said.

"We've got five angles on you, sir, but yes. Green is looking directly into their eyes. Thirty seconds."

David Halstram positioned himself at the back of the TV studio, taking in the whole scene. The President stood tall at the podium, utterly calm, waiting for the light to come on. In the small amphitheatre facing him sat some of the most important and influential people in the country.

Congressmen and Senators from both sides of the aisle made up much of the audience—mostly liberals like the President, but also plenty of the loyal opposition. The Secretary of State was here, as was the Secretary of the Treasury and the Secretary of Education. The Directors of NASA, the National Science Foundation, and the National Park System sat in a row, surrounded by their senior staff.

Halstram's heart raced. To say he was excited would be to badly underestimate his state of mind. He felt like he was in a rocket ship, accelerating through the Earth's gravity field. These were the moments he lived for.

He was born to do this job. He didn't drink alcohol, and he had never done drugs. He barely had any need for caffeine. He worked eighteen-hour days without blinking, dropped to sleep for

163

four or five hours, got up and did it all over again. What kind of rush was coffee compared to the life that David led?

President Thomas Hayes was about to give one of the most important speeches in American history, and David Halstram, his chief-of-staff, his confidant, his trusted advisor, was standing thirty feet away.

"Twenty seconds, Mr. President."

A brief disturbance flickered across David's awareness. Luke Stone. They had vetted him this afternoon. Of course they had. He had saved the President, but... you had to know who you were dealing with. There was a lot in the man's file. Red flags waved like crazy. Combat stress. Questionable use of force. Abuse of authority. Forgeries. Apparently, he had entered the West Wing today with faked Yankee White security clearance. How did he manage that? What would have happened if he hadn't managed it?

"Ten seconds. Good luck, sir."

Now he wanted them to leave the facility. Okay, David would talk to him about it. Maybe in the morning, they would... what? Go to Camp David?

On the podium, Hayes looked straight at the camera.

The voice came back one last time. "We are live in four..."

"Three..."

Hayes smiled. It seemed faked, forced, but then it faded into something else.

"Two..."

It became a look of determination.

"One."

"Good evening, my fellow Americans," the President began, with a broad, confident smile. "I am here to tell you—"

BOOM!

A light flashed, and for a split second, David thought it was the green light the President was waiting for. But it wasn't green. It was white, and huge, and blinding. It came from somewhere behind the President.

It swallowed the President whole.

David was blasted off his feet by the force of it. He flew through the air, hit the wall ten feet behind him, and fell to the ground. Everything had gone dark. He could not see. The ground beneath him was shaking.

Suddenly, another light flashed, bigger this time, more intense. Everything was rumbling. The entire facility was moving. The ceiling above him caved in. He heard it go, and for a very brief second, he felt it. A large chunk of masonry landed on his lower back and on his legs. It hurt, and then it didn't.

David had a very quick mind. He knew instantly that his legs were crushed, and that he was, in all likelihood, paralyzed from the waist down. He suspected that although he couldn't feel it, he was probably hemorrhaging blood.

In the darkness all around him, invisible people were screaming.

I am ten stories below the surface. No one is coming to rescue me.

He thought backwards, rewinding events several seconds. That first blinding flash of light. He saw it now, more clearly than before. The light hadn't swallowed the President.

It had obliterated him.

The President—and likely everyone underground with him—was dead.

Chapter 37

"And now…" a quiet voice said. "The President of the United States."

Luke was just merging onto the highway as the President's speech was about to start. Luke's thought was that if the President spoke for an hour, by the time the speech was over, he would be entering the gates at Mount Weather.

He heard the President's first words—and then the radio went silent.

A woman's voice came on.

"Uh…we seem to be having technical difficulties. We've lost communication with the President's bunker at Mount Weather. We're working to correct the problem. In the meantime, a few words from our sponsors."

Luke punched in another station. The story was the same.

He tried another station. They had put on a rock song.

Finally, a man's voice came on the radio.

"Ladies and gentlemen, we are getting word that an explosion of some kind seems to have struck the Mount Weather government facility. We do not have any details at this moment. There is no contact with the facility, but first responders are converging on the scene. We caution you that this doesn't mean—"

Luke switched off the radio.

For a moment, Luke felt nothing. He was numb. He remembered the morning on that long-ago hill in Afghanistan. It was cold. The sun rose, but there was no warmth to it. The ground was rugged, and hard. There were dead bodies everywhere. Skinny, bearded men lay all over the ground, with eyes wide and staring.

At some point in the night, Luke had ripped off his shirt. His chest was painted red. He was soaked in their blood. He had chopped them up. Stabbed them. Sliced them. And the more he killed them, the more they kept coming.

Martinez was sprawled on his back nearby, low in a trench. He was crying. He couldn't move his legs. He'd had enough. He wanted out. "Stone," he said. "Hey, Stone. Hey! Kill me, man. Just kill me. Hey, Stone! Listen to me, man!"

166

Murphy was sitting on an outcropping of rock, staring into space. He wasn't even trying to take cover.

If more enemies came, Stone didn't know what he was going to do. Neither one of these guys looked like they had much fight left in them, and the only usable weapon Stone still had was the bent bayonet in his hand.

As he watched, a line of black insects appeared in the sky far away. He knew what they were in an instant. Helicopters. And then he knew he was still alive. He didn't feel good about that, or bad. He felt nothing at all.

Like now.

He snapped out of it as, to his left, an ambulance roared by at a hundred miles per hour, headed west, lights flashing, siren blaring. Luke got off the highway at the next exit. At the bottom of the ramp was a commuter parking lot. Luke pulled in and slowed the car to a stop.

He put the car in park and turned off his headlights. He thought that maybe if he screamed, he would feel something, so he tried it.

He screamed. He did it for a long time.

It didn't work.

Chapter 38

9:35 p.m.
Fairfax County, Virginia - Suburbs of Washington, DC

Whiskey on ice.

There was something exquisite about the way it was cold in his mouth and then ignited a fire inside him when it reached his stomach.

Luke sat on the sofa in his own living room. He had just walked in the door moments ago. He glanced at the clock, thinking back. He hadn't been here in almost exactly twenty hours. He had gone out with purpose, and full of energy. He had worked hard to avert disaster, he had risked his own life again and again, and for what? Disaster had happened anyway.

He turned on the TV set and set it on MUTE. He flicked through the channels, watching the imagery. Mount Weather, where he had been earlier today, on fire. The distraught First Lady being interviewed at a resort in Hawaii. She broke down and wept in front of the cameras. Spontaneous candlelight vigils in many places. A hundred thousand people in Paris, a hundred thousand in London. Deserted streets in DC and Manhattan. Rioting in Detroit and Los Angeles and Philadelphia, places where the President had been beloved. Talking heads talking, talking, talking, some teary-eyed and sincere, and some angry and gesturing emphatically. Someone had to pay, of course. Someone always had to pay.

Now the news changed. Somewhere, fighter planes were being scrambled. Bombs were hitting targets in the Middle East. Nuclear submarines in the North Sea. The American fleet in the Persian Gulf. The Russian president addressing a news conference. Chinese cabinet members in Beijing. Iranian mullahs. Chanting crowds, men in turbans and sandals brandishing AK-47s, kissing babies and hoisting them up to God. A riot in the alleyways of an ancient city, soldiers firing tear gas, people running, being trampled in the darkness. A man, a traitor of some kind, being stoned to death in a dusty town.

All of this flowed past, image after image after image. The American President had been murdered, and the whole world had gone mad. It was impossible to grasp the magnitude of what had happened.

Luke reached down, untied his boots, and kicked them off. He sat back. Less than twenty-four hours ago, he had been on the verge of retiring from the intelligence game. It had been almost unbelievably pleasant these past six months, teaching a couple of classes, playing some pickup basketball with the students, relaxing here with his family. Maybe his days as a soldier and a spy and a kamikaze really were over.

He glanced around the house. They had a great life here. It was a beautiful home, modern, with floor to ceiling windows, like something out of an architectural magazine. It was like a glass box. In the winter, when it snowed, it was just like one of those old snow globes people used to have when he was a kid. He pictured Christmas time—just sitting in this stunning sunken living room, the tree in the corner, the fireplace lit, the snow coming down all around as if they were outside, but they were inside, warm and cozy.

God, it was nice.

He could never afford this place on his government salary. Becca could never afford it on a university researcher salary. The two of them together couldn't afford this place. It was her family money that bought it.

And that told him all he needed to know about the job. It didn't matter if he worked two days a week or if he never worked again. They were set, probably for life.

A dark thought occurred to him. If war broke out among the great powers, it would be almost impossible to stop it. Even so, maybe he could let these gigantic forces fight it out amongst themselves. He didn't have to participate. Maybe, if given enough time away, he could put the whole thing out of his mind. The worst atrocities could be something that happened to other people, somewhere far away.

He picked his phone up off the coffee table and called a number.

The lines were open now. The cell towers weren't overwhelmed anymore. People had given up.

The phone rang. On the third ring, she picked it up.

Her voice was thick with sleep. "H'lo?"

"Babe?"

"Hi, baby," she said.

"Hello. What are you doing?"

169

"Oh, I was tired, so I decided to go to bed early. Gunner was running me all day long. So I hit the hay right after I hung up with you. How did everything go? Did you watch the President?"

Luke took a deep breath. She went to sleep before the President's speech. Which meant that she didn't know. He couldn't bring himself to tell her. Not now.

"Nah. I was too tired. I decided to take a night off, and unplug from everything. No TV, no computer, nothing. I'm sure people will fill me in tomorrow."

"Now you're thinking," she said.

Luke smiled. "Okay, sweetheart. Go back to sleep. I'm sorry I woke you."

She was already falling asleep again. "I love you."

He sat on the sofa and smiled to himself for a moment. He took another sip of the whiskey. It made him happy to think of Becca and Gunner running around all day, and now sleeping in the deep quiet of the country house. Luke was going to enjoy retirement, he really was.

Just not yet.

He dialed another number.

A clipped female voice answered. "Wellington."

"Trudy, it's Luke."

"Luke, where are you? Everything's gone haywire."

"I'm home. Where are you?"

"I'm at headquarters, where the hell else would I be? Luke, half the Congress was at Mount Weather. The President and his aides and his chief of staff. The Vice President, the Secretary of State, the Secretary of the Treasury, the Secretary of Education. They are all down there. The place is on fire and no one can put it out. There was a firestorm in the elevator shafts. The emergency stairwells were blown up. The firemen can not get down to the fire."

"Is there any contact at all?"

She made a sound. It was almost a laugh. "The President's chief of staff, David Halstram, managed to call out. He called 911, if you can believe that. There's a 911 dispatcher tape. I heard it a little while ago. He sounded terrified, talking very fast. He said his legs were pinned and he was afraid the President was dead. He said you called him just before it happened, and told him to get the President out. He..." Trudy's voice shook... "said he wished he had listened to you."

Luke didn't say anything.

"Did you call him?" Trudy said.

"I did, yeah."

"How did you know? How did you know what was going to happen?"

"Trudy, I can't tell you that."

"Luke—"

He cut her off. "Listen, I need you to do something for me. Is the Secretary of Defense alive? David Delliger?"

"He's alive. He's at Site R."

"I need a direct line for him. Some way to contact him."

"Why him? Shouldn't you talk to the President instead?"

Luke shook his head. "There is no President."

"Not yet. But they're swearing the new one in... ten minutes from now."

"Who is it, if not Delliger? Who's even alive to become President?"

"Luke, don't you know? It's Bill Ryan, the Speaker of the House."

Luke thought back to the various Representatives and Senators he saw gathering at Mount Weather earlier in the day. "Ryan? How did he survive?"

Trudy's voice sounded unsure. "They say it was dumb luck. He didn't go to Mount Weather."

Ryan, Luke thought, flabbergasted. A hawk among hawks. That could only mean one thing: they were going to war.

*

10:02 p.m., Site R - Blue Ridge Summit, Pennsylvania

It was a nightmare from which he could not awake.

His name was David Delliger, and he was the United States Secretary of Defense. He had been appointed to this role by his longtime friend and college roommate, Thomas Hayes, the former President of the United States.

Delliger was a surprising choice for the position, by any standard. He was a professor of history at the Naval Academy, and an attorney who had spent much of his career as a third-party mediator. In the years before he took this job, he had consulted with the Carter Center, monitoring elections in new democracies,

171

countries with long histories of despotic rule. That job was the opposite of making war.

And that's why Hayes the liberal had chosen him. Thomas Hayes was dead now, and had been for an hour. There was currently no way to tell who else was alive and who was dead in the wreckage of what had been the Mount Weather facility. The Vice President was missing and assumed dead. Fires still raged on several floors deep underground. Hundreds of people were trapped inside, including many of the members of Congress, and at least some of their family members.

Delliger stood in a concrete room, also deep underground, but more than sixty miles from the disaster. About thirty people were in that room with him. A blue curtain had been pulled across the concrete walls to mask the sheer ugliness of the room. On a small dais, two men and a woman stood. Photographers snapped pictures of them.

One of the men on the dais was short and bald. He wore a long robe. He was Clarence Warren, Chief Justice of the United States. The woman's name was Karen Ryan. She wore a bright blue suit with a red rose in her lapel. She was holding a Bible open in her hands. A tall, good-looking man in a dark blue suit and tie stood with his left hand on the Bible. His right hand was raised. Until this moment, the man had for years been the Representative from North Carolina, and the Speaker of the House.

"I, William Theodore Ryan," he said, "do solemnly swear that I will faithfully execute the Office of President of the United States."

"And will to the best of my ability," Judge Warren prompted.

"And will to the best of my ability," Ryan said.

"Preserve, protect, and defend the Constitution of the United States."

Ryan repeated the words, and with less ceremony than many local moose lodges employed to induct their new members, abruptly became President of the United States. Delliger was in something like shock. Yes, his good friend was dead. Thomas Hayes was a great man and his loss was a tragedy, both personally for Delliger, but even more profoundly for the people of America.

But even worse, one of the President's most formidable enemies in government had just taken over his job. The very man who had threatened the President with impeachment this morning was now President himself.

172

It didn't make sense. How had both the White House and Mount Weather been destroyed on the same day? Why had the President and Vice President been evacuated to the same facility? They should have been separated as soon as the Secret Service realized they were together.

As Delliger watched, Ryan and his wife, Karen, shared a kiss. Then, for a brief moment, Ryan mugged for the cameras, and several people in the room laughed. Delliger glanced around to see who the people were. He recognized many of the people in attendance. They were the most rabid war hawks in government. Members of the Joint Chiefs. The Director of the CIA. Congressmen with close ties to defense contractors. Lobbyists from the defense industry, and from the oil industry.

How did they all wind up here? No, a better question was how did he wind up among them? He was an alien to them, an outsider. He was the Secretary of Defense, but he had been appointed by a dove, a man who was doing everything in his power to avoid a war. *A man who was dead.*

This was the military bunker. These people felt at home here. David Delliger, even with his military background, would feel more at home in the civilian bunker, which was a place…

…that had just been destroyed.

A strange feeling came upon Delliger. For a moment, the faces of the people in the crowd seemed distorted, like funhouse faces. Everyone was smiling. The biggest disaster in American history had happened an hour ago, and people here were smiling. Why shouldn't they smile? They were in charge now.

Delliger glanced around the room again. No one was paying any attention to him. Why would they? He was the Defense Secretary of a dead President. He was a joke to them, part of a regime that had swept away.

On the dais, Ryan was serious again. He faced the gathering.

"No one wants to become President the way that I have. But I'm not going to stand up here and pretend I didn't want this job. I did want it, and I still do. I want it because I want to make America great again. Thomas Hayes was a great man in many ways, but he was also a weak man. He could not stand firm against our enemies, and as a result, he paid the ultimate price. Those policies, the policies of weakness, stop now."

A cheer went up from the crowd. Someone let loose a long wolf whistle. The clapping went on for an extended period. Ryan raised his hands to ask for quiet.

"Tonight I will address the American people, and by extension, the people of the entire world. What I tell them will give hope to those who have been terrorized by the events of the past day, and of the past several months. I plan to tell them that we are going to war, and that we are going on the offensive, and that we will not stop until the perpetrators of this terrible atrocity are brought to their knees. And even then, we will not stop. We will not stop until their palaces and towers are consumed by fire, and their people run screaming in the streets. And even then, we will not stop."

The cheering was so loud now that Ryan had to stop speaking. There was no sense continuing. No one could hear him.

He waited. Slowly the sound died down. Ryan stared directly at Delliger.

"We will avenge our losses," he said. "And we will avenge our loved ones. And we will not stop until the country of Iran can never project its power in the world again. We will not stop until they cannot feed themselves unless we feed them, and clothe themselves unless we clothe them. Eventually, there will be a time for mourning, and for remembering. But not yet. The time now is for vengeance!"

As another cheer went up, and the phone in Delliger's pocket vibrated. He took it out and glanced at it. He had a text message. This was his private phone. He rarely got texts. He opened it.

My name is Luke Stone. I know why the President died. Meet me.

174

Chapter 39

10:47 p.m.
Davis Memorial Hospital - Bethesda, Maryland

The three men entered his room like shadows.

They were quiet, almost silent. They had turned the lights off out in the hallway. So when they opened Ed Newsam's door a crack, and slid into his dark room, almost nothing about the light changed.

It didn't much matter. Ed Newsam didn't believe in sleep. Not at a time like this. He had been prescribed a powerful morphine-based painkiller for his bullet wounds and his cracked hip. The painkiller would make him sleep. Ed believed in pain. This pain was all too real not to believe in it. And he didn't refuse the painkiller. He palmed it. And when the nurse left the room, he slipped it under his mattress.

He could have refused it instead, but he wanted them to put it on his medical chart. He supposed that somewhere in the back of his mind he had expected a visit just like this one. Men such as these, they would take a look at Ed's chart before they came in here.

Ed was knocked out. Ed was on painkillers. Ed was getting some well-earned rest.

He breathed deeply, like a man long gone in never-never land. His eyes were open only a sliver. Lots of people slept that way. His hands were under the sheet. In his right hand he held a Beretta M9. A full magazine was loaded. A round was in the chamber. It was ready to rock.

The men approached the bed. They wore dark pullover shirts, dark pants, and black hoods that covered everything but their eyes.

It was safe to say they weren't doctors.

Two men were on his right side, one on his left. One of the men pulled out a syringe. In the half-light, Ed watched him hold it up and remove the cap. A tiny pop of fluid squirted out. He looked at the other two men and nodded.

The two men moved fast. But Ed was faster. They darted to the bedside and tried to pin his arms. He slid his gun out the instant before the man on the right moved. He swung the gun up into his face. The muzzle was an inch from the man's forehead.

BAM!

The noise was deafening in the close confines of the room. Stars were imprinted on Ed's eyes from the muzzle flash.

The man's head cracked apart. Blood and bone and brains sprayed backwards across the room. The man fell forward across the rails of the hospital bed. Ed pushed him back with the gun, and the corpse fell to the floor.

He swung the gun upward. He pointed the gun into the middle of the syringe man's chest. The man held both hands up, his eyes wide behind the mask. The syringe was still in his right hand.

BAM!

The gun's muzzle was a foot from the man's chest. The shot blew his heart and half his lungs out through his back. The man dropped to the floor like a trap door had opened beneath him.

The third man had backed to the other side of the room. He was so surprised, he hadn't even tried to run for the door. If he had gone right away, he might have made it. Now, he was in a corner, ten feet from Ed. Ed pointed the gun straight into his body mass. The man glanced at the window. Eight stories up, Ed remembered, with no fire escape. Good luck.

"Nice gun, right?" Ed said. "I call it Alice. You want to ask it something?"

The guy raised his hands. "Hey. I think you're making a big mistake."

"No, you made the mistake, motherfucker. You want to kill me? Don't come in here and try to pretend it's a drug overdose. If you want to kill me, you better come in here and kill me dead, right away." He shook his head and lowered his voice. "Otherwise, you see what happens to you."

Somewhere in the hospital, alarms were going off. Security would be here in another minute.

"Who are you?" Ed said.

The man smiled beneath his mask. "You know I'll never tell you that."

Ed was a crack shot. It was another of his skills that he kept sharp. At ten feet, he could hit anything he wanted. He changed his aim and shot the man in the right leg, just above the knee.

BANG.

Ed knew what the shot did. It shredded the large bone there. Blew it to pieces.

The doctors had told Ed the right tip of his own pelvis was cracked, probably from a bullet that had ricocheted and lost most of

176

its energy before it hit him. The treatment was bed rest, painkillers, and physical therapy. He would have to use a walker for a little while, then crutches. In eight weeks or so, he might still have some soreness, but he should be almost good as new. In six months, it would be like it never happened.

In contrast, the man now shrieking on the floor would never walk normally again. And that was if Ed let him live.

Ed dropped the railing from the side of the bed. There was a hospital walker near the chair, with wheels in the back and half a tennis ball on each of the front knobs. Ed pulled it close, and worked his way to a standing position by the side of the bed. He gritted his teeth against the pain.

Jesus. If this was what old age would be like, he wanted no part of it.

He looked at the man sprawled on the floor in the corner. Ed used the walker to gimp his away around the two corpses, careful not to slip in all the blood. The polished floor was awash in it. He headed toward the injured man.

"We don't have much time," he told the man. "Let's see if I can get that name out of you in a minute or less."

Chapter 40

11:05 p.m.
Fairfax County, Virginia - Suburbs of Washington, DC

Luke was drifting.

The phone was ringing.

He snapped awake, lying flat on the sofa. He'd had another drink while waiting for David Delliger to call him. Then he'd fallen asleep. This must be Delliger now.

He picked up the phone.

"Hello?"

"Luke? It's Ed Newsam. Did I wake you?"

Luke was disoriented. "No. What time is it? No, you didn't wake me. Ed. How are you doing? I'm planning to come see you tomorrow. I'll bring you some flowers. You want a sandwich? Like a real one, not hospital food."

"Don't bother," Ed said. "I'm leaving in the morning. Listen, we got trouble. Three men just tried to kill me."

Luke sat up. "What? Where are you?"

"I'm still in the hospital. I've got about ten cops in here right now. They're going to move me to another room, post some guards at the door."

"Where are the killers?"

There was a pause. "Uh, they're here on the floor. They didn't make it. I tried to get an ID on one of them, but he wasn't into talking. There really wasn't anything I could do. Turns out they killed the nurse at the nurse's station, stuffed her under the desk. They came in here wearing masks. If I had to guess, I'd say these guys are not going to come back identifiable. Spooks is what I'm saying. Ghosts."

Luke ran a hand through his hair. "You killed them all?"

"Yeah. I did."

There was a long silence over the line.

"You need to watch yourself, Luke. That's why I called. This thing with the President... it's all wrong. And these guys sure don't look Iranian. They look like surfer boys from San Diego. If they tried to get me, they'll be coming for you, too."

Luke killed the TV set, then leaned over to the end table and turned off the light. He crouched low and ran to the kitchen. He turned off that light as well. Except for the faint orange glow of the

178

wall switches, and a red LED light on the stereo in the living room, it was now dark on the first floor. Luke crawled into the dining room.

"Luke? You with me?"

"Yeah. I'm here."

"What are you doing?"

"Nothing, man. I'm good."

Luke took a corner of the blue dining room carpet and rolled it up. Underneath was a hinged trapdoor built into the hardwood floor. Luke nestled the phone in the crook of his ear, and pulled his key ring out. There were tiny locks left and right, embedded into the trapdoor. He found the small silver keys that fit each lock, slid them in and unlocked the door.

"You going to talk to me?" Ed said.

"I'm getting ready right now, Ed. I think I should hang up."

"That's probably a good idea. Good luck, brother."

"Thanks for the tip."

Luke let the phone fall to the floor. He opened the trapdoor and pulled a long metal box up and out of it. Another toy chest. Luke kept them salted around the house. He punched in the code from memory and opened the box. This was a bigger box than most.

An M16 rifle. A Remington 870 pump shotgun. A couple more handguns. A hunting knife. Three grenades. Various boxes of ammo, plenty of rounds for the guns. He ran his hand over the grenades. He would try, really try, not to blow up the house. With hands trembling just slightly, maybe from fear, but maybe just from hunger, he began to load up the guns.

The phone rang again. He looked at the readout this time. The caller was blocked. He sighed. He might as well talk to whoever it was. He answered it, hoping for David Delliger, or maybe a late-night telemarketer.

"Luke? It's Don Morris."

Luke pressed nine-millimeter rounds into an empty magazine, his fingers moving fast and automatically. As he worked, a piece of the puzzle fell into place with a thud. Don knew something about what was going on. Of course he did. He and the new President were fly-fishing buddies.

"Hi, Don. How do you know the former Speaker?"

"We were at the Citadel together, Luke. Many years ago. After graduation, I joined the real military, and Bill went to law school."

"I see."

179

"Luke, we need to talk."

"Okay." Luke filled a magazine and put it aside. He started on the next one. "But if we talk, let's be honest, shall we?"

"That's fair," Don said.

"So why don't you start?"

Don paused before speaking. "Well... By now, I suppose it's clear to you what happened today."

"I'd say it's crystal clear, Don. It's suddenly become even clearer as a result of this phone call."

"I'm glad about that, Luke. That way we don't have to play footsie here. We can get right to the facts. You're an old battle-scarred warrior, just like me. You must see that this had to be done. It was for the good of the country. It was for the future of our children, and our children's children. We cannot allow our enemies to push us around on the world stage. The man in question would have handed over the whole fort without firing a shot. All that's over with."

Luke finished another magazine. He started loading a third.

"What happens now?" he said.

"We set some things to right. We put a few people in their place, and we remind everyone out there who's in charge."

"After that? What happens with the government?"

"The same thing that happened last time. President Ryan serves out the existing term, in this case three more years. He runs for re-election, or he doesn't. I imagine he will, but that's up to him. The people decide who the next President is. Nothing has changed, Luke. The Constitution is still in effect. All we did is press the reset button."

"The entire civilian government has been decapitated," Luke said.

"So we'll fix it."

"Just a little do-over, eh, Don? Like when we were all kids?"

"Sure. A do-over, if you like."

"How many people have died for your do-over so far?"

The line was quiet.

"Don?"

"Luke, I'd say about one percent of one percent of one percent of the population. Three hundred and fifty people out of a total of three hundred and fifty million. That's an estimate, but it's probably accurate. We'll know more in the morning. Not a very high price to pay, if you think about it."

Luke crouched in the darkness. He shrugged into a shoulder holster on his left side, then another on his right. He would strap the M16 to his back. The grenades would go in his cargo pockets. He'd carry the shotgun in his arms and fire that one off first.

He glanced into the living room. Those floor-to-ceiling windows were looking pretty silly right about now. He lived, quite literally, in a glass house. There was no way he could defend this place. He would have to get out of here, most likely through a hail of gunfire.

"Luke?"

"I'm listening, Don."

"Do you have any questions?"

"Sure. Here's one. Why did you wake me up in the middle of the night to be part of all this? I hadn't even clocked in for six months. I hadn't worked a case in ten."

Don laughed, and that slow Southern drawl came flowing out like syrup. "It was just a mistake on my part. You're one of the best operatives I've ever seen, but I figured you'd be slow and out of practice after so much time away. And you were a little slow last night, but you caught up quickly. I underestimated you, that's all. You were supposed to get as far as the Iranian and stop there."

"So when the White House blew up, we could just blame it on the Iranians?"

"Yes. It could have been that simple."

"And Begley? What about him?"

Don laughed again. "Ron Begley can't find his ass with both hands."

"So he wasn't in on it?"

"Oh my, no."

Now Luke almost laughed. That figured. Poor Ron Begley was up there safeguarding Ali Nassar's rights for reasons he didn't even understand. He probably thought he was protecting the sanctity of diplomatic immunity. *If we don't respect it here, they won't respect it over there.* Or maybe he was just trying to break Luke's balls.

"Why are you calling me, Don?"

"Now we get to the meat of it, son. There's been another warrant issued for your arrest. The chief of staff of the former President managed to call out of Mount Weather before he died. He implicated you in the disaster. You're wanted for questioning about that. Also, that murder in Baltimore this morning? That's back on

181

again. It seems that you were in league with the terrorists all along. You led the President to his doom. That little dalliance in Baltimore was you killing off one of your partners to cover your tracks. And we've found an off-shore account that we've managed to trace to you. There's more than two million dollars in there."

Luke smiled.

"Surely you can do better than that?" Luke asked. "Putting money into a fake account in my name."

"I think that will suffice," Don said.

"And Ali Nassar?" Luke asked.

"Your paymaster? He died about an hour ago. It was a suicide. He jumped from the balcony at his apartment. Fifty stories, can you imagine? Luckily, he hit a concrete overhang on the third floor. No one on the street was injured."

Luke shrugged. He was no fan of Ali Nassar. Whatever Nassar thought he was doing, he had to know it was wrong. And he had to know his own death was a distinct possibility. If he didn't, then he was a bigger fool than he seemed. "That's convenient," Luke said. "Another one bites the dust."

"Indeed."

"And now you want me to surrender peacefully, I suppose."

"I would like you to, yes."

"Not much hope of that, is there?"

"Luke..."

From Luke's location in the dining room, he could see out the big south and west facing windows in the living room. The house sat up on a little rolling hillock of grass. The height extended his vantage point. It was a quiet neighborhood. Most residents parked in their own driveways or garages.

To the south, two unmarked squad cars were parked nose to nose at the next corner. They were fast cars, the kind that the government confiscated from drug dealers. Their windows were dark. They looked like spiders crouched there, waiting. To the west, at the far northern corner of the window, he could see a black van parked up at the next street. That was all he could see from here. There were probably others.

"If there's a warrant out for me," Luke said, "then why not just send some cops? All I see are spooks."

Don laughed. "Ah, well. Warrant might have been a strong word. Let's just say we'd like you to come in and have a chat."

Of course. There were no police involved at all. If Luke went out there and surrendered, they would just get rid of him. He would drop into a black hole and never be heard from again.

That wasn't going to happen.

"I can promise you a bloodbath, Don. If you come after me, I will put all of the men outside my house, plus ten, or twenty, or thirty more, in the ground. That's a lot of widows and orphans. Test me on this."

Don's voice was quiet. "Luke, I want you to listen to me very carefully. This is the most important thing I've ever had to tell you. Are you listening? Can you hear me?"

"I'm listening," Luke said.

"They've taken your wife and son."

"What?"

"None of this concerns you, Luke. It never did. You were window dressing, a bit player in a much larger drama. If you had gone home when I suspended you this morning, none of what followed would have happened. But you didn't go home, and as a result you've put Rebecca and Gunner at terrible risk. They're fine and they haven't been harmed, but you have to listen to me. If you quit now, just stop what you're doing, and walk out of the house with your hands in the air, it will all be fine. If you insist on continuing with this… foolishness…" He paused. "I don't know what will happen."

"Don, what are you saying?"

"It's not your fight, Luke, or mine. This is bigger than we are."

"Don, if you hurt my family—"

"It isn't me. You know I would never hurt your family. I love them as though they were my own. I'm just the messenger. Please remember that."

"Don—"

"It's your choice, Luke."

"Don!"

The line went dead.

183

Chapter 41

Rebecca lay upright in bed, staring into the darkness. On the end table next to her, the telephone started to ring. She looked at it. She could see the readout from here. It was Luke calling. But she could not move. It would give her away. Someone, she knew, was inside her house.

She lay there, frozen in place, her heart thumping in her chest. She had awakened to their footsteps downstairs, heavy bodies stepping carefully. This was an old, old house, and the floorboards creaked. There was almost nowhere to walk that wouldn't creak at least a little.

There it was again. A heavy step downstairs, trying to be quiet, trying to be stealthy. Another one came, across the living room from the first. At least two people were down there. Outside her bedroom window, she heard more footsteps padding on the grass below. People were moving around outside the house.

A realization came to her. It took a moment because she had been asleep when the sounds started. Gunner was here in the house with her.

Oh God. She had to get him out.

What could she do? Luke kept his weapons locked away. She had made him do that so Gunner could never find them one day when he was alone.

She slid out of bed, careful where she put her feet on the floor. She yanked her nightie over her head and off. She pulled on the same pair of jeans and the shirt she had worn in the daytime. A plan started to form in her mind. She would go to Gunner's room, wake him very quietly, then open his window. They would both climb out and silently cross the low sloping roof outside his bedroom. If no one spotted them, they would climb down the gutter downspout, then run like hell to the nearest neighbor's house, a quarter of a mile away.

That was it. That was the entire plan.

She looked up and gasped. Gunner came in, wearing his *Walking Dead* T-shirt and his pajama pants. He rubbed his eyes.

"Mom? Did you hear something?"

Approaching out of the dark just behind Gunner was a very tall man. He had a prominent Adam's apple. His face was flat and blank. His expression did not seem to reach his eyes. His eyes were dead. He grinned at her.

His voice was pleasant. He sounded amused.

"Hello, Mrs. Stone," he said. "Did we wake you?"

Gunner screamed, startled by the deep voice just behind him. He ran to her. Becca slid him behind her. Her breath seemed trapped in her throat. Her breathing sounded like a locomotive. Then an odd thought occurred to her.

"That's okay, little lady," the man said. "We're not going to hurt you. Yet."

The thought was about Luke. He was so paranoid, probably because of the terrible things he had seen. In the days when he was still deploying overseas for weeks at a time, he had taught her to defend herself. But what he showed her wasn't like kickboxing or karate. He didn't teach her to flip or punch anyone.

No. He brought home these very lifelike, heavy, anatomically correct dummies. Luke taught her how to gouge their eyes out by plunging her fingers deep into the eye sockets. He taught her to bite their noses off. Off! All the way off, just dig her teeth in deep, and rip the nose right off the face. He taught her to crush, not squeeze, their testicles. He taught her to shove her hand all the way into someone's mouth and down their throat. He showed her how to permanently damage another human being, especially one that was bigger and stronger than she was.

She remembered Luke's sunny smile while talking about this. "If a time comes when you have no choice but to fight, then you have to hurt the other person. And not just a little. Not even a lot. You have to hurt them all the way, so that they can't get up and do the same or worse to you."

Could she do it? Could she hurt this man? If left on her own, she thought not. But Gunner was here.

The man walked up to her. He came very close. He wore boots, khaki pants and a T-shirt. He pressed his body against hers, but didn't touch her with his hands. His chest lightly touched her face. She could feel his body heat. He pressed his hands against the wall behind her. The man's body pushed her backwards.

"You like that?" he said. He breathed deeply. "I can tell, you're not going to miss your husband at all."

185

Gunner made a sound behind her, like an animal squeal.

Becca screamed, just like Luke taught her to do. The scream unleashed her energy. She rammed both hands up and into the man's balls. She grabbed for them and through his pants, she squeezed as hard as she could. She took them in a death grip. Then she tried to rip them away from his body.

The man's eyes went wide in shock. He made a gasping sound, then fell to the floor with a thud. His mouth was agape in a silent shriek. His hands were at his groin. His pants were staining with blood. She had hurt him. She had hurt him very badly.

She turned to Gunner. "Come on! We have to get out of here."

Chapter 42

"Hi, this is Becca. I can't answer your call right now. Please leave a message after the tone, and I'll call you back as soon as I can."

Luke hung up. There was no sense leaving a message.

He had moved downstairs. The house had a finished half-basement. It opened to a walkout at the bottom of the little hill, between his house and the neighbor's house. That door was a vulnerable spot, and at first, this was the reason Luke went to it. Luke crouched at the door, in near pitch-darkness, staring at his neighbor's house. That house gave him an idea.

The question was: Did he dare act on it?

Throughout his career, he had done everything in his power to shield Becca and Gunner from the realities of his work. Becca knew what he did for a living, but she knew very little of what that actually meant. Gunner, in his own way, was closer to the truth. He thought his dad was James Bond.

Luke grunted. He saw, in a flash of insight, that he was the one who didn't understand. All these years, he had *compartmentalized* like a good agent. That's how they taught you to think about it. On the one hand, you had the job, and everything you did as part of the job. The secrets you learned and then quickly forgot, the people you met, or arrested, or killed. On the other hand, you had your real life. You kept the two as far apart as possible.

But it was a lie. The work was dangerous and it was dirty. Luke routinely dealt with some of the worst people on Earth. They didn't draw arbitrary distinctions like work life and home life. It was all the same to them. It was all fair game.

How did he not see this until now? Or had he seen it all along and ignored it?

There was a terrible thought in his mind, one he didn't want to think. He had been doing this a long time. When people were kidnapped, mostly they were killed. Letting them go was dangerous. They knew too much. They saw too much. It was easier and smarter just to kill them.

This business was full of people who killed for a living. It was nothing to them. They could kill in the morning and then go to Applebee's for a ten-dollar lunch.

Luke clenched his teeth against the scream that raged in his throat. Abruptly, he started crying, and that surprised even him. But it hurt. It hurt so bad, and it had hardly even started yet. He knew that. He knew how bad it was going to be. He had seen it many times. Innocent people wrenched from this life, ripped away. The survivors like shadows, empty, alive and dead at the same time. His body was wracked by sobs.

His phone beeped. He looked down at it, hoping it was from her. It wasn't. It was from David Delliger.

I can meet you. Annapolis?

Okay. That decided him.

Across from his basement door was his neighbor Mort's house. Mort was a funny guy, mid-fifties, single. He was a lobbyist for the casino industry. Not the established casino industry in Las Vegas. The weird casino industry, which kept popping up with slot machine houses at old rundown harness racing tracks, and dismal "riverboats" moored in man-made lakes in the middle of Nowhere, Indiana.

Mort was headquartered here in Washington, but he spent a lot of time flying around the country to grease the palms of state legislators. He wasn't around very much.

Like tonight. Luke could always tell when Mort was away by the timing patterns of his indoor automatic lighting. It was consistent from one night to the next. It would never fool a burglar, but it probably gave Mort peace of mind, which was more important to a man like Mort anyway.

Mort made a lot of money. He made so much money that last year he had built an addition onto his house. The addition was big. And it was garish. It was a post-modern tumor, a mix and match of various architectural styles, growing out of the side of Mort's stately colonial. It came within bare inches of the real estate setbacks on Luke's side of the property. Luke liked Mort, he really did, but that addition was obnoxious. It was beyond the pale.

And Mort wasn't home.

From his crouch, Luke opened the basement door about halfway. Mort's house was close, easy throwing distance. Luke pulled the pin on one of his grenades and tossed it down the small hillock toward Mort's house. The grenade bounced twice and nestled perfectly against the wall.

Luke ducked back and hit the deck.

BOOM!

A flash of light and sound ruptured the darkness. After a few seconds, Luke got up and went back to the door. The grenade had blasted a hole into the side of Mort's house. A small fire had started there around the ragged edges of the hole.

Luke opened the door all the way this time, stepped outside, gambling there were no snipers, pulled the pin on his second grenade, and threw it like a baseball right through the middle of that flaming hole. He dashed inside again.

The light was different this time, and the sound was muffled. Luke looked out. The side of Mort's addition had caved in. There was debris all over the grass between the two houses. The fire was starting in earnest. Once the furniture and the paperwork and the rugs and all the various junk got going, it was going to get nice and warm over there.

One more? Sure. One more would do it. Luke stepped out and tossed the last grenade into the already flaming house. In the distance, sirens were already approaching. The local police, fire engines, ambulances—they'd be here in minutes. Once all the neighbors came out onto their lawns in their robes and slippers, it was going to be quite a scene. It would be hard to quietly disappear someone with so many citizens round.

Luke went back upstairs as the final blast rocked Mort's house. He looked out the windows. Burning embers were flying everywhere, black smoke funneling into the sky against the red and orange glow.

The two dark squad cars started up and silently pulled away. The van was already gone. It was time for Luke to go as well. He looked at the burning house again. He shook his head.

"Sorry, Mort."

Chapter 43

11:19 p.m.

Queen Anne's County, Maryland - Eastern Shore of Chesapeake Bay

The tall man was done. He writhed on the floor in agony.

He wasn't getting up again.

Becca took Gunner by the hand. She led him to the window and pushed the screen out. It clattered away and slid down the tiles. Behind her, heavy footsteps pounded up the stairs.

She crouched in front of Gunner. "Honey, climb out, run to the other side, carefully, and shimmy down the drainpipe. Just like we do in fire drills, okay? I'm right behind you. When you hit that grass, you run. Run to the Thompsons' house as fast as you can. Okay?"

She thought of the Thompsons, an old couple who were eighty-five if they were a day.

"Who is that man, Mom?"

"I don't know. It doesn't matter. Now go!"

Gunner climbed head first out the window, jumped up, and ran.

Now it was her turn. She glanced at the door. Two more men came barreling into the room and ran toward her. She dove through the window. She scrabbled across the slate tiles, but one of the men grabbed her leg. She was three quarters of the way onto the roof, one quarter still in the room. The men had both her legs now. They started to pull her back inside.

She kicked crazily, as hard as she could.

She heard herself making sounds. "Aahh! Anh!"

She kicked free, then rolled backwards. She was all the way onto the low slanted roof. A second later, one of the men dove through the window. He was with her then. They rolled together, toward the end. He tried to pin her, but she scratched and tore at his eyes. He rolled away to escape her, rolled too far, and went right over the edge. She heard him hit the cement walkway with a thud.

She jumped up and started to run. Another man was climbing onto the roof. Up ahead, Gunner was already at the drainpipe. He sat on the lip of the roof, his legs dangling. He grabbed the pipe, pushed himself off, then swung around to the left and disappeared.

Becca reached the edge.

Gunner slid down the pipe, landed on the grass, then rolled backward onto his butt. A second passed, and he was still on the ground.

"Get up, Gunner! Run!"

He pushed himself up, turned, and ran down the hill toward the Thompson house.

Becca looked back. A man approached her across the roof. Behind him, another one was just climbing out the window. Below and to her left, she saw men on the ground turning the corner of the house and coming this way.

There was no time to climb down. She just turned and jumped.

She hit hard, and she felt a sharp pain in her ankle. She rolled forward over her shoulder, came up limping, and ran anyway. Each step sent a shockwave of pain up her leg. She ran on. Ahead of her, Gunner was running, his arms and legs pumping. She was gaining on him.

"Run, Gunner!" she screamed. "Run!"

Behind her, she heard the pounding footsteps of the men. She heard their heavy breathing. She ran and ran. She saw their shadows in the grass ahead of her. They came closer, closer, then mingled with hers. Arms reached for her. She fought them off.

"No!"

A man dove for her. She felt the weight of his body. They crashed to the ground and went sliding along the grass. She fought him, scratching and clawing. Another man came, and then another. They held her down.

Two men ran by, after the boy.

"Run!" she shrieked. "Run!"

She craned her neck to see what was happening. A hundred yards away, Gunner was almost to the Thompson house. Lights came on inside the house. The porch light came on outside. Gunner bounded up the steps just as the door opened.

The two men were just behind him. They stopped running and walked to the porch. Slowly they climbed the steps.

Becca could see Mr. and Mrs. Thompson standing in the doorway, framed by the light. Suddenly there was a burst of light, then another. Muzzle flashes, but Becca couldn't hear a sound. This close, but she couldn't hear the guns.

Mr. and Mrs. Thompson dropped to the floor. There another flash, then another, as the men finished them off.

"Oh no," Becca said.

Now the men were coming back, walking with Gunner. They flanked him, each one holding one of his wrists.

There was a man on top of her. He had a bad shave and coffee breath.

"Did you see that?" he said. "Did you see it? You did that, not us. If you had come quietly, that never would have happened."

There was nothing left to do. Becca spit in the man's face.

Chapter 44

11:27 p.m.
Mount Weather Emergency Operations Center –
Bluemont, Virginia

Chuck Berg drifted in and out of consciousness for hours, until another explosion woke him. The sound was deep, like faraway thunder. It made an impression in the air, like a wave on the ocean. He seemed to swim underwater for a long while, then he rose to the surface.

He broke through and opened his eyes. Thirty-seven years old, Chuck had been in the Secret Service for almost twelve years. He had spent two of those riding a desk, and nine of them as part of an advance security team. Six months ago, he had been awarded the plum assignment of a lifetime, working as one of the Vice President's personal bodyguards. It didn't feel so plum right now.

Chuck pieced together what he could remember. They had exited the elevator and were moving down a narrow corridor to the TV studio. They were a couple minutes late, and were walking fast. He was behind the Vice President. Two men, Smith and Erickson, were in the lead.

Suddenly the steel door in front of them blew inward. Erickson died instantly. Smith turned to come back up the corridor. His face was lit with the firelight as the flames burst through the shattered doorway. He saw a shadow stagger through the bright orange and yellow of the flames. It was Smith, lit up like a torch. He screamed for only a second, then went silent and keeled over. Berg pictured Smith inhaling fire. His throat ruptured, the scream had died almost before it began.

Chuck tackled the Vice President and held her down.

A shockwave moved through the hallway. The entire facility seemed to tremble. Something hit Berg in the head. He remembered thinking: *Okay, I'm dead. Okay.*

But he wasn't dead. He was still here, in the same corridor, in pitch-darkness, on top of the Vice President. The pain in his head was bad. He ran a hand along his scalp and found a wide slice tacky with dried blood. He pushed into it. A cracked skull should make the pain worse the more he probed. It didn't happen.

He was alive, and he seemed to be operational. And that meant he had a job to do.

"Mrs. Hopkins?" he said. She was tiny, so small compared to him that lying on top of her was strange.

"Ma'am, are you with me?"

"Call me Susan," came her surprisingly resilient voice. "I hate all that ma'am shit."

"Are you hurt?"

"I'm in pain," she said. "But I don't know how bad it is."

"Can you move your arms and legs?"

She squirmed beneath him. "Yes. But my right arm hurts a lot." Her voice was shaking. "The skin on my face hurts. I think I was burned."

Chuck nodded. "Okay." He did the math. She could move her extremities, so no important nerves had been severed. They had been down here a long time. Internal injuries or severe burns probably would have killed her by now. So her injuries, while painful, were probably not immediately life threatening.

"Ma'am, in a moment, we're going to see if you can stand, but not yet. I'm going to crawl away just for a minute, then I'll be right back. I don't want you to move at all. I want you to stay exactly where you are in exactly the position you are in. It's very dark and I need you right where you are. Do you understand? Please say yes or no."

"Yes," she said in a little girl voice. "I understand."

He left her behind, moving like a snake along the floor. He had noted an emergency kit stored behind glass directly across from the elevator doors. If that part of the hall was intact, he would be in business. He moved slowly, touching everything in front of him, looking for sharp edges and possible drop-offs. There was a lot of debris. He also felt along the wall. After a time, his hand touched the indent in the wall which told him he had reached the elevator.

Chuck worked his way to a kneeling position. Three feet above the ground, the air became fetid and smoky. He ducked back to the floor.

"Mrs. Hopkins?" he called out. "Are you still there?"

"I'm here, all right."

"Continue to stay on the floor, please. Do not stand up for any reason, okay?"

"Okay."

194

Chuck took a deep breath then stood up. His knees popped. His hands moved along the wall until they found the glass case. He had no idea how to open it, so he punched it as hard as he could. It was breakaway glass, and it shattered instantly.

The case was deep. His hands roamed inside of it, feeling familiar shapes. There were ventilator masks in here. He would need those. There was a gun—unnecessary, given the circumstances. He found a flashlight secured to the wall with a strap. He undid the snap, brought the flashlight out, and turned it on. It worked.

Oh my God. Light.

Quickly now he found water and a stack of meals-ready-to-eat. A first aid kit. A hatchet and a universal tool. He dropped to the floor just before his breath ran out.

He leaned against the wall. They were alive, and they had supplies. They were moving forward, and it was time to start thinking ahead. The facility had been attacked. It was a hardened facility, so it should withstand any missile or bomb attack from above. That suggested the attack had come from down here. And that, in turn, suggested that Chuck needed to find a way to the surface.

But...

He had to be careful. Nearly a decade ago, when he had first gone in the field, they had paired him an older agent, a man named Walt Brenna, who was months from retirement. Walt had a funny way about him. The other agents said he was a curmudgeon. They told Chuck not to listen to him. But he and Walt spent a lot of time together. Some days, there was nothing to do but listen to him.

Walt was obsessed with a concept he called "White on White."

"They'll tell you that this job is watching out for Islamic terrorists or Russian assassins or what have you," Walt would say. "But it really isn't. You think those guys are going to get anywhere near the President of the United States? Think again. The entire point of what we do is to neutralize a White on White attack."

Chuck Berg took Walt's ramblings with a giant grain of salt. But they stuck with him over the years, and he sometimes thought about them. To Walt Brenna, a White on White attack was one where the government attacked itself. The Kennedy assassinations were examples of this. So was the attempted assassination of Ronald Reagan in 1981.

195

Walt Brenna on Reagan:

"The Vice President, first in the line of succession, is the former CIA Director. The father of the man who tries to kill the President is the head of World Vision, a CIA front group. The Vice President's family are friends with the would-be assassin's family. The Vice President's brother and the assassin's brother are scheduled to have lunch together while the murder is taking place. Very little of this makes the newspapers. None of it is ever investigated. Why? Because the assassin is crazy and that's all we need to know? No. Because White on White is an accepted part of the game. Their job is to do it, and our job is to stop it. Offense and defense, that's all."

As the years passed, Chuck learned that Walt wasn't the only one in the Service who thought this way. No one talked openly about it, but he had heard whisperings. How could you identify a White on White? What would it look like if one was coming?

Chuck nodded to himself. *This* is what it would look like. A bomb had gone off inside a secure facility, hours after an attack on the White House. The explosions at the White House also came from inside the building, or most of them did. Outsiders couldn't plant bombs in either place, and definitely not in both places. The only ones who could have done this were the military, the intelligence community, or the Secret Service itself.

With the benefit of the flashlight, he crouched low and duck-walked quickly back to the Vice President. She hadn't moved at all.

"Ma'am? You can sit up now, if you can manage it. I have food, water, and a first aid kit. We're going to need to wear these masks when we move out, and I'll show you how. It will seem cumbersome and confining at first, but I promise you'll get used to it."

She moved slowly to a sitting position. She winced at the pain in her arm. Some of the skin on her face had peeled away. To Berg, the burns looked superficial, although she might get some scarring or discoloration. If that was the worst thing that happened to her, Chuck would call that lucky.

"Shouldn't we try to call someone?" she said.

He shook his head. "No. We can't call anyone. We don't know who the enemy is. For the time being, we're going to operate in secret."

She seemed to think about that. "Okay."

"Now, the way to the surface may be difficult," Chuck said. "We might have to climb, and it may be frightening, and painful. So I'm going to ask you to do something for me. I'm going to ask you to reach down deep inside, and be as tough as you can. Find that tough person inside you. I know she's in there. Can you find her?"

The woman looked at him, and suddenly her eyes were hard. "Buddy, I was in the fashion industry, surrounded by predators, when I was a young girl. I was living in New York and Paris and Milan, by myself, at sixteen years old. I am as tough as they come."

Chuck nodded. That was exactly what he wanted to hear.

Chapter 45

11:57 p.m.
The United States Naval Academy - Annapolis, Maryland

It was a strange place to meet.

Luke was dressed entirely in black. He wore black gloves. There was a black hood stuffed in his pocket.

The dark football field of the Navy Marine Corps Memorial Stadium spread out in front of him. The vast empty stands towered above him. GO NAVY was painted in massive letters across the upper tier of seats. In the night, the words looked white, but he knew that in the daytime they were yellow against a dark blue background.

He hung back, lingering in the shadows of the end zone concourse ramp. He watched the darkened broadcast booth at the top of the stadium, looking for the slightest movement. If he were a sniper, that was where he would be.

A man walked across the field toward him. Gradually, the man became clearer. He was tall, heavyset, walking as though he was carrying more weight than he once had. He wore a long overcoat. He came closer still, and now Luke could make out the dark suit under the man's coat, and the soft, almost doughy features of the man's face.

He entered the darkness of the concourse ramp.

Luke moved, only slightly. "Mr. Secretary?"

The man started, just a touch. It was clear he hadn't seen Luke there. His eye was drawn immediately to the black matte Glock in Luke's hand. Luke holstered it for the moment, to put the man at ease.

"Yes," the man said. "I'm Dave Delliger."

"I'm Luke Stone."

"I know who you are. I was on a call with the President today. You're the man who saved his life."

"Temporarily," Luke said.

"Yes."

"I'm sorry things happened this way."

Delliger nodded. "I am, too."

"I hate to ask you this, sir, but is there any chance you were followed here?"

198

Delliger nodded again. "There's every chance. I attended the new President's swearing in two hours ago at Site R. I took a Navy helicopter here. Site R is a hundred miles away, in the mountains. In the dark, with my failing night vision, it would have taken me until tomorrow morning to get here."

Luke faded back against the wall. That was the wrong answer. Certainly not the one he was hoping for.

"Don't worry," Delliger said. "There's nothing out of the ordinary. They have no reason to suspect me. This is my alma mater, and I taught here for many years. I still keep an office and a bedroom on campus. The Navy lets me do it because they're so proud of me. I am what you might call a fixture here. I told the people at Site R that if we're all going to die, I would prefer to do it here than in a hole in the ground."

"I was under the impression," Luke said, "that you once roomed with President Hayes at Yale."

"Law school," Delliger said. "I did, and we really were best pals, like everyone says. But that was later, after I performed my military service." He raised his arms and gestured at their surroundings. "This is my true home."

"President Hayes was murdered," Luke said.

"I know he was. It was a coup d'état. I was there when Bill Ryan took the oath of office. Everyone was quite pleased with themselves, believe me. Now we're going to have a war with Iran. Ryan's going to make the declaration tonight, if he hasn't already made it. Why wait for the *Today Show* to come on? And since most of the Congress is dead, there's no sense asking them to declare it. Makes me wonder how the Russians are going to feel about all this."

"We can stop it," Luke said.

"What, the war?"

"The coup."

"Mr. Stone, as far we know, time only moves forward. You can't stop something that has already happened."

Luke was silent.

"The President and the Vice President are dead," Delliger said. "The next two in line are Bill Ryan and Ed Graves, both hawks, both alive. After that, the entire line of succession is gone. They were all at Mount Weather. If you were going to stop this, assuming such a thing were possible, and topple Bill Ryan, who would you

199

replace him with? At this point, who is the legitimate heir to the throne?"

"I don't know," Luke admitted.

All day, he had been so focused on stopping it from happening that it hadn't yet occurred to him the whole thing was already over. He was only now beginning to grasp the sheer scale of the operation. Don had told Luke he was window dressing, but that was wrong. He wasn't window dressing. He was a bug on the windshield.

For a second, Luke's mind flashed backwards to tonight's meeting with Paul.

Paul had described Luke as a kamikaze flying a toy plane into an aircraft carrier. It would seem spectacular, but it would actually be pathetic.

"I don't know either," Delliger said. "But it doesn't really matter, does it? They have people everywhere. Can you imagine who had to be involved to make this happen? Can't you see how high this goes? If you were somehow able to undo this, who could you ever trust again? You'd have to root the conspirators out of every department and agency. This government is a corpse riddled with maggots."

He paused. "I wish I had known all this five years ago. I never would have accepted the position. I would have thanked Thomas for the honor, politely declined, and gone about my business. Secretary of Defense? It's a joke. They humored me. I was never in charge of anything."

"We can find evidence," Luke said. "We could bring a case. Anything, a toehold, something to offer the media. You're still on the inside."

Delliger shook his head softly. "I've been informed that President Ryan anticipates my resignation first thing in the morning. If he receives it, he will publicly thank me for my service and my dedication. If he doesn't receive it, he'll fire me for gross incompetence. It's my choice."

Luke was thoughtful. "Why did you agree to meet me?"

Delliger shrugged. "I think you're a good man. You're obviously a brave one. I thought I should tell you that if it isn't too late, you ought to walk away from this. Just walk away. Maybe they'll leave you alone. Life is a beautiful thing, Mr. Stone. And there's more to it than fighting battles you can't possibly win."

Luke took a deep breath. There was no point in telling this man that it was already too late, at least for Luke himself.

"Is that what you're going to do?" he said. "Walk away?"

Delliger smiled. It was a sad, rueful smile. "I'm going to walk over to my office right now and draft my resignation. Then tomorrow I'm going to get my old life back. You know I'm a pretty good gardener? It's a favorite hobby of mine, and one I haven't been able to indulge in years. I just haven't had the time. I know, it's already June, so I'm a little behind the curve this year. But the growing season is long and forgiving in this part of the country."

Luke nodded. "Okay. Goodbye, Mr. Delliger."

"Goodbye, Mr. Stone. And good luck to you, whatever you decide."

Delliger turned and started off across the field again. Luke stayed against the wall. He watched Delliger dwindle into the distance. When Delliger reached the fifty-yard line, a single gunshot rang out.

CRACK.

It echoed off the grandstands of the stadium, and through the tree-lined streets of the surrounding area.

Luke's eyes scanned the empty stadium, trying to spot the shooter. He hadn't noticed a flash, even a suppressed one, so the shot hadn't come from the broadcast booth. He would have seen it from the corner of his eye. He realized that bullet might have come a long way. The best shooters could make that shot from two thousand yards, even longer. The United States military trained some of the best shooters alive.

He gazed back across the field. Delliger's body was out there, a dark lump halfway across. It occurred to him that they hadn't even bothered to silence the shot. They could have, and they didn't.

Luke removed the black hood from his pocket and pulled it on over his head. The only thing showing was his eyes. He slid down along the concrete wall toward the concession concourse. A moment later, he had disappeared into the shadows.

Chapter 46

June 6th
12:03 a.m.
On the Road

The world around him was black.

The man was a long-haul trucker driving through the night. He was below Florence, South Carolina, in that part of the state where the exits were few and far between. The dark highway stretched away in the glare of his headlights. His plan was to reach northern Florida before he got off the road, maybe Jacksonville, maybe St. Augustine if he could make it that far.

It had been a terrible day, maybe the worst in his memory. But life went on. He was moving a truckload of canned Virginia pork products destined for the docks at Port Everglades. It wasn't going to drive itself there.

He lit a cigarette and turned on the radio. The new President, a man the trucker had never heard of before tonight, had just been introduced. He was going to make an announcement.

The trucker sighed. He hoped this one didn't get blown up too. Then the President came on.

"My fellow Americans," he said.

"Yesterday, June fifth, the United States of America was suddenly and deliberately attacked by undercover agents and provocateurs of the Islamic Republic of Iran. The United States was at peace with that nation, and was still in conversation with its government, looking toward the maintenance of peace in the Middle East.

"Indeed, less than twenty-four hours before an Iranian airborne drone strike on our White House, the Iranian Ambassador to the United Nations delivered to our United Nations Ambassador a formal reply to a recent American message. And, while this reply stated that it seemed fruitless to continue the existing diplomatic negotiations, it contained no threat or hint of war or of armed attack.

"You will note that the nature of the attack makes it obvious that it was deliberately planned many days, weeks or even months ago. During the intervening time the Iranian government has deliberately sought to deceive the United States by false statements and expressions of hope for conciliation.

"The attack tonight has caused severe damage to the Mount Weather Emergency Operations Center, where the former President, Vice President, and many members of the sitting government had gathered. I regret to tell you that very many American lives have been lost. The exact number is not known at this time, but we anticipate confirming, in the days ahead, at least three hundred American deaths.

"Iran has therefore undertaken a surprise offensive on American soil. The facts of yesterday and today speak for themselves. The people of the United States have already formed their opinions and well understand the implications to the very life and safety of our nation.

"As Commander-in-Chief of the Army and Navy I have directed that all measures be taken for our defense. No matter how long it may take us to overcome this premeditated attack, the American people will win through to absolute victory. I believe that I interpret the will of the people when I assert that we will not only defend ourselves to the uttermost, but will make it very certain that this form of treachery shall never again endanger us.

"Hostilities exist. There is no blinking at the fact that our people, our territory and our interests are in grave danger. With confidence in our armed forces, and with the determination of our people, we will gain the inevitable triumph, so help us God. I therefore inform you that ever since the unprovoked and cowardly attacks of June fifth, a state of war has existed between the United States and Iran."

Chapter 47

12:35 a.m.
Queen Anne's County, Maryland - Eastern Shore of Chesapeake Bay

Luke arrived at the house knowing how late he was.

It was dark. The nearness of the water seemed to add electricity to the air.

At first, he parked his car a hundred yards from the property. He killed the headlights, then waited and watched. No one was moving on the road. TV lights flickered from a home far to his left. Closer, a quarter of a mile away, the Thompson house was dark.

His sense of dread was so complete that he felt he might vomit. All along, he had made mistakes, and now it had probably cost Becca and Gunner their lives. He should have told Becca long ago about the risks his work entailed. Scratch that—he shouldn't have become involved with Becca, or anyone, in the first place.

He let the car roll down the hill to the house. Her Volvo was here. He parked next to her. He got out and checked her door. He didn't try to hide. Better they should come for him than kill his family. He wished he had made that trade when he could have. He knew it was a lie, but…

The car was unlocked—she never locked her car doors out here. There was nothing in the main cabin of the car. He popped the trunk, and steeled himself for what he might find. Nothing. A jack, a lug wrench, an air pump, and two tennis rackets.

He walked over to the house. The door was unlocked. He went in.

Nobody here.

He could feel the old house's emptiness. The light in the bathroom was on, throwing shadows through the living room. The coffee table in there had collapsed, as though someone had fallen on top of it. That was the only sign of struggle he could see.

He stood for a moment, holding his breath, looking and listening.

No sounds. None at all.

His breath came out in a long, low groan. Okay. He had come this far. Now he would take a moment, gather his emotions, and

204

then search the rest of the house. If anyone was here, they were dead.

I'm so sorry, Becca.

He stood there for several minutes. Out the back window, and far away, a boat went by on the dark water. He couldn't see the boat at all. He could tell it was there by the red running light at its stern.

He began his search. He walked through the rooms absently, checking the rest of the house. Shadows loomed all around him. He went into the master bedroom. He searched the bathroom and the closet. Becca wasn't here. Whatever they had done with her, they hadn't left her body behind.

He went into Gunner's room. There was a life-sized zombie poster above the bed. It startled him. For a split second he had thought a man was standing there. The bloodied zombie, clothing in rags, gore dripping from his mouth, accused him:

You murdered the child. You did it.

There was nothing Luke could say in his own defense.

A searing pain ripped through him. It had nothing to do with the violence he had endured today. It was the pain of separation, the impotent fear for their safety. They had been ripped from him, and he had no way to get them back.

His mind raced. He couldn't breathe.

He could call Don. He could beg. It would be abject, it would be disgusting. Just one impossible favor for old times' sake. Luke would do anything, anything at all, to trade places with them. But Don would never do it. He knew Don. When Don gave an ultimatum, that was the end of it. No turning back. Hell. Don probably couldn't stop this if he wanted to. He probably had no contact with the kidnappers, and the kidnappers themselves were probably operating in a vacuum. Once they were set in motion, they carried out their task with no further contact.

Becca and Gunner were probably already dead.

Luke was about to cry again. It was okay. There was no reason not to. And there was nothing left to do.

His phone rang. He answered it.

A woman's voice spoke. "Luke?"

"Trudy."

"Luke, the Vice President is alive."

Within three seconds, Luke was out of Gunner's room and bounding down the stairs. Then he was out the door and in the night air, walking fast to the car. It was instinct. His body knew it before his mind. Vice President Susan Hopkins, and everything she represented, was his one chance of saving his family.

"Tell me," he said.

"ECHELON," Trudy said. "It's been looking for any signs of life, from cell phones, email addresses, tablets, any communications devices associated with people who were at Mount Weather. Just about ten minutes ago, it picked up a signal—the cell phone of a Secret Service agent named Charles Berg, a member of the security contingent for Susan Hopkins. The system alerted the Real Time Regional Gateway at NSA headquarters, and they monitored a call Berg was making."

Luke started the car, put it in drive, and stomped on the gas pedal. The tires screeched as he peeled out of the driveway.

"I'm listening," he said.

"Berg phoned a retired Secret Service agent named Walter Brenna. They worked together at one time. The long and the short of it is Berg has Hopkins, she is injured but alive, and he is driving her back to Washington. He doesn't plan to tell anyone else about this. Apparently, Brenna was a Marine Corps medic before he joined the Secret Service. I'm talking about thirty years ago. Berg is going to bring the Vice President of the United States to Brenna's house in the eastern suburbs, and they're going to see if they can treat her injuries there. Then they're going to hide her."

"What's the extent of her injuries?"

"Unclear. The conversation lasted just over one minute."

"Where does Brenna live?"

"Uh… I have that. They tracked the call to a landline. He lives in Bowie, Maryland, at 1307 Third Street."

Luke was already punching the address into the GPS unit on his dashboard. He watched the unit draw a route map. He was thirty minutes away, less if he gunned it.

"Where are Berg and the Vice President now?"

"Also unclear. Berg's phone stopped moving on a back road in Eastern Virginia. Attempts to call it have gone unanswered. Agents from various organizations are moving toward the location, but they can only pinpoint it to within two hundred yards. Satellite data shows a grassy and woody area long the side of the road. There are no cars parked in the vicinity. It seems like Berg might have made the one call to Brenna, and then threw the phone out the window. No one even knows what Berg is driving."

Luke nodded. The man was clever. He knew people might be watching. What he didn't know was just how many people were watching, and to what extent.

"Does Don know about any of this?"

"It's very strange. He does know. He went racing out of here when the intel came in. Don is not himself."

"Did he say anything about me?"

"He said he talked to you. You had an argument. You told him you were going to bed. He said not to bother you, but I guess I knew better than to think you were actually sleeping. I don't think I've ever seen you fall asleep for any reason."

"Trudy, Don is trying to kill me."

The words came out before he knew they would. Once they were out there, he was okay with it. It was a fact, and Trudy was a big girl. He couldn't protect her from the facts. There was a long silence over the phone.

Luke zoomed past a sign for the Chesapeake Bay Bridge. Five miles. In ten minutes, he would go racing by David Delliger's corpse again.

"Trudy?"

"Luke, what are you talking about?"

"If I tell you, I'll be putting your life in danger."

"Tell me," she said.

So he told her. At the end, there was more silence. Luke was moving fast, ninety miles an hour, climbing the on ramp to the bridge. The roads were empty. He hadn't so much as glimpsed a cop.

"Do you believe me?" he said.

"Luke, I don't know what to believe. I know that Don and Bill Ryan were friends at the Citadel. They used to take their families on vacation together."

"Trudy, they've taken my wife and son."

"What?"

He told her about it. He kept his voice firm. He stuck to the facts of it, the things he knew for sure. He didn't cry. He didn't scream.

"It was a coup," Luke said. "There are people in the intelligence apparatus and the military who want a war. Probably the defense contractors, too. Don was in on it. A bit player, but in on it nonetheless."

207

Trudy's voice shook. "Just over half an hour ago, Bill Ryan declared war against Iran. Immediately afterward, the airwaves went berserk. ECHELON, all the listening stations, Fairbanks, Menwith Hill, Misawa Air Force Base in Japan, a bunch of others… they're picking up Russian chatter. The Russians haven't announced it yet, but they are prepared to treat an attack on Iran as an attack on Russia. They are getting missiles ready. I can't believe Don would want any of this to happen."

"Here's what I want you to do," Luke said. "Get Swann… Is Swann still there?"

"Swann never goes home," she said.

"Get Swann to access Don's computer. Look for any evidence that Don knew about the attacks beforehand. Emails, files, anything. Don didn't organize the attacks, but he knew they were coming."

"What good would that do, even if we found something?"

"It might give us an angle on prosecuting Ryan and whoever was behind this. If we get Don, then maybe we get Ryan, then the next one and the next one. We knock them down like dominoes. If we can keep the Vice President alive, we can force Ryan to step down. Once he does, he's no longer protected by his position. If we have any evidence against him, he is as good as toast."

"Okay, Luke. I'll have Swann see what he can find."

"I know he'll find something," Luke said. "Call me as soon as he does."

"Anything else?"

"Yeah. Call Ed Newsam and tell him to get dressed. I can't have him lying around in bed at a time like this."

"What will you be doing?"

"Me? I'm going to save the Vice President—if it's not already too late."

Chapter 48

8:56 a.m. (Moscow Time)
Strategic Command and Control Center - Moscow,
Russian Federation

Yuri Grachev, twenty-nine, aide to the Defense Minister, walked briskly through the hallways of the control center, on his way to the large situation room. His footsteps echoed along the empty corridor as he pondered the situation. The worst-case scenario had arrived. It was a disaster about to happen.

For reasons no one had explained, in the past forty-five minutes the Minister's black nuclear suitcase, his *Cheget*, had been handcuffed to Yuri's right wrist. The suitcase was old, it was heavy, and it forced Yuri to lean to his left side as he walked. It contained the codes and mechanisms to launch missile strikes against the West.

Yuri didn't want this horrible thing attached to him. He wanted to go home to his wife and young son. Most of all, he wanted to cry. He felt his entire body trembling. His impassive face threatened to crumble and break.

Four hours ago, the American government had been toppled in a coup. An hour ago, a new President had emerged on radio and television and declared war on Iran. In Russian government circles, the new President was widely understood to be a madman, and a front for war-mongering elites who hid in the shadows. His possible rise to power had long been thought of as a worst-case scenario.

The coup, and the declaration of war, had triggered a series of long-dormant protocols here in Russia. The protocols were known by several names, but most people called them the "Dead Hand."

Dead Hand sent Russian defense systems into a state of high alert, and gave far-flung missile stations, airplanes, and submarines semi-independent decision-making authorization. It decentralized command.

The idea was that Dead Hand gave Russian defenses the ability to counterattack after a surprise American first-strike wiped out the leadership in Moscow. If communications were severed and unusual seismic signatures or radar readings were detected, then regional commanders and even isolated bunkers could decide for

209

themselves if an attack had happened, and whether to launch retaliatory nuclear strikes.

But the system didn't work. It had been deteriorating for more than two decades, nearly Yuri's entire life. Eight of the original twelve monitoring satellites had fallen into the ocean during that time. None had been replaced.

Communications were constantly severed to outlying stations. There were always unusual seismic readings—at any given moment, small and even large earthquakes were happening across the globe. Worst of all, radar routinely misidentified missile launches. No one in the leadership would admit this, but it was true.

Yuri himself had been on hand here in the control center three years ago, when the Swedes launched a scientific rocket into orbit. The early-warning system mistook it for a missile launched from an American submarine stationed in the North Atlantic.

The nuclear suitcase (at that time, thankfully not attached to Yuri's wrist) began to sound an alarm. It sent alarm messages to combat stations, yes, but it also made an audible sound, an ugly clarion screeching

Missile silos across the Russian heartland reported combat readiness. If the rocket was an American first strike, it would make impact in perhaps nine minutes. Was it an electromagnetic pulse weapon that would disable Russian response capacity? Would it be followed by a larger attack?

No one knew. To their credit, the General Staff held their breath and waited. Long minutes passed. At the eight-minute mark, a radar station reported that the rocket had left Earth's atmosphere. A tentative cheer went up. At the eleven-minute mark, the radar station reported that the rocket had assumed a normal orbital pattern.

No one cheered after that. People simply went back to work.

Dead Hand was not in effect that day. Combat stations waited for orders from the central command. But today Dead Hand was in effect. A mistake, a downed communications system, a rat chewing through wires, could put nuclear decisions in the hands of faraway people who were drunk, or tired, or bored, or insane.

The Americans had done something no one expected. A dangerous cabal had seized the government in Washington, and their next moves were unpredictable. In response, Russia had activated unreliable and unsafe procedures that put the entire world at risk.

210

Dead Hand was a "fail-deadly" deterrent. It was mutually assured destruction. It might have been a good idea once, during the glory years of the great Soviet Union, when the communications and warning systems were robust and modern and well-maintained.

But now, it was a terrible idea. And it had become a reality.

Chapter 49

1:03 a.m.
Bowie, Maryland - Eastern Suburbs of Washington, DC

Luke parked a hundred feet away. The house was a raised ranch, sitting on top of a two-car garage. Just about every light in the house was on. One of the garage bays was open and lit up. The place looked like Christmas.

There was nothing in the open garage bay—just some tools hanging along the wall, a garbage bin, a couple of rakes and shovels in the corner. Luke guessed that Brenna had moved his own car out of there so that Chuck could pull straight in when he arrived. These guys had no idea who they were dealing with.

Luke glanced at the sky. It was an overcast night. With everything that was at stake, he wouldn't be surprised if at any second, a drone strike obliterated the house. They would do it and claim it was lightning. Only they would probably wait for Susan Hopkins to get here before they did.

The game was winner take all.

Luke's phone rang. He glanced at it and answered.

"Ed."

"Luke, I'm glad you're still alive."

"Me too. Thanks for the heads-up. It saved me."

"Trudy told me to call. She told me your family is missing. Is that true?"

"It is," Luke said. "Yes."

"Are you going to stand down?"

"I'm afraid it's too late for that. My best hope is to keep going forward."

"I want to tell you something in confidence," Ed said. "I once kept a man alive for a week while I killed him. It was a private matter, not work-related. I would do it again. If someone hurts your family, I will do it for you. That's a promise."

Luke swallowed. The day might come when he took Ed up on that offer.

"Thank you."

"What can I do for you now?"

"I have a friend," Luke said. "He's an Iraqi doctor and he works at the Chief Medical Examiner's office down on E Street.

212

His name is Ashwal Nadoori. I blew my cover for him in-country once upon a time. Saved his ass. He owes me. When we hang up, I want you to call him. Okay?"

"Got it."

"Tell him I'm calling in the favor. No uncertain terms. He doesn't have a choice. He told me he would walk across the desert on his knees for me. Something like that. Remind him of it. This is his one chance to repay me. Then go meet... Can you walk?"

"No. Not really. But I can gimp."

"Then gimp over to his office. When you get there, call me back, but don't use the phone you're using now. Steal somebody's phone. I'm answering all my calls tonight. If I see a call from a number I don't recognize, I'll know it's from you. By then, I'll have picked up another phone. We'll do a call between the two stolen phones. I'll give Ashwal his instructions at that time. You might have to help him do what I need done. You might have to twist his arm a little."

"All right, Luke. I'm pretty good at arm-twisting."

"I know you are."

Luke hung up and got out of the car. From his trunk he took a metal box and a green satchel. He walked through the dark neighborhood up to the front door of the house. He had a hunch the neighborhood wasn't really sleeping. Who could sleep on a night like this? He pictured dozens of people all around him, lying awake in bed, maybe talking quietly with loved ones, maybe crying, maybe praying.

If there was a sniper positioned out there, they could take him out now. He braced for the shot, but nothing came.

He climbed the stairs and rang the doorbell. It made a musical chime throughout the house. A few moments passed. Luke put his bags down. He turned and gazed out at the night. House upon house, street upon street, stretching several blocks over to the little Main Street area. For many people, this was probably the worst night of their lives. He was one of those people.

The door opened behind him. He turned and man stood there. He was a tall man with silver hair and a craggy face. He looked like the kind of sixty-five-year-old who had never smoked, and still put five sessions a week in at the gym. He stood in a shooter's crouch. His hands held a large pistol. The business end was in Luke's face.

"Can I help you?" the man said.

Luke put his hands up. No sudden moves, no getting shot pointlessly. He spoke slowly and calmly. "Walter Brenna, my name is Luke Stone. I'm with the FBI Special Response Team. I'm one of the good guys."

"How do you know my name?"

"Walter, everyone—and I mean *everyone*—knows your name. They all know who you are and what you're trying to do. I'm here to tell you it's not going to work. The bad guys heard your little chat with Chuck Berg, and they are converging on this spot as we speak, if they aren't here already. You're not going to hold them off."

Brenna smiled. "And you will?"

"I was a Delta Force operator on the ground in Afghanistan, Iraq, Yemen, and the Democratic Republic of the Congo, among other places. No one even knows we were in the Congo, you understand?"

Brenna nodded. "I do. But that doesn't mean I care, or that I even believe you."

Luke gestured with his head. "You see that box and that bag behind me? They're filled with weapons. I know how to use them. I stopped counting my confirmed kills at a hundred. If you want to live through this night, and if you want to see the Vice President live through this night, you should let me in."

Brenna wanted to play twenty questions. "And what if I don't?"

Luke shrugged. "I'll wait out here. When Chuck shows up, I'll tell him the Vice President is coming with me. If he disagrees, I'll kill him. Then I'll take her with me anyway. She has to be kept alive at all costs. Chuck doesn't matter and neither do you."

"Where do you think you'll take her?"

"To see some friendlies. I have a doctor waiting, along with another former Delta operator. He's my partner. Not for nothing, but he's killed six men in the past twelve hours. Three of them were government assassins. When was the last time you killed anyone, Walter?"

Brenna stared at him.

"Do you suppose you're going to make it through this without killing people? If so, you might want to think again."

The gun wavered.

"I rang the doorbell, Walter. They're not going to do that."

Brenna lowered the gun. "Come in."

214

Luke grabbed his bags and entered the house. He followed Brenna down a narrow hallway. They passed through an old galley kitchen. Luke took charge instantly, and Brenna accepted Luke's command.

"Are there any women here?" Luke said. "Children?"

Brenna shook his head. "I'm divorced. My wife went to Mexico. My daughter lives in California."

"Good."

Brenna led Luke into a bare room with no windows. There was a wooden table in the middle. Medical equipment was laid out—scalpels, scissors, antiseptic, bandages, tourniquets. "This room is double steel-reinforced. It's in a dummy placement, several feet back from the walls of the house. From the outside, you don't see its location."

Luke shook his head. "No. They'll use infra-red, heat seekers. We had goggles like that in Afghanistan. You can see heat signatures right through the walls. They'll start a firestorm in here and we'll be trapped."

Luke raised a hand. "Listen, Walter. We're not going to win this by being cute. They're going to drop all pretense. There is no rule of law. There are no negotiations. There's too much at stake. When they hit, they're going to hit hard. We need to be prepared for that. They won't hesitate to torch this place, and then tell everyone a gas main blew. Personally, I'd rather die in a shootout on the street."

Luke put his bags down on the table. The man was obviously a hobbyist, one of these so-called "preppers," building cockamamie devices like this panic room, and storing canned food to survive the coming apocalypse. It wasn't Luke's cup of tea, but it was better than someone who wasn't prepared at all.

"What else you got?" Luke said. "Give me something good."

"I have an M1 Garand rifle, and maybe twenty magazines loaded with .30-06 armor-piercing incendiary rounds."

Luke nodded. "Better. What else?"

Brenna took a deep breath.

"Come on, Walter. Out with it. We don't have much time."

"Okay," Brenna said. "I have a GMC Suburban completely redone in after-market armor. It's in the garage. It doesn't look like anything, but the doors, body, interior, suspension, the engine, all of it is wrapped in steel plates, ballistic nylon or Kevlar. The tires are modified runflats—you can ride on them for another sixty miles

215

after they're blown out. The glass is two-inch-thick transparent polycarbonate and lead. The weight is immense, two thousand pounds more than a stock Suburban. The engine is a jacked-up V8, and the front bumper and grille are reinforced steel—you could drive that thing through a brick wall."

Luke smiled. "Beautiful. And you didn't want to tell me."

Brenna shook his head. "I put a hundred thousand dollars into that car."

"No better time to use it than now," Luke said. "Show me."

They moved through Brenna's house to the garage. Luke held Brenna back from entering. They stood near the kitchen door, mindful of the possible sniper angles coming through the open garage bay. Across the way from them was the black Suburban. Brenna was right. It looked like a typical late-model SUV. Maybe the windows were a little darker than normal. Maybe the truck glowed a little more than it should. Or maybe that was all Luke's imagination.

"Gassed up?" Luke said.

"Of course."

"I need to borrow it."

Brenna nodded. "I figured. Maybe I'll ride with you."

"That's a good idea. Do you have any old Secret Service buddies, ones who are still able-bodied, and who you know you can trust?"

"I have a few I can think of. Yeah."

"We need them," Luke said. "Hell, the country's still paying them a pension, right? They might as well put their bodies on the line one last time."

Just then, the rumble of a large motorcycle came to them from the street. It was coming fast. It appeared out of nowhere, made a crazy low turn into Brenna's short driveway, and rambled uphill into the garage bay. It skidded to a stop, the front tire crashing into the far wall. The rider managed to keep it upright.

Luke pulled his gun, thinking it was the start of the attack.

Brenna ran for the garage door. He leapt, grabbed a cord, and yanked the door down. He locked the door by hooking it into a heavy clasp on the ground.

The man on the bike removed his dark helmet. A woman was on the back, holding him around the waist. Luke looked closer. In fact she wasn't holding him at all. Her wrists were handcuffed around the man's waist. She was also tied to him with two large

216

leather straps. Brenna produced a knife and immediately started cutting them apart.

Once her wrists were freed, the woman's left arm fell to her side. She used her right hand to remove the helmet. Her short blonde bob fell almost to her shoulders. Her face was dirty with soot. Her jaw was clenched. The left side of her face, nearly to the chin, was an angry, peeling red. Her blue eyes belied her exhaustion.

Susan Hopkins looked around the garage. Her eyes caught Luke.

"Stone? What are you doing here?"

"Same thing you're doing," Luke said. "Trying to get my country back. Are you okay?"

"I'm in pain, but I'm all right."

The man put down the kickstand and climbed off the bike. He was very tall. His face was tired, but his body language was erect and his eyes were alert.

"Charles Berg?" Luke said.

The man nodded. "Call me Chuck," he said. "The Vice President has been a trouper. We've had a rough night, but she hung in there. She's as tough as they come."

"She's the President," Luke said, and the truth of that hit him for the first time. "Not the Vice President." He looked at her. She was small. He couldn't get over that part. He always thought supermodels were supposed to be tall. She was also beautiful, almost ethereal in her beauty. The burn on her face somehow added to the effect. He felt like he could look at her for an hour.

He didn't have an hour. He might not have five minutes.

"Susan, you are the President of the United States. Let's everybody try to remember that. I think it'll help. Now we have to get out of here."

Luke's phone started ringing. He looked down at it. He didn't recognize the number. Ed was calling.

"Walter, this is a crazy question, but do you happen to have an extra cell phone you've never used?"

Brenna nodded. "I have five or six prepaid phones. I keep them on hand in case I want to make fast calls that can't be monitored in real time. I use a prepaid phone once, then I destroy it."

The guy was a jackpot. "You're a little paranoid, aren't you?" Luke said.

217

Brenna shrugged. "Can't really blame me at this point, can you?"

Luke answered his phone. "Ed? You with my friend there? Good. I'm going to call you right back."

Chapter 50

1:43 a.m.
Office of the Chief Medical Examiner - Washington, DC

Ashwal Nadoori hung up the telephone.

He sat thoughtfully at his desk for a moment. A large black man sat across from him in a wheelchair. The sight of the man, and the type of man he was, brought back bad memories for Ashwal.

"Did he tell you what he wants?" the man said.

Ashwal nodded. "He wants a corpse, preferably intact. A woman, late forties, blonde hair. Someone who appeared healthy before she died."

"Can you do that?"

Ashwal shrugged. "This is a big place. We have many, many bodies. I'm sure we can find one that fits that description."

Once upon a time, in another life, Ashwal had been a doctor. Here in America, they did not accept his Iraqi education, so now he was only a medical assistant. He worked in this giant morgue, processing bodies, assisting with autopsies, whatever they assigned him. It could be unpleasant work, but it was also peaceful in its own way.

The people were already dead. There was no struggle for life. There was no pain, and there was no terror of dying. The worst that could happen had already happened. There was no need to try and stop it, and there was no need to pretend it wasn't a foregone conclusion.

Ashwal had a sick feeling in his stomach. Stealing a corpse was risking his job. It was a decent job. He was frugal, and the job more than paid his bills. He lived in a modest house with his two daughters. They lacked nothing. It would be a terrible shame to lose the things they had.

But what choice did he have? Ashwal was Bahá'í. It was a beautiful faith, one of peace, unity, and a longing to know God. Ashwal loved his religion. He loved everything about it. But many Muslims didn't. They thought Bahá'í was apostasy. They thought it was heresy. Many thought it should be punishable by death.

When he was a child, his family had left Iran to escape the persecution of the Bahá'í in that country. They moved to Iraq, which at the time was mortal enemies with Iran. Iraq was run by a

219

madman, one who mostly left the Bahá'í alone. Ashwal grew to manhood, studied hard, and became a doctor, and enjoyed the fruits and privileges of that calling. But then the madman was toppled, and suddenly it was not safe to be Bahá'í.

One night, Islamic extremists came and took his wife. Perhaps some of them were his former patients, or his neighbors. It didn't matter. He never saw her again. Even now, a decade later, he did not dare to imagine her face or her name. He simply thought "wife," and kept the rest blocked. He could not bear to think about her.

He could not bear to think that when she was taken, there was no one he could turn to for help. The society was no longer functioning. The worst tendencies had been set loose. People laughed, or looked away, when he passed on the street.

Two weeks later, in the night, another group came, a dozen men. These ones were different, unfamiliar to him. They wore black hoods. They took him and his daughters into the desert on the back of a pickup truck. They marched the three of them out onto the sand. They forced them to their knees at the lip of a trench. His girls were crying. Ashwal could not bring himself to cry. He could not bring himself to comfort them. He was too numb. In a sense, he almost welcomed this, the relief that it would bring.

Suddenly gunshots rang out. Automatic fire.

At first, Ashwal thought he was dead. But he was wrong. One of the men was shooting all the others. He killed them and killed them. It took less than ten seconds. The sound was deafening. When it was done, three of the men were still alive, crawling, trying to escape. The man calmly walked up to each and shot them in the back of the head with a pistol. Ashwal flinched each time.

The man removed his hood. He was a man with the full beard of the mujahideen. His skin was dark from the desert sun. But his hair was light, almost blond, like a Westerner. He walked up to Ashwal and offered a hand.

"Stand up," he said. His voice was firm. There was no compassion in it. It was the voice of a man accustomed to giving orders.

"Come with me if you want to live."

The man's name was Luke Stone. He was the same man who had just instructed Ashwal to steal a corpse. There was no choice. Ashwal didn't even ask why he wanted it. Luke Stone had saved his life, and his daughters' lives. Their lives were far more important than any job.

The last thing Luke Stone said into the phone decided him, if he hadn't decided already.

"They've taken my family," he said.

Ashwal looked at the black man in the wheelchair. "Shall we go in the back and see what we can find?"

Chapter 51

1:50 a.m.
Bowie, Maryland - Eastern Suburbs of Washington, DC

A motorcade of vehicles had sped through the night to arrive here.

There were more than a dozen vehicles, mostly Jeeps and SUVs. All were black, with no markings of any kind. The last was a sort of paddy wagon, on hand in the unlikely event that any prisoners were taken. The vehicles parked quietly, two blocks from the house. The neighborhood was a suburban cul-de-sac. On the streets at least, there was only one way in or out. Two SUVs parked face to face across that entrance.

Meanwhile, a twenty-man assault team closed in on the house.

Eight men approached from the front, five each from either flank. Two men, the team leaders, hung back, kneeling behind parked cars half a block away. They would use their spot as a viewing and command post. The men all wore Kevlar body suits and helmets. All the helmets had internal radios.

The eight men crossed quietly in front of the two car garage. The lead man carried a thirty-pound steel battering ram, which should take the front door out in one or two swings. Each man after that had a flashbang stun grenade. Each man carried a shotgun. The plan was to blow the front door, then throw the flashbangs in. If the team was lucky, the blasts and the blinding light might disable the subjects, or might get them running from the house, where the rest of the assault team could easily take them down.

The third man in line, a young guy named Rafer, wiped some sweat out of his eyes. Truth be told, he was nervous.

He had a feeling in his bowels, a loose feeling like how it was before he went into a firefight. He could easily soil his pants. He smiled. Loose bowels were his good luck charm. Three tours of duty in Iraq and Afghanistan, and he'd never gotten so much as a scratch in combat.

Stop it. Pay attention.

He brought his mind back to the present moment. The line of men leaned up against the garage door. The front stairs were a right turn ten feet ahead. This had to happen fast. He pictured it in his mind. BAM! The door came down, and they threw their flashbangs.

222

His would be second. Fall back, wait for the explosions, then rush in.

Somewhere nearby, there was a sound.

It was muffled, but it sounded like a car engine. And it sounded like it was right on the other side of this garage door.

The guy in front of him looked back at Rafer. His eyes widened. They both turned and looked at the door.

* * *

Luke sat in the driver's seat of the Suburban inside Walter Brenna's closed garage. Brenna sat next to him. In the back sat Susan Hopkins and Charles Berg. Brenna had his M1, lying across his knees. Chuck had a nine-millimeter Beretta. Susan had nothing. Luke was like the dad up here in the front. They were like his little family.

His hands gripped the steering wheel. It was almost silent inside the SUV. In the corner of the garage was a small video display. It showed what was happening outside the garage doors. Men were out there, outfitted like a SWAT team. Luke had no idea who they were or what they thought they represented.

Did they know there had been a coup? Did they know the real President was in here? Maybe they thought they were about to take down some terrorists.

He shook his head. It didn't matter. They were about to hit the house, and that meant they were bad guys.

"They're not going to expect this," he said quietly. "So we have the initiative. But it's not going to last."

"Are you planning to kill those men?" Susan said.

"Yes."

He turned the key in the ignition and the engine barked into life. There was no turning back now.

He put the car in gear and took a deep breath.

"Ready?"

"It's a really heavy car," Brenna said. "You have to punch it."

Luke stomped on the gas.

The tires shrieked on the concrete floor of the garage, and the Suburban screamed forward, blasting through the door, knocking it down, splintering it into pieces. The SUV erupted into the night. They bucked over something, pieces of the door, speed bumps, men, Luke didn't know, and he didn't care.

223

To his right and left, men in black were running.

He turned left, never letting off the gas. Men crouched and fired, spraying the side of the car with bullets.

DUH-DUH-DUH-DUH-DUH…

Susan screamed.

"Susan!" Luke said. "Get your head down, all the way in Chuck's lap. We don't know how long those windows are going to last. I don't want you sitting upright when they fail."

The SUV gained speed. Luke felt the acceleration.

Two blocks ahead, two dark SUVs were parked nose to nose in the middle of the street. Men took up positions behind them. Luke saw the muzzle flashes of their guns. They were already firing.

"Where are we going, Walter?"

"Straight ahead. It's the only way out."

"I guess we're going to find out how bulletproof this glass is right away."

Luke stomped on the gas again, pressing it all the way. He watched the parked trucks zoom toward them. Closer, closer. A dozen men in black fired their weapons. Bullets strafed the windshield like wasps.

Two men leaned across the hoods of the SUVs, still firing.

"Here we go!"

BOOM!

The Suburban smashed between the two SUVs, metal rending metal. It burst through them, spinning them, knocking them away like toys. The two shooters were sucked under and crushed.

The Suburban barely slowed.

Luke floored the gas pedal again. The car burst forward, gathering speed.

A burst of gunfire hit the back windshield. Susan yelped again, but not as loud this time. Then they were out of range, moving fast. Luke glanced in the rearview the mirror. Men were running, jumping into SUVs.

"Okay," Luke said. "That went pretty well. Where's the highway entrance?"

"Up ahead," Walter said. "One mile, on the right."

The car ripped through the quiet town. Luke barely slowed for the highway entrance, taking the sharp curve hard. They merged into four nearly empty lanes of traffic, running west toward the city.

The car was still gaining speed. The digital readout hit 80, then 90, then 100. The car burst forward, its ride smoothing out. Luke took the curves of the road effortlessly. He embraced the speed, the exhilaration. For a moment, he smiled. The Suburban had blown right through them.

Behind them, the first pursuit vehicles appeared. Luke could see their headlights in the rearview. Could he outrun them in this car? He didn't think so.

He pushed the car on. 120 now.

130.

Inside the cabin, it was quiet. No one cheered. No one war-whooped. They hadn't won anything yet, not even close. Everyone must have understood that.

Ahead of them, cars were signaling and pulling off the road. Luke glanced at the rearview again. Flashing red and blue lights now, coming fast.

"We're about to have a lot of company," he said.

Behind them, the pursuit vehicles were closing in. They passed an entrance ramp. Three more black SUVs raced onto the highway next to them. Two hundred yards ahead of them, two more had slowed almost to a stop. Their brake lights lit up in the dark.

"Stone!" Chuck Berg said. "They're going to box us in."

"I see that."

Susan poked her head up. "What would happen," she said, "if we just gave up?"

"They'd kill us," Brenna said.

"Do we know that for a fact? I mean, this is crazy. If they saw me in here, are they just going to shoot me?"

Brenna shrugged. "Do you really want to find out?"

Every few miles, they passed little turnarounds, where state troopers would normally park to monitor traffic with radar, or simply turn around and go the other way. They were due to pass another one in a moment.

An SUV pulled even on Luke's left. A gunman leaned from the rear passenger window.

"Get down!" Luke shouted.

The man fired at the back of the Suburban. Bullets strafed the side of it. Susan screamed. The rear window smashed, but didn't break. Luke spun the wheel hard to the left. The armored car hit the black SUV and drove it into the concrete sidewall. The car crumpled, its tires shredded, and it flipped. The Suburban kept going.

Luke looked back at her. "Susan, I told you to stay down. I didn't mean sometimes. I meant all the time. They don't care about us. They're shooting at you. I'd prefer if you didn't show them where you are."

They were surrounded by SUVs now. Three in front, one to the side, two behind. The three in front slowed down, and slowed down some more. There was no way around them. Their rear lights went light and dark, light and dark, as they tapped their brakes. Luke looked at the speedometer. 60. 55. 50. 45. Falling fast. They were trapped. There was no way out of here.

"I'm about to do something really unpopular," Luke said. "I'd put it up for a vote, but I doubt anyone would vote with me."

"What is it?" Brenna said.

The next turnaround was coming.

"This," Luke said, and spun the wheel hard again.

The big Suburban veered through the turnaround, bounced over some rough road, and into the eastbound lanes of the highway. Traveling west.

Headlights loomed ahead, a sea of them.

"Jesus!"

Luke plunged straight at the headlights, jaw set. He stomped on the gas again.

They plowed through the traffic, oncoming cars scattering like leaves.

A tractor trailer went by on his left. The entire car shuddered with the wind of it.

"Luke!" Susan screamed. "Stop!"

The Suburban accelerated into the traffic. Cars veered by. The headlights were nearly blinding. There was no time to look behind him. He gazed ahead, both hands gripping the wheel, his concentration supreme.

It was a long straightaway, cars coming in droves. Luke plowed through like a boat cutting the waves. He began to get that confident feeling—that humming, buzzing feeling he associated with taking Dexies. He had to be careful. Overconfidence could kill.

Cars zipped by like missiles.

"Did anyone make that turn with us?" Luke said.

Brenna looked back.

"No. No one else is crazy enough."

"Good."

Luke veered all the way to the left and zoomed off the highway at the next entrance ramp.

Chapter 52

Luke spotted Ed Newsam leaning up against the wall of the building, his M4 rifle cradled in his arms.

The building was four stories tall, with a glass front. It was located just outside the half-mile radiation evacuation zone around the White House. The streets were entirely deserted. It looked like most people had decided that a half mile wasn't nearly far enough.

Luke let the car roll to a stop on the sidewalk in front of the building.

"What now?" Susan said.

"Now you get out. You stay with Ed, Chuck, and Walter inside that building. No matter what happens, or who comes, you stay with them. Stay as close as you can to Ed. Chuck and Walter are very good, but Ed is a killing machine. Okay?"

"Okay."

"Then let's do this fast."

Luke popped out of the car. Smoke rose from the radiator. All of the doors were stove in with bullet holes. Three of the four tires were shredded. All in all, the car had held up exceptionally well. Luke needed to get one of these.

"Took some heat, huh?" Ed said.

Luke smiled. "You should have been there."

Behind him, they were climbing out.

"Ed, you remember the President, don't you?"

"Of course."

Ed pushed the door to the building open. He had very little leverage and had to use his body weight to do it. They entered the main foyer. Ashwal was there with a wheelchair. He was a dark man, balding, with glasses. Years had passed since Luke had seen him. Strapped upright in the wheelchair was a dead woman with a blonde bob haircut. She wore a white spring sweater and slacks. Her skin was gray and slack, but otherwise she might just be sleeping.

"Ashwal," Luke said.

The man stared at him. "Luke."

Luke gestured at Susan with both hands. "Ashwal, this is Susan Hopkins, the President of the United States. She's injured. I

228

need you to diagnose her injuries and treat her with whatever you have on hand here. We can't bring her to the hospital. People are trying to kill her."

Ashwal stared at Susan. Something slowly dawned behind his eyes.

"I'm not a doctor anymore."

"You are tonight."

Ashwal nodded, his face severe. "Okay."

Susan was staring at the corpse.

"Is that supposed to me?" she said.

"Yes."

"What are you going to do with her?"

Luke shrugged. "I'm going to kill her."

Chapter 53

2:30 a.m.
Streets of Washington, DC

They must be looking for this car. The easiest thing to do was help them find it.

Luke was in the Suburban, alone now. He had Brenna's M1 Garand rifle with him in the front seat. It was loaded with an eight-shot magazine of the high-powered .30-06 armor-busting incendiaries. Ten more mags were on the floor in front of the seat.

In the back seat, the corpse sat where Susan had been. The seatbelt kept the body upright. Its head bobbed and moved with the movement of the car.

Luke rolled slowly through the empty streets near the National Mall and the Capitol. He was right on the edge of the radiation containment zone. Somewhere around here, the DC cops should have the streets blocked off.

There it was, flashing lights, down a side street to his right. He passed the intersection, then pulled over to the curb. There were no cars or people anywhere.

Cops were good. They were a start. But what Luke needed were bad guys. The cops didn't know anything about what was going on. This car would be meaningless to them. He sat for a minute, thinking about it. Could he have lost them so thoroughly back there on the highway that they had no idea where he was? He didn't think so.

He still had his cell phone with him. He knew it was stupid to keep it, but he was hoping against hope that he'd get a call or a text from Becca. He brought the phone out and stared at its eerie glow in the darkness.

"Oh, hell," he said. He speed-dialed her number.

Her phone was off. It didn't ring at all.

"Hi, this is Becca. I can't answer your…"

He hung up. He sat quietly for a few moments, trying not to think about anything. Maybe they would find him, maybe they wouldn't. If not, he was going to have to go out and find them. He closed his eyes and breathed deeply. He sank into the driver's seat for a moment.

Gradually, he became aware of a sound. It was the heavy rumble of a large helicopter. It didn't alarm him. There could be a million reasons why a helicopter, even a military chopper, was in the sky over Washington, DC, right now. He sat up and looked out his windshield. It gave him a view down the wide boulevard in front of him.

The chopper was approaching dead ahead. It was flying low and slow. After a few seconds, its shape resolved into something familiar to him.

It couldn't be what he thought it was, not here in the middle of the city.

But it was...

...an Apache helicopter gunship.

"Oh no."

Luke slammed the car into gear and stomped on the gas. He spun the wheel hard to the left and did a giant, screaming U-turn in the middle of the street.

The chopper fired its mini-gun.

Thirty-millimeter rounds strafed the top of the SUV, ripping up the car's armor.

Luke flinched, but kept driving. He spun another hard left, making the turn down the side street. The chopper passed behind him.

Up ahead, four street cops stood in front of a low concrete barrier. They were watching the sky, their attention suddenly grabbed by the chopper. Two police cruisers were parked on either side, lights silently flashing. Luke took a deep breath.

Real cops! He couldn't imagine a group of people he'd rather surrender to right now. A hundred yards out, he stomped on the gas. The Suburban picked up speed. He accelerated toward the cops.

The four of them scattered.

Three seconds later, he plowed through the concrete barrier, cracking it in half, driving the two crumbling pieces ahead of him. He skidded to a stop, reversed a few feet, then peeled out around them.

Behind him, the cops had jumped in their cruisers. Seconds later, the familiar siren wail began.

Luke took a left on Independence Avenue. He scanned the sky for the chopper. He could hear it, but couldn't see it. The Suburban was smoking from the rounds it had just taken. He had badly underestimated them. An Apache! They were going to kill this car and they didn't care who knew about it.

He pushed the Suburban up as fast as it would go. It had lost some power, and topped out just under 80. He sped along Independence, on the south side of the Mall. The tidal basin was to his left. Street lights shimmered on the water.

Behind him, the cops were coming hard.

The Apache swooped in from his right. It was four stories up. The mini-gun fired again. The bullets hit. It sounded like a jackhammer. The right side rear window shattered, spraying the corpse with glass.

Luke swerved the car crazily, his foot still pressing the gas to the floor. The roadway zipped past him. Far ahead and to his left, he could see the Lincoln Memorial, lit up in the night.

The chopper came back around. It gave up on the mini-gun. It started launching its Hydra rockets instead. A line of rockets whooshed out from the right side of the chopper. Three, four, five.

Ahead of him, the roadway blew up in shades of red and yellow. BOOM... BOOM... BOOOM.

He spun hard to the left. The SUV broke through a chain-link barrier and bounced over the grass. Luke was thrown around in his seat. His hands gripped the wheel. He barely let up off the gas.

More rockets came. One lit up a line of cherry blossom trees. The small hills blew up all around him.

The car took a direct hit, in the back.

Luke felt the back of the car go up in the air. He pushed open his door and jumped.

He hit the grass and rolled away to the left. The car's rear wheels bounced back down and the car kept going, downhill toward the water.

Luke saw the spark as another Hydra rocket took off. It zipped through the air, penetrated the SUV's armor, and hit home. Flames shot out an instant before the entire car blew.

BOOOOOM.

Luke hit the deck and covered his head as heavy armor flew. A moment later, he looked back. The car was still rolling, red and orange flames reaching like arms into the night sky. Inside the car, a woman in her late forties burned, unclaimed, a person with no name. Luke could see her silhouette.

The car, utterly on fire, rolled slowly to the edge of the water. The lip of the tidal basin was a drop-off. The car went off the side and in. It hung there for a few seconds, half in the water, half out, before it fell all the way in. It burned, even as it sank.

The chopper veered off and away. Seconds later, it was a dark and distant shadow against the night sky.

Luke lay on the grass, breathing heavily. A Capitol District police car skidded to a halt behind him, its siren howling. Two cops got out, one white, one black. They approached him with flashlights and guns drawn.

"On your face. Arms out."

Luke did as the man said. Rough hands searched him. They pulled his arms behind his back and cuffed his wrists tight.

"You have the right to remain silent," a cop began.

Chapter 54

3:23 a.m.
Municipal Detention Center - Washington, DC

Everything was white.

The walls and the floors were white. The overhead lights were bright and white. The sliding electronic metal gates that slid open and clanged shut behind him were painted white.

They processed Luke and put him in a holding cell with half a dozen other men. The room was large. It was white, with dirty handprints all over the walls. The floor was white, going toward dingy gray from the bottoms of a thousand pairs of sneakers. There was a urinal and a toilet built into one wall. The floor sloped very gradually toward the middle, where there was a small, round open drain.

A dirty white bench ringed the walls of the cell, reaching almost halfway around. Luke paced the cell for several minutes while the other men watched him. He was the only white man in the room. That didn't bother him. He barely noticed the other men. It was just being trapped in here. It was not being in motion. He couldn't stand it.

Somewhere out there, Becca and Gunner were in the hands of bad people. Luke might be kidding himself, but he sensed that they were still alive. If so, he needed to get out of here and find them. He would never stop, never, until he found them again. And God help the men who had them.

No. That was wrong. No one could help them.

If they laid so much as a finger...

Now that he was stuck in here, he could feel the rage begin to boil inside him. The Vice President, the car chase, all of it—it had taken his mind off things. But now there was nothing to distract him.

Then, of course, there was Susan Hopkins. He had left her with Ed, and Brenna and Berg. They were capable men, especially Ed. But if Luke was still alive, he should really be there with them.

He felt like screaming.

He walked over to the bench and sat down. Within a minute, a guy had peeled himself off the bench along the far wall and ambled over to Luke. He was a big young guy, well-muscled, with a

Chicago Bulls jersey on. He had a crazy tangled mass of Afro atop his head. He smiled, and one of his front teeth was gold.

He crouched down in front of Luke.

"Hey, bro, you okay?"

A quiet round of titters and chuckles went around among the men in the cell.

Luke looked at him. "The President died tonight. Bro."

The guy nodded. "Heard about that. I guess that don't really bother me. Never voted for the man."

Luke shrugged. "Can I help you?"

The guy gestured with his chin. "I noticed your boots. They're nice."

Now Luke nodded. He looked down at his own feet and the leather boots he was wearing. "You're right. They are nice. My wife gave them to me last Christmas."

"What kind are they?"

"They're Ferragamo. I think she paid about six hundred bucks for them. My wife likes to buy me nice things. She knows I'd never buy them for myself."

"Give them to me," the young guy said.

Luke shook his head. "I can't do that. They have sentimental value. Anyway, I don't think they would fit you."

"I want them."

Luke looked around the cell. Every set of eyes was on him. He could imagine how for someone, this might be a tense and frightening situation.

"I think you better go sit down," he said. "I'm not in a very good mood right now."

The kid's eyes flashed anger. "Give me those shoes."

Luke rolled his eyes. "You want them? Take them."

The kid nodded and smiled. He glanced around the cell. Now there was outright laughter. The big tough thug was going to steal the white man's shoes. He leaned in and reached for Luke's feet.

Luke paused a beat, then kicked the kid in the mouth. It was a lightning strike. The kid's head snapped back. Teeth went flying, maybe three of them in all. One was the gold tooth in the front. The kid fell backwards. He ended up on his knees, bent over, his hands to his mouth.

Luke sighed. He stood up, stepped up behind the kid, and punched him hard in the back of the neck, right where the spinal column attached to the bottom of the skull. The kid collapsed to the

235

grimy floor. His eyes rolled back. In a few seconds, he was unconscious. A few seconds later, he started making an odd snoring sound.

Luke looked around the cell. He had been in a bad mood before. The young shoe robber had only made it worse. Luke would beat every man in here half to death, if that's what they wanted from him.

"The next man who fucks with me loses all his teeth," he said, loud enough that everyone could hear him.

They all stared back, mouths agape, then all finally looked away. Their eyes, so filled with bloodlust but moments before, were now filled with something else: fear.

Chapter 55

5:45 a.m.
United States Naval Observatory - Washington, DC

His name was William Theodore Ryan.

He was the great-great-grandson of plantation gentry. His people, for generations, were proud Confederates and rebels. And here he was, the President of the United States of America.

He was as tired as he could ever remember. He had barely slept last night. Before first light, he had insisted they fly back to Washington from Site R. There was no sense staying underground, was there? The threat was over. And it would show the American people how courageous he was. He wasn't going to hide in a hole in the ground while more than three hundred million people had to go on with their lives above ground, vulnerable to foreign attack.

He smiled at the thought of it.

He sat in sitting area of the upstairs office of the Vice President's official residence. Outside the windows, weak light was entering the sky. The house itself was beautiful, a huge white Queen Anne with gables and a turret on the lovely, rolling grounds of the Naval Observatory. It dated to the mid-1800s and generations of Vice Presidents had called it home. Now it would serve as the White House until the original could be rebuilt.

On the sofa across from him sat Senator Edward Graves of Kansas. Later today, at the age of seventy-two, Ed was going to become the oldest Vice President in modern U.S. history. Ed Graves was a military expert, and had been chairman of the Congressional Armed Forces Committee since the world was young. Ed had been one of his mentors for almost twenty years now.

Between them a black speaker phone sat on the table. It squawked, as an undersecretary from the Joint Chiefs gave them a quick update on events in the Middle East. Things were tense, but seemed to be going well.

"Sir," the voice said, "on your orders, two American F-118 fighter jets entered Iranian airspace at approximately 1:45 p.m. local time, just about half an hour ago."

"Status?" Bill Ryan said.

"Within two minutes, they were intercepted and engaged by three Iranian jets, we believe them to be outdated Russian Mig fighters. The F-118s destroyed the Iranian jets after a brief dogfight. Radar picked up the presence of at least a dozen more Iranian fighters converging on the area, so the F-118s retreated to Turkish airspace. The Iranians turned back at the border."

"Okay," Ryan said. "What else?"

"Two listening stations, one in Japan and one in Alaska, have reported that as many as half a dozen Russian missile silos in eastern Siberia have switched to a state of full combat readiness in the past twenty minutes. The silos have as primary targets major metropolitan areas along the West Coast, including Seattle, Portland, and San Francisco. They have acquired and locked on to their targets."

"Jesus. Why are they doing that?"

"We're not sure, sir. The timing seems related to the Iranian airspace incursion, but the chatter we're picking up suggests some confusion at the Russian Central Command. We don't believe those silos have gone rogue, but they do seem to have misunderstood their orders."

Ryan looked at Ed. It was typical of the Russians to have their heads that far up their own asses. What were they going to do, start a nuclear war over Iran? He had to admit, though, there was something exhilarating about all this brinksmanship. He had been President less than eight hours.

Ryan addressed the voice. "Do we have missiles that target those Russian silos?"

"Yes sir, we do."

"Then ramp those missiles up to combat readiness, and make sure the Russians know about it. They need to get their boys in line. If we show 'em our guns, maybe they'll see we mean business over here."

The voice on the other end hesitated. "Yes sir."

"Anything else?"

"Not at this moment, sir."

Ryan turned off the phone. It was very quiet in the room. He looked at Ed Graves.

"Thoughts?"

Ed's hands rested on his knees. They were gnarled and liver-spotted hands, like old tree trunks. Ed's face was craggy and lined.

238

His nose was bulbous, and crisscrossed with broken blood vessels. But his eyes were like twin laser beams.

"It's silly," he said, "to send two planes across the border. Why are we testing them? We know what they can do, and we know what we can do. They attacked us first, right? They killed our President."

Here, Ed made an outrageous wink. Bill was almost embarrassed for him.

"If that's true, then we need to hit them and hit them hard. We need to retaliate. We have the Fifth Fleet in the Persian Gulf. Let's take out the Iranian guns in the Strait of Hormuz. We don't want to give them a chance to lay mines there. Just take them out. Poof. Then, send bombers all the way to Tehran. Give them a full complement of fighter escorts so they get there. I would start all of this today."

Bill nodded. "They'll have to fight their way to Tehran."

Ed shrugged. "Our boys are the best. And isn't that what we pay them to do? Fight? A week or two of heavy bombing in the city center and I think our whole Iranian problem will go away."

"What about the Russians?"

Ed Graves seemed to think about that for a moment. Finally, he shrugged. "Fuck the Russians."

A knock came at the heavy oak door.

"Come in."

The door opened. A young aide came in. His name was Ben, and he had been on Ryan's staff for a couple of years. He was an energetic kid in general, but today he seemed positively electric with excitement. The whole team was moving up in the world.

"What can I do for you, Ben?'

"Sir, we just got an identification on the woman found in the SUV that blew up and went into the Tidal Basin last night. You asked me to report to you when I heard anything about that."

"Yes, I did. What have you got?"

"Dental records indicate it was a woman named Liza Redeemer."

Those were not words Bill Ryan wanted to hear. "Redeemer?"

"Yes sir. She was a 33-year-old vagrant. Long history of mental illness, schizophrenia, bipolar disorder, the works. She had her name legally changed from Elizabeth Reid when she turned 18. There's no indication here what she was doing in that car."

Ryan nodded. "Okay. Thank you."

When the aide went out, Ryan looked at Ed Graves again. "We need to get Don Morris on the phone."

Chapter 56

7:15 a.m.
Municipal Detention Center - Washington, DC

"How did you sleep?"

"Like a baby. I was in the lockup with about six other men. Nice guys. I never knew how many innocent people there were in jail."

Luke stepped into the sunlight outside the detention center. It was bright out. His hands were still cuffed. He was led along by Don Morris. He, Don, and two agents Luke didn't recognize walked down the steps and headed toward a late-model black sedan parked up the street.

"That was quite a trick you pulled. They had to use dental records to figure out it wasn't Susan Hopkins in the car with you. And that was barely an hour ago. They still don't know who it is."

"Oh?" Luke said. "I could have sworn it was Susan."

Don stopped walking. He looked at Luke. "Cut the shit, Stone. I'm not in a funny mood today, and I didn't think you would be, either. You're going to talk, and you're going to tell us where Susan is. You realize that, don't you? Oh, I know. Luke Stone is unbreakable. It'll take days to get the information from him. Personally, I don't think so. I think you're going to talk very fast. We've got some leverage on you, in case you've forgotten."

"You said you would never hurt my family."

Don smiled. "I won't. Your family is alive and doing fine. You need to know that. But we need to know where Susan Hopkins is."

"Don, Susan is the President of the United States."

He shook his head. "You don't decide that, Stone."

"No. The Constitution does."

Don made a sound. It was something like a harrumph. He looked at the two agents with them. "Can you men give Agent Stone and me some time alone?"

The two men walked perhaps thirty yards away. They stood near a parked car and stared at Luke and Don. They didn't pretend to do anything but watch. Luke supposed they must know that he could kill Don with his arms and his legs tied.

Don leaned back against the black sedan. "Son, what are you doing?"

241

Luke stared at him. He had known Don a long time, and yet, had never really known him at all. "What are you doing, Don? What are you doing? I'm not the one who just helped engineer a coup."

Don shook his head. "Luke, whatever you prefer to call it, it's already over. Things are moving forward, not backwards. Bill Ryan is President of the United States, whether you like it or not. Your family is in jeopardy, but they're not dead, and they haven't been hurt. You can get them returned to you. You just need to play ball here a little. I can't even believe your reluctance. You're not holding any cards."

"What's in this for you, Don? Surely you didn't do this just because Bill Ryan is your old college buddy."

Don nodded. "Okay. Fair question. If it helps you do the right thing, I'll answer it. I'm tired of America being weak. I'm tired of America being hesitant. That kind of thing was never in my training as a military man, and frankly, it isn't in my DNA. I can't stand it. And I'm tired of begging for resources to keep the Special Response Team afloat year after year. We were doing great work, you saw it, you were part of it, and the whole thing was going down the tubes."

Luke was beginning to see. "So Bill Ryan is going to give you the budget you want for SRT?"

Don shook his head. "No. Bill Ryan is a figurehead, as I'm sure you're aware. There are other powers at work here. And they would like to see America restored to greatness, just as I would, and you would. So this afternoon, Bill's going to announce that I'm his nominee for Secretary of Defense."

Luke stared at him. He thought back to the night before, David Delliger taking a bullet at the 50-yard line inside the Naval Academy football stadium.

"You sure you want that job? I was with your predecessor last night. His tenure ended pretty abruptly."

Don smiled. "Dave wasn't a good pick for that job. He was a military man, but he wasn't a warrior. These times call for a warrior. I'm sure you of all people can understand that."

"Don, if we go to war with Iran, the Russians…"

Don raised a hand. "Luke, don't lecture me about the Russians. I was killing Russians when you were shitting in your diapers. I know what the Russians are going to do. Nothing, that's what. They're going to stand by and watch. Now tell me where Susan is. Please."

Luke didn't say anything.

"Rebecca and Gunner are going to die today, Luke. That's what is going to happen. And you won't have anyone to blame but yourself."

Luke turned his head away. "You're a traitor, Don."

Up the street, in the direction Luke was looking, something strange was happening. The two agents were walking quickly back this way. Behind them, a group of men in suits and wearing sunglasses followed them along on the sidewalk. Luke counted seven men. He turned and looked in the other direction. Maybe they were all headed somewhere else.

No. Another half a dozen were coming up the sidewalk the other way. Luke glanced back at the agents who were with Don. Suddenly, they bolted. One darted into the street. He ran halfway across before a car hit him. The car screeched to a halt. The agent rolled over the hood and fell to the street. Three men ran toward him, guns drawn.

The other agent ran across a lawn toward a parking lot. Five men chased him.

Three men approached Don and Luke from one side, two from the other side. They drew their weapons. A man held up a badge.

"Secret Service," he said.

They put Don on the ground, face first. They took his guns and cuffed him.

"What are the charges?" Don said.

"Where to even begin?" the man said. "Treason. Domestic terrorism. Murder. Kidnapping. Conspiracy. Those will do for a start."

They cut Luke's wrists free. He massaged his wrists, getting the feeling back in them. "Some of those sound like death penalty offenses."

The Secret Service man nodded. "They are."

"My wife and son have been kidnapped. This man knows where they are."

Luke stared down at Don.

"If I were you," he said, "I'd start talking, and fast."

Chapter 57

7:45 a.m.
United States Naval Observatory - Washington, DC

A black SUV pulled up the circular driveway in front of the Vice President's official residence.

The back door opened, and Susan Hopkins stepped out. The Iraqi doctor had set her arm and her wrist in the night. Her face was beyond his abilities—he had merely put a topical painkiller on the burns so she could sleep.

She had talked to Pierre just fifteen minutes ago, after she was assured it was safe to do so. He had cried, and she almost did, too. She still hadn't talked to the girls.

She walked up the path toward the big white house wearing full body armor under her suit. Chuck Berg walked with her, as did Walter Brenna.

The house was beautiful, and it had never looked more beautiful than it did this morning. She loved that house. It had been her residence for the past five years.

They entered the foyer.

About a dozen men in Army dress blues and business suits stared at them as they came in. She recognized a few of the men. They were Secret Service agents. All Ryan's people.

They stared at her as if they had seen a ghost. One of the men shook hands with Chuck Berg. A low murmur went through the crowd.

"Can I help you?" a man in Army dress said.

"I'm here to speak with William Ryan."

"Who may I say is calling?"

"My name is Susan Hopkins, and I'm the President of the United States."

More people came into the foyer. Many of them were tall men in blue suits, with guns strapped under their jackets. A small woman in a maid's uniform walked in. Susan recognized her. Her name was Esmeralda, but people called her Esa, and she had worked in this house for more than twenty years. She seemed puzzled. She looked at Susan as if Susan were one of those Catholic miracles that believers sometimes flocked to. She could have been a weeping Virgin Mary in the sheer face of a stone cliff.

"Mrs. Hopkins?" Esa said. "You're alive."

She walked up to Susan as if in a dream. The two women hugged. It was tentative as first, but then Susan pulled Esa closer. Abruptly, Susan started to cry. It felt so good, so good, to be here with this woman, at this moment.

"I am," she said. "I'm alive."

She closed her eyes and let the hug go on.

"You're not the President," a booming voice said.

Susan let Esa go. Coming down the grand marble staircase was none other than William Ryan. He looked hale and hearty, fit and energized, much younger than his years. "I am the President. I took the Oath of Office last night. It was administered by the Chief Justice of the United States."

He reached the bottom of the stairs and walked directly to Susan. He was very tall. He towered over her. She looked up at him. Chuck Berg was on her right. Walter Brenna was on her left.

"Susan," Ryan said. "It's nice to see you. But I'm going to have to ask you to leave. You've obviously been under terrible strain during the past twenty-four hours. I'm pretty sure you're in no frame of mind to take the Oath."

A crush of military men and Secret Service agents had gathered in the foyer now.

Ryan gestured to a couple of military men near him. "Will you escort Mrs. Hopkins out, please? We have work to do here."

Susan pointed at him. "Arrest that man. For treason, and for the murder of President Thomas Hayes, and more than three hundred other people."

There was a moment when she didn't know what would happen. Everyone simply stood and stared. Somewhere, a clock ticked. Three seconds, four seconds.

Five.

Chuck Berg stepped forward. He took a pair of steel handcuffs from his belt.

He moved toward Ryan. "Sir, you have the right to remain silent."

An Army man stepped in front of him. Chuck pushed the man. Suddenly, there was pushing and shoving everywhere. Susan was jostled as big strong men moved each other back and forth. Then she felt a sharp pain.

Someone had stepped on her foot.

245

The Secret Service agents outnumbered the military three to one. All of the Secret Service men upheld their jobs.

In the end, Ryan fought them. He went down swinging, but down was where he went. In seconds, he was face first on the polished wooden floor, two Secret Service men pressing him down.

The Secret Service stood Ryan to his feet. His face was red from exertion. He glared at Susan as they led him toward the front door.

"I am the President of the United States!" he shouted.

Susan waved a dismissive hand at him.

"Get out of my house," she said.

*

Pierre and the girls were flying in to see her. The thought of it gave her hope, and happiness. She needed a little of that.

This being President was going to be a tall order. The conspiracy against Thomas Hayes had been far-reaching. At this juncture, it was impossible to know everyone who was involved, and what branches of government they were in. For the foreseeable future, the domestic threat level against her would be considered the highest level. She would wear body armor during all public appearances.

The problems in the Middle East would not go away overnight, but maybe she was already making some headway. She had spoken briefly today with the President of Russia. He told her, through an interpreter, that he was very glad to hear she was alive. He assured her they could work together to smooth out the problems with Iran.

But there were even darker problems on the horizon. In the afternoon, she sat in her office with two visitors.

"I want to keep funding the Special Response Team," she said. "But I'd like to take it out from under the umbrella of the FBI."

Luke Stone stood at the window, staring out at the grounds of the Naval Observatory. "Whose umbrella would you like to put it under?"

She shrugged. "It could be a branch of the Secret Service. Or it could simply be its own organization that reports directly to the President."

"That sounds nice," Ed Newsam said. He sat in a wheelchair with his bad leg up on the desk. He held an unlit cigar in his hands. "I like the ring of that."

Stone turned around. "Until yesterday, I was on an extended leave of absence. I don't know if I even work for the Special Response Team anymore."

"That's funny," she said. "I kind of had you tapped for Director. I was wrong about you, Stone. That's what I'm telling you. In the past twenty-four hours, you've saved my life again and again."

Stone shook his head. "I need to find my wife and son. The plot has unraveled, and the conspirators don't need them anymore. Every minute that passes..."

Susan nodded. "I know. We've got every available resource working on finding them. I promise you we will find them. But in the meantime, I can't have you walk away from the SRT. There are only a handful of people I can trust right now, and you two are at the top of that list."

She walked to the door of the office and looked outside. Chuck Berg and another agent were ten feet away. She quietly closed the door.

She turned back to Stone and Newsam.

"The truth is I have another urgent mission for you. I only heard about it in the past half hour. Unfortunately, our enemies see us in a weakened position, and they're taking this moment to strike. The next forty-eight hours will be crucial."

Now Stone and Newsam stared at each other.

"Come on, guys. I need you."

"Do we even get to know what it is?"

She nodded. "I'm about to tell you. But I want you to say yes first."

A long moment passed.

"Yes."

*

Luke walked the manicured grounds of the Naval Observatory toward the parking lot. Next to him, Ed Newsam rolled his wheelchair along, his massive arms giving the wheels a spin every once in a while.

"Are you ever going to get out of that thing?" Luke said. "I feel like you're slacking off. Can't you do physical therapy or something?"

"Stone, I've only been in it since last night."

Luke shrugged. "Well, I can't help the way that I feel. It's seems like you've been in it for a month already."

Luke's phone rang. He pulled it out and glanced at the number. For a split second, he had been hoping that...

He answered it. "Trudy. What do you got for me? What's going on with Don's computer?"

Her voice was musical, upbeat. She probably hadn't slept in close to forty-eight hours. She probably hadn't even been home in all that time, and she was probably on her twentieth cup of black coffee. But there was something about winning, even winning ugly, that brought out the music in people.

"Swann finally managed to break the encryption on Don's files. Luke, he knew about it all along. He was in on the plot from the beginning. In fact, he was in on it since before the beginning. There are emails between him and Bill Ryan about seizing power that date to before Thomas Hayes was even President."

"You think you know a guy," Luke said.

"I thought I knew him better than most," Trudy said.

Luke ignored that statement. He and Trudy had a complicated history. He didn't feel like dealing with that right now.

"What else?" he said.

"Luke, Don talked. He gave the address of a CIA safe house. The people who run it are ghosts. They're not on the official payroll. Don thinks it's where your wife and son might be."

Luke stopped walking. His heart began to pound in his chest.

"What?"

Instinctively, he felt for the gun strapped inside his jacket. He looked down at Ed Newsam. Ed stared up at him. He picked up on Luke's body language. Ed's hand strayed to his own guns.

"I have the address of a safe house. We're sending agents there. They're going to hit hard, and without warning. If your family is there, the agents are going to do everything they can to keep them safe."

"Trudy, give me the address."

"You can't go there, Luke. You have no objectivity. You'll be a liability to the operation. And you'll put everyone in danger."

"Trudy..."

248

"Luke…"

"Trudy, tell me the address."

There was a long pause over the line. His entire body was on fire with the searing pain of losing Becca and Gunner.

"Tell me," he pleaded.

A long silence followed.

And then she did.

Coming in February!

Book #2 in the Luke Stone series

Please visit www.Jackmarsauthor.com to join the email list and be the first to know when it releases!

Jack Mars

Jack Mars is an avid reader and lifelong fan of the thriller genre. ANY MEANS NECESSARY is Jack's debut thriller. Jack loves to hear from you, so please feel free to visit www.Jackmarsauthor.com to join the email list, receive a free book, receive free giveaways, connect on Facebook and Twitter, and stay in touch!

CPSIA information can be obtained
at www.ICGtesting.com
Printed in the USA
LVOW03s1503021017
550635LV00001B/1/P

9 781632 914644